What the critics are saying...

"DEMONIC OBSESSION will thrill, excite, and enthrall readers as they delve between the pages of this book and meet the intriguing characters, Eric and Ellie. Ms. Adams does an excellent job with the plot and characterization. I look forward to reading more from this author." ~ *Sinclair Reid for Romance Reviews Today*

Rated 5 Roses "The sex is hot. The story is wild and exciting. The characters are very believable. There's not much more to say. Elisa Adams beings us a wonderful story of passion, fantasy and mystery. If you enjoy vampire stories, then this book is for you. A definite keeper for my e-book collection." ~ *Debbie for A Romance Review*

"DEMONIC OBSESSION is full of adventure, suspense, and heated sensuality...a definite must read for lovers of the paranormal, shape shifters, vampires, and suspense." ~ *Vikky Bertling Road to Romance*

"The sexual scenes in this book are amazing. It doesn't take long for Eric and Ellie to get together physically and when they do, wow! There is so much intensity, you feel as though you are right there, going through everything with Ellie. Elisa Adams has done an excellent job in writing this book. The plot and characters all combine to create one dynamite book I'm sure will be a keeper." ~ *Angel Brewer Just Erotic Romance Reviews*

Elisa Adams

Demonic
Obsession

ELLORA'S CAVE
ROMANTICA PUBLISHING

An Ellora's Cave Romantica Publication

www.ellorascave.com

Demonic Obsession

ISBN #141995217X
ALL RIGHTS RESERVED.
Demonic Obsession Copyright© 2003 Elisa Adams
Edited by: Martha Punches
Cover art by: Darrell King

Electronic book Publication: November, 2003
Trade paperback Publication: June, 2005

Excerpt from *Midnight* Copyright © Elisa Adams, 2003

Warning:

The following material contains graphic sexual content meant for mature readers. *Demonic Obsession* has been rated *S-ensous* by a minimum of three independent reviewers.

Ellora's Cave Publishing offers three levels of Romantica™ reading entertainment: S (S-ensuous), E (E-rotic), and X (X-treme).

S-ensuous love scenes are explicit and leave nothing to the imagination.

E-rotic love scenes are explicit, leave nothing to the imagination, and are high in volume per the overall word count. In addition, some E-rated titles might contain fantasy material that some readers find objectionable, such as bondage, submission, same sex encounters, forced seductions, etc. E-rated titles are the most graphic titles we carry; it is common, for instance, for an author to use words such as "fucking", "cock", "pussy", etc., within their work of literature.

X-treme titles differ from E-rated titles only in plot premise and storyline execution. Unlike E-rated titles, stories designated with the letter X tend to contain controversial subject matter not for the faint of heart.

Also by Elisa Adams:

Demonic Obsession
Dark Promises

Chapter 1

Ellie sat on an old wooden bench, her sketchpad resting on her lap. The sunset just visible over the tops of the trees washed the sky in brilliant hues of orange and pink. The rustling of the summer wind through the leaves and the faint breaking of waves against the nearby shore calmed her nerves like nothing else could — on most nights.

Just not tonight.

She tucked a few stray strands of hair behind her ears and took a sip from her water bottle, making an attempt to ignore the strange sensations that prickled the hair on the back of her neck. The air crackled with an electrical tension, sending a shiver through her despite the warm temperature.

Something was different.

Something had disturbed the peaceful, sleepy quiet of Stone Harbor. Something she couldn't define — maybe didn't want to. A knot of anxiety formed in the pit of her stomach and her gaze landed on a man leaning against a tree a few dozen feet away. Did he have something to do with the disturbance?

"Yeah, right," she muttered to herself, turning her attention back to her sketchpad. He looked about average height, with an average build and average dark hair — nothing spectacular about him, at least from this distance. He wore khaki pants and an off-white polo shirt — nothing impressive there. He looked more like the married-with-three- children type than the bad-to-the-bone and out-to-cause-trouble type.

So why couldn't she shake the feeling that his presence signaled danger?

She blew out a breath, frustrated with her paranoia. So her ex-husband had turned out to be a first-class jerk disguised as a successful businessman. That didn't mean that every other man who dressed nicely meant her emotional harm. If she didn't get over what happened with Todd, she'd never get the chance to meet a nice guy and settle down. Three years had passed since her divorce—plenty of time to get over her silly insecurities.

She had to stop pasting Todd's face on every man who walked into her life. They weren't *all* like him—she wasn't naïve enough to believe that—but her luck with men seemed to really suck lately. This poor guy hadn't done anything to her, he probably hadn't even noticed she was alive, and she'd already pegged him as some kind of deranged mass murderer.

His head was turned toward the small pond in the center of the park, but every so often, he looked in her direction. From the distance, she couldn't be sure if he was looking at *her*, but the fact that he might be married unsettled her. Her fingers smoothed over the totem that hung from a silver chain around her neck—a small panther carved in black onyx—in a reaction that was more automatic than calculated. She closed her eyes briefly, calling to the animal the totem represented for guidance. She tried to focus on the sleek grace of the creature, the control and strength it exuded, but her powers of concentration were severely lacking tonight. It was all *his* fault.

She tried to keep her eyes off him, but she couldn't help stealing little glances every so often. Something about him compelled her, even when she knew it was impolite and possibly dangerous. The man was a complete stranger in a town where she recognized most people on sight, and that fact alone made her wary. She knew she shouldn't stare, yet she couldn't pull her gaze away.

That frightened her the most. An odd fixation on a complete stranger was something she thought she'd outgrown years ago, once she'd hit puberty. What made him so special that she couldn't draw her gaze away, even with exercised concentration? As far as she could tell—*nothing*.

But there had to be *something*, or else she wouldn't be spending her evening observing him when she'd come here to sketch the sunset in preparation for her next painting.

His head swung in her direction and she didn't have time to look away. This time she had no doubts—he was looking right at her. She drew in a deep, shaky breath, her palms suddenly growing damp. A smile spread across his face and he nodded slightly—just enough to let her know he'd caught her staring. The thought unnerved her, but not enough to make her drag her gaze from his. A dog barking in the distance finally broke the spell. She looked quickly back at her sketchpad, not wanting to encourage him in any way, but afraid it might already be too late.

She tried to make a rough sketch of the flowers lining the banks of the pond, but her traitorous hands instead drew the shadowy form of a lean, dark-haired man. After three attempts, she slammed her pencil down on the pad and sighed in disgust. It figured. She'd never felt a pull this strong—not even when she'd been with Todd. She prided herself on being independent, level-headed to a fault, and suddenly she felt like the world had tilted on its axis.

She was being such an idiot! Ellie was the calm one. Her sister, Charlotte, was the dramatic one. Always had been. But now it seemed like Ellie had switched places with her younger sister. The whole situation made her feel off balance, like she couldn't quite get her footing right. This had to be some kind of a sign that she needed to make some changes in her life. Either that, or she needed some kind of psychological counseling. She blew out a breath and muttered to herself, "Normal, healthy women don't obsess about complete strangers."

And all the while, the stranger in question was probably leaning against that tree, laughing to himself about the skinny girl who kept staring at him. He'd probably go home later to his house with a white picket fence and a couple of Volvos in the driveway and have a good laugh with his equally yuppy wife.

Yeah, she was definitely nuts. Time to get back to work. That was, after all, her purpose for being in the park.

She picked her pencil back up and tried her best to focus on her sketching, but it was no use. Her mind was on that man, not on her work. She slammed her pencil down on the pad yet again, this time with a lot more force. If she wasn't going to get anything done tonight, she might as well just pack up and go home. No sense wasting time sitting around gaping at strangers when she could be home in her studio—alone—getting some actual work done.

"Why did you stop?"

She nearly jumped a mile at the voice behind her. She spun around so quickly the pad and pencil slid out of her lap and hit the grass below.

It was *him*.

She opened her mouth to chastise him for sneaking up on her, but she couldn't form a single coherent sentence. Up close, he was even more fascinating than he'd been at a distance—and he certainly wasn't as *average* as she'd first thought. His hair was thick and shiny, a rich, deep brown nearly as dark as hers, and without a hint of gray. The light-colored shirt contrasted sharply with the golden bronze tone of his skin.

A half-smile played on his full lips, and she caught a glimpse of gleaming white teeth. "Are you an artist by trade?" he continued, his gaze snagging hers and holding tight. She couldn't look away, even if she'd wanted to. His eyes were a clear emerald green with small flecks of gold threaded through, almost hypnotic in their beauty. She'd never seen eyes that color in her life.

He cleared his throat and she realized she'd been staring. "You do speak English, don't you?" he asked, his tone laced with humor.

"What? Oh, English. Yeah." She cursed herself for sounding like a complete airhead, but she couldn't help it. They just didn't make them like this in Stone Harbor, and seeing him must have short-circuited something vital in her brain.

"I asked if you were an artist."

She could do this. He was just a man. Nothing to fear.

"Yes." She paused and took a deep breath. At least she'd been able to make some sense this time. A little calmer, she launched into an explanation. "A painter, but I work with charcoal from time to time when I need a change, which now I—"

She clamped her mouth shut and let a breath out through her nose. *Geez, Ellie. Think you can give him any* more *information he didn't ask for?* She mentally berated herself for nearly boring him to death. What would he care about her humdrum life? The only interesting things about her were things she only told her closest friends. The rest of her life—the public part—wasn't even worthy of a mention. Bending down, she scooped the pad and pencil off the ground and settled them back in her lap, covering the picture with her arms to block it from his view.

She lifted her gaze to him again, ready to excuse herself and make a quick exit before she humiliated herself further. He focused his eyes on her lap, presumably trying to get a glimpse of what she'd been drawing. It gave her a chance to get a better look at near-perfection. His face reminded her of a sculpture— all smooth lines and clean angles. She placed him somewhere in his late thirties or early forties from the faint lines around his eyes and mouth. And all that bronze skin looked unusually soft. She had the strange desire to run her fingertips over his cheeks to find out.

What a painting he'd make. She'd never ask a complete stranger to pose, but the thought intrigued her. A face like that would keep her hands—and eyes—busy for hours. The fading sun glinted in his eyes, and for a second they flashed gold. The sight made a shiver run down her spine, both from anxiety and something she hated to label as arousal.

"Who are you?" she asked when she finally got her mouth working properly. She supposed if he planned to stand there and let her gape at him all night, he at least owed her an introduction. And if she knew his name, he wouldn't be a *complete* stranger anymore, and she wouldn't feel so guilty about staring.

"Eric Malcolm." He held out his hand and she took it hesitantly, expecting a handshake. When he brought her hand to his lips and brushed a kiss over her knuckles, she blinked in surprise. His palm was warm and soft, and the fleeting touch of his lips against her skin had her drawing a sharp breath.

"And you are…?" he continued, her hand still firmly in his grip.

Think. She mentally knocked herself on the head, trying to get her brain to function. "Ann Elizabeth Holmes."

Stupid! No one called her Ann Elizabeth. What was she thinking?

"Well, Ann Elizabeth—"

"Ellie." She smiled weakly. "Please. Call me Ellie. I hate Ann Elizabeth."

"Why?" He raised an eyebrow at her as he spoke.

"It's boring." *Oh, yeah. Like Ellie is any better.*

He frowned and studied her for a minute. "You don't strike me as a boring woman."

She had to laugh at that. "Stick around. I'll prove you wrong in a matter of days. Maybe even hours."

He nodded slowly, his eyes darkening almost imperceptibly. "I might just do that."

"Oh, no, I didn't mean…" She sighed, not willing to finish the thought. She felt a little like a moth drawn to flame. His gaze sucked her in, entranced her, but if she got close enough, she'd be fried to a crisp. He could do that to her—she had no doubts about it.

"I think you did." He glanced at the pad in her lap, his head cocked to the side. Self-consciously she brushed her hair back behind her ears again. He took full advantage of the moment, reaching over her shoulder and lifting the pad off her lap before she even had time to react.

"Hey! Give that back!" She made a grab for her sketchpad, but he held tight with one hand as he leafed through a couple of the pages with the other. He had to have noticed the sketches of him, but he didn't show any kind of a reaction.

"Why are you trying to hide this from me? Surely a woman as talented as you is used to showing off her work?"

The subject matter, rather than the work as a whole, caused her the most distress. She didn't need him thinking she was some kind of obsessed mental case. *Normal women didn't go around drawing pictures of complete strangers.* Yeah. If she kept repeating that, she might actually start to believe it.

She shrugged, failing miserably at casual. "I have a few in a gallery downtown. This," she yanked the pad out of his hands and closed the cover, "is too raw to share. I make it a policy never to let anyone see my work when it's in the beginning stages." Especially if the work was of a man who had no idea she'd used him as an artist's model.

"That's too bad. It seems like such a waste to *not* share."

His compliment caught her off guard. She didn't know how to answer. "I guess I have doubts about that. Most artists do."

"Don't doubt your talent. If you consider these sketches rough, I'd be very interested in taking a look at some of your finished work."

"Why?" she asked, incredulous. Suspicion rose in her. That was taking the whole flattery thing a little too far.

"I'm redecorating my house, and I'm very interested in New England artists." He put his hands in his pockets and leaned a hip against the back of the bench. Everything about his manner said "casual", yet she detected a faint...restlessness about him that practically screamed "ulterior motives".

"Is that why you're in town? To acquire *art*?" She resisted the urge to tell him that the words "woman" and "stupid" were not synonymous. When people wanted art, they went to the big galleries in New York City. They didn't come to Stone Harbor. Sure, there were a couple of galleries downtown, but they were mostly for the tourists who flocked to the town in late summer to invade the beaches.

He elegantly shrugged one shoulder, the casual façade firmly in place. "Art is one of the reasons for my visit."

Business, perhaps? He didn't strike her as someone who traveled to the edge of nowhere for fun. She waited for him to elaborate on his other reasons, but he didn't. He just stood over her, his gaze boring into hers, until she couldn't take the silence anymore. "The gallery at the Art Association downtown has a few of my paintings. You could always go down there if you wanted to take a look. It's a little red brick building on the corner of Main and Washington. You can't miss it."

"I don't get a personal tour?" He smiled down at her and something quivered low in her stomach.

She almost gave in then and there. *Almost.* But then she remembered that, even in a tiny town like Stone Harbor, getting too friendly too quickly with strangers was a bad idea. "No, I don't think so. You look like a smart guy. I think you can find your way around a gallery all by yourself."

She had to get out of there—*now*, before she forgot all her common sense. She stood and left the bench, stuffed the pad and pencil into her tote bag, and started toward the parking lot without glancing back. If she looked, even a tiny bit, she knew part of her would want to stay. Funny, she'd always thought of herself as a rational woman. Talking to a complete stranger the way she had certainly wasn't rational. It bordered on insane.

"Would it change things if I told you I'm more interested in the artist than the art?"

She stopped in mid-stride and pivoted. "No. Definitely not. I—" The words she'd meant as a forceful denial came out as no more than a squeak that ended in a gasp when she realized he stood less than two feet away.

"How did you get there?" He'd been all the way back by the bench, and she hadn't heard his footsteps behind her.

"The same as you. I walked." He shrugged and smiled, fixing that incredible green gaze on her and turning her body to jelly. She felt like he'd stepped even closer in the seconds that followed, but he hadn't moved at all.

"Sure you did." Yeah, and she was Mary, Queen of Scots. Thoughts in her head began sliding together like pieces in a puzzle, and she didn't think she'd like the final picture. "Listen, I really do have to go. I have things to do."

"That's too bad. It would be a shame to waste such a beautiful night. I'm sure, without all the lights of the big city, the night sky here is fabulous."

"It is. It's also dark. Very dark, and I have to get home before the sun sets." She had a feeling that she didn't want to be stuck alone with him after the sun went down. He made her nervous, suspicious—*tense*.

And aroused.

The last thought hit her like a slap in the face. The only thing she knew about him was his name, and somehow he conjured such strong emotions within her that she couldn't control them.

"It will be a beautiful sunset, if you just stay a few more minutes," he continued with that deep, hypnotic voice.

She smiled nervously, shifting from foot to foot. The combination of unease and attraction was a powerful combination. "Yeah. It will. I hope you get a chance to enjoy it. If you'll excuse me…"

"Of course." He smiled ruefully. "If you insist on leaving, I won't stop you."

Then why did it feel like her legs were leaden, and she couldn't drag herself away without some serious effort? "I-I have to go." She repeated the words like a mantra, one her body refused to acknowledge. Despite her best intentions, her feet remained planted to the ground as if she'd grown roots.

"You're unsure of me, aren't you?" He didn't look upset. Instead, his gaze held sparks of humor and curiosity, and a healthy dose of the crippling arousal currently assaulting her.

She nodded slowly, nervously wetting her lower lip with the tip of her tongue. She backed up a step, then another, to put some much needed distance between them.

"I wouldn't expect a beautiful woman like you to be all alone. Do you have a man waiting at home for you?" His eyes darkened at the question.

He didn't know the half of it. Sometimes she *wished* she were all alone. One day with her family, and he'd understand. She shook her head. "It's just...I... Never mind." She should leave before this got any worse, but her stubborn feet refused to move.

He stepped closer and raised his hand, a set of keys dangling from his fingers. *Her* keys. She thought her heart stopped for a beat before starting again with a thud. "Where did you get those?"

"On the ground by the bench. They must have fallen out of your bag." He held them in front of him as if daring her to come and get them.

She swallowed hard. She always kept her keys in her pocket or purse. *Always*. She never put them in her bag. That thought was enough to release her from whatever held her to the spot. "Thanks for bringing them to me." She held out her hand and waited for him to place them in her palm.

He laughed softly as he walked to her. "Here you are. Have a safe drive home." His fingers brushed her palm as he gave her the keys. She felt the contact all the way to her toes. His voice was a husky whisper, one that had her thinking illicit thoughts about naked, sweaty bodies tangled in satin sheets, moving together in —

"Thanks," she said sharply, trying to pull herself out of her lust-induced haze. What was wrong with her? It was like some wanton flake had crawled into her mind and set up residence.

"My pleasure." He lowered his head a little, his gaze meeting hers dead-on. His deep voice had her practically panting at his feet. "I meant what I said about your talent, and your beauty."

The sincerity in his gaze made her face flame. "Well, thanks. I really do have to go now. Again."

"I'll be in town for a while, and I plan to take a trip to the gallery you mentioned to see your paintings," he said as she turned to walk away. "Maybe I'll see you later."

"Maybe," she said without turning back to him.

She virtually ran toward her car. He didn't follow, and she didn't care. The pull he had over her rattled her, and if she hadn't walked away that second there was no telling what stupid things she might have done. She shifted her tote bag on her shoulder and walked faster. When she glanced up after she opened her car door, he hadn't moved an inch. Funny, but it felt as if he were standing right next to her.

It took about five minutes for everything to click firmly into place. She'd known, subconsciously, almost from the beginning of their meeting, but she hadn't dared acknowledge it until now. The truth hit her all at once when she paused at a stop sign. She didn't know *who* the stranger in the park was, but she knew *what* he felt like.

A vampire.

Just what she needed in her life, another vampire. She leaned forward and banged her head on the steering wheel a few times. *"Wonderful."* She had a serious case of lust, and the guy wasn't even *human*.

And she'd bet her entire year's commission that the real reason for his visit had nothing to do with art.

* * * * *

Eric sat at the tiny round table, the blue light from the screen of his laptop the only illumination in the hotel room. He shifted in his chair and glanced at the glowing green digits on the alarm clock. Twelve-fifteen. The night had just begun. He rubbed a hand down his face and thought about the woman in the park. Ellie. She might prove to be a distraction if he wasn't careful. He had a job to do, and he'd be wise not to forget it.

He'd shaken her. That much had been obvious—barely. She was strong. Getting close to her wouldn't be as easy as he'd previously thought. He'd tried his hardest to bend her mind to his will, but he'd scarcely been able to get inside. Every time he thought he had her, she mentally locked him out. Sam had told him the woman was an ordinary human. Obviously, that was not the whole truth. But he'd do what it took to bend her—out of necessity. She might be his last chance at catching a killer before he destroyed another life. He had a personal stake in this job since three of his closest friends were dead.

He might be next, if he wasn't careful.

He'd have to be. Tracking the killer while having to constantly look over his shoulder had become tedious work. It had been months, and it was time to end this for good, no matter what it took. But he didn't want Ellie hurt.

Where that thought came from, he had no idea. He'd need to remember that he was here in Stone Harbor to do a job, *not* pursue a woman—at least no more than the job entailed. If he could get close to her, he'd be able to get the information he needed. It was quite possible, given her friendships with the few vampires who lived in town, that she already knew the killer's identity. On the other hand, those vamps were a secretive bunch, so she might not know anything at all. That was why he'd have to get close to the human woman, get her to relax around him enough that he could get inside her head.

And he was fooling himself if he thought that was his only reason for wanting to get close to her. The second she'd looked up at him with those big blue eyes, lust had hit him with the force of a hurricane. He *wanted* to get to know her better, both mentally and physically, in a way that had absolutely nothing to do with work. But getting closer to her might mean putting up with her vampire friends for a little while too, and that thought turned his stomach. The last thing he needed were a bunch of vamps to ruin his life, especially those vamps in particular.

God, he hated bloodsuckers.

Chapter 2

Ellie pulled into her driveway, gave a quick glance toward the garage apartment where her grandmother had moved to last summer, and let herself into her house. Still uncertain about her encounter in the park, she poured a glass of water and downed it in one gulp. She didn't need another vampire in her life. The three she had were enough. She'd known Marco so long—since she was eight years old—that he'd become a permanent fixture in her world. She'd instantly bonded with Amara, his wife.

And then there was Royce.

She hated to call him her boyfriend. The term usually inferred some sort of deep emotional bond, of which the man wasn't capable. He was more of a friend, one she slept with on occasion. And even those occasions were lessening with time. He didn't do anything to turn her *off*, he just didn't turn her *on*. She'd been trying to break it off with him for a week or so now, but couldn't think of a way to do it without hurting Amara's feelings. She was the one who pushed Ellie to get to know her brother-in-law better, and Ellie had agreed to at least give the man a chance. But like every other man she'd dated since her divorce, he didn't do a thing for her. None of them ever did.

Except Eric Malcolm.

No. She wouldn't think about him now. She'd never see him again, and it was time to get back to her real life—the one that didn't include seductive vampires in public parks.

She'd just started fixing supper when the doorbell rang. She ran down the hall to answer it, knowing it was only a matter of time before her grandmother had some kind of an emergency. But it wasn't her grandmother she saw through the narrow windows next to the door.

Royce. This was *not* what she needed after the incident in the park. She opened the door, even though she would have pretended she wasn't home if she'd thought she could get away with it.

"Hi." She smiled weakly.

"Can I talk to you about something?" He walked in without being invited, but that was nothing new. She'd gotten used to his way in the past couple of months he'd been staying in Stone Harbor—but that didn't mean she had to like it.

"Um, okay." She sighed as she shut the door behind him. *Men.* What was it about them that made them think they owned the world?

He walked into the living room and sat down on the couch, looking way too comfortable in her house. She bit back a snippy reply, knowing it wouldn't do any good to get him angry now. She couldn't really blame her mood on him, even though she'd like to. Eric Malcolm had set her off-balance, and she wanted to lash out at the loss of control. Royce had picked a bad night to visit.

She took a deep breath and sat down in a chair across from him. "What's up?"

He leaned back and propped his arms behind his head. "I'm going to South Africa."

"Excuse me?" His reply floored her. She didn't know what she'd been expecting, but that wasn't it. "You're going *where*?"

"South Africa. I got a job offer to travel to a couple of countries in need of a doctor, and I've decided to go." He paused and frowned. "That doesn't upset you, does it?"

"Why should it?" she asked slowly. Why did she think there was some kind of a catch here?

He continued, ignoring her question. "I was hoping you'd come with me."

Her mouth fell open. Come with him? Was he out of his mind? "*Why?*"

Her sharp answer got his attention. He sat up on the couch, his eyes narrowed. "What do you mean, why? I thought we had something going here. I *thought* you might want to spend a couple months seeing other parts of the world."

She thought carefully before she answered, not wanting to do any more damage to his fragile male ego. "Royce, I can't. I have a life here, a family that needs me. I can't just pack up and leave them."

He shook his head and ran his hand through his long, blond hair, looking shaken for the first time since she'd known him. When he finally spoke, defeat was evident in his voice.

"I'm sorry about this," he said softly.

That took her by surprise. She'd expected anger, or even a guilt trip, but she hadn't expected an apology. It was probably the first time in the history of her life that a man had bothered to apologize to her, and she didn't know how to handle it. "What in the world do you have to be sorry for?"

"I'm trying here. I've done nothing but try to get this thing between us to work out. You know that, right?"

She nodded. "Of course I do."

"And you're not interested."

Royce was an attractive man. She just wasn't attracted *to* him. His lifestyle and sometimes careless attitude didn't lend themselves to deep, emotional connections. "Deep and emotional" didn't even have a place in his vocabulary. She needed connections, and he couldn't provide them. They just weren't compatible in that way, and to her, that was everything.

She took a deep breath, not sure what to say next. She didn't want to hurt him, but she couldn't keep letting him think there would ever be more between them than friendship. He knew it, too, even if until now he'd refused to admit it.

He spoke when she remained silent. "Don't feel bad. Just tell me the truth. Honestly, I've been trying to find some kind of a spark between us, but it's just not there."

"I didn't think men needed a spark."

That got a laugh out of him. "I've been getting the feeling you're looking for something I can't give you. Your response to my request proved it. I can't do the commitment thing, Ellie. I haven't been able to in so many years. I think maybe we should stop this relationship stuff and just try to be friends, for Marco and Amara's sake."

She breathed a sigh of relief, for both being free of the weight that had been suffocating her, and for not having to do the dumping herself. *No* was not a word that came easily to her, and she hated more than anything to hurt people. "That's probably a good idea."

Of course, she'd miss the sex. It had never been mind-blowing—which only happened in books, as far as she was concerned. But pretty good sex was better than no sex at all. She'd get over it. She'd find someone else, someday. Unbidden, Eric's face flashed through her mind.

"You're not upset?" Royce asked, looking a little confused.

Upset? She was ecstatic. Now she could get on with her life, and not feel guilty. She shook her head. "Are you?"

His smile was nothing short of rakish. "I'll be okay. In time."

For the first time in months, she felt like she could get to know him without the commitment angle thrown at them at every turn. She should have known better than to try to force something that never would have worked. "Well, good. You know this means we're not going to bed together anymore, right?"

"What?" He gazed at her, mock-wounded. "Why not? What's wrong with a little sex between friends?"

She smiled at his half-joking tone. "I'm looking for commitment, not casual. Besides, you'll be in South Africa. When do you leave?"

"In a couple of weeks. Maybe until I go..." He let his sentence trail off, the look in his eyes completing the thought better than words ever could.

She shook her head and frowned at him. "Give it up, because it's not going to happen. I don't think you'll have any trouble finding some other woman to satisfy your needs during the weeks before you go."

He just smiled. He didn't need to answer that. They both knew he never had trouble finding a woman when he needed one. "What about you?"

"Don't worry about me." She didn't indulge in casual affairs, usually, and with Royce she'd pretended they had a commitment to justify her behavior. In truth, she'd been bored, a little lonely, and in need of something new in her life. Now she knew without a doubt that flings weren't her style. She'd wait until she found a man who could make a commitment to her, and *not* run away screaming when he learned the truth about her family.

She was starting to believe that she'd never find one man who fit those criteria. Royce, being what he was, accepted her just fine but balked at the idea of commitment. Todd was all for commitment—or at least she'd thought he'd been—but he'd failed in the understanding department. He'd *said* he accepted her lifestyle, but now she wondered if it was more a novelty for him than true love. Once the newness had worn off, and he'd seen that witchcraft was a real part of her life and not some silly phase she'd grow out of, he'd packed his things and moved in with his "normal" girlfriend.

"What are you thinking about?" Royce asked, leaning forward on the couch. "Are you sure you're not upset about this?"

She smiled at the genuine concern she saw in his eyes. "We're better off as friends. We both know that, and it would be wrong to push for more. Are *you* upset?"

He laughed. "No. I'm sorry I waited this long to bring it up, but I didn't want to hurt you like your ex-husband did." He paused, frowning. "You know, someday you're going to make some guy very happy."

"Maybe." Her smile wavered and she pushed the lingering doubts out of her mind. Someday she *would* find the right man. Maybe she already had. She'd just have to wait and see what the future held. "And someday you might realize that living alone isn't all it's cracked up to be."

He shook his head, denial plain on his face. "*Right.* I've been alone for too long. It's too late to break this habit, Ellie."

"I wouldn't be so sure about that. You just need to find the right woman."

His expression saddened a little. When he spoke again, his voice was soft. "I'm not looking. I never will be." His expression changed again, like a door closing in his mind, and the cheery visage slipped back into place. "I'm having too much fun on my own. Why would I want to weigh myself down with another wife? That would be a moronic thing to do. Look, I have to go. I told Amara I wouldn't be long, and you know how she gets. I'll be in touch before I leave, okay?"

Just like that, she'd chased him away. Amara was only an excuse, the set of his jaw and the darkness in his eyes told her he'd had enough conversation for the night. Wanting to kick herself for bringing up his painful past, she walked him to the door. "If you ever want to talk, you know you can call me, right?"

He looked down at her for a while before he answered, his gaze unreadable. Tenderness sparked in them for a few seconds before it disappeared behind the hurt and anger. "You've really got to stop taking care of everyone else and start taking care of yourself, Ellie."

She smiled as he bent down to kiss her forehead before he walked out the door. Whether he knew it or not, he was a good man. He deserved to find someone to make him happy. Unfortunately, she wasn't the person to do that.

After Royce drove away, she went back to fixing dinner for herself and her sister Charlotte, who'd moved back home after her divorce a couple of months ago. What a track record her family had—both she and Charlotte had been married and divorced before they were thirty. But Ellie knew better than anyone that it was hard to find a good man these days. The Holmes family had been practicing witchcraft for generations, and they weren't prepared to give it up for the sake of a man with conformist ideals—at least most of them weren't.

Their youngest sister, Becca, didn't get it, either. All her life she'd questioned their practices, refused to participate in every aspect of witchcraft, and berated them all—especially her mother and grandmother—for carrying on with what she termed old and outdated traditions. Ellie knew her discomfort with living in a family of witches played a big part in Becca's decision to move out, and it hurt a little. But she couldn't change Becca's opinions. Of course, it didn't stop her sister from visiting several nights a week at suppertime. Becca swore her visits were just that, but Ellie suspected the girl was hungry. Becca's job at a novelty shop downtown barely made her enough to pay the bills, and her jerk of a live-in boyfriend was too lazy to go out and get himself a job.

Ellie wanted so much to go over to their apartment and throttle the guy, but she'd promised Becca she'd stay out of it. Her little sister wanted a chance to live her own life, and Ellie had to respect that. Still, it was hard to sit back and watch the young woman's life fall apart around her while the jerk did *nothing*.

"Smells good." Becca came through the front door just as Ellie set the table. She set an extra place for Becca's boyfriend, knowing it was useless. He wouldn't set foot inside their house even if he had to, and he'd probably rather Becca didn't either. Tony hated how close she was to her family, and he constantly tried to find ways to separate them. He'd been in town for a month, and already he had her living with him and supporting both of them on her salary.

How he'd done it so fast, Ellie could only guess. She'd met him once, and she hadn't seen the appeal. With shabby clothes, shaggy hair, and an unshaven face, he looked like a vagrant. She'd decided on the spot that she didn't like him one bit. It didn't have to do with his appearance as much as it did the creepy vibe she'd gotten from him. Something with him wasn't quite right, but Becca wouldn't listen to reason. Since that first meeting three weeks ago, he'd stayed away from everyone in Becca's life — and he'd nearly managed to get her to do the same.

"How are you doing, kiddo?" Ellie asked her, smoothing one of her sister's dark curls away from her forehead. At eighteen, Becca's maturity level was falling fast. She thought she was all grown up, but Ellie still felt the need to watch over her. Becca didn't show any signs of abuse — yet — but that was only a matter of time. If things kept going this way, she thought about asking Royce to have a talk with Tony. *He'd* probably get him to stay away from Becca, but she'd promised to give her sister a fair chance. It hadn't quite been a month. A few more like this one, and she'd come running home before Ellie had to interfere at all.

"Fine." Becca smiled. "I can't stay long. I just wanted to drop in and see how you're doing."

"Do you have time enough to stay for supper, or will *he* get angry with you?" As soon as the words left her mouth, she winced. When it came to Tony and the way he treated her sister, sometimes she just couldn't control her temper. She had to keep in mind that Becca was her *sister*, not her daughter. If their mother wanted to run interference, she was more than welcome to try. But Ellie really had no right to step in, at least not quite yet.

"*Ellie*," Becca moaned in typical teenage fashion. "He's a nice guy. Leave him alone."

Calling Tony nice was like calling a gunshot wound pleasant. Still, Becca was eighteen years old, still a child, but recognized by the government as an adult. Ellie's hands were tied. "Sorry. I'm sure he's wonderful." *Gag.* "Why don't you sit down? I made spaghetti." She had to force the next sentence out. "Do you want to take some home to Tony? I could make a plate..."

"No thanks. Tony doesn't like spaghetti." Becca dug in as soon as Ellie set the plate in front of her. Ellie's heart clenched at the sight. The girl was skinny enough already, and in the past few weeks had started looking borderline anorexic. According to their mother, Becca and Ellie took after their father with their tall, lean frames. Charlotte, the lucky one, got all the curves. Ellie knew she was sometimes self-conscious of her body, but she didn't have any reason. At least she didn't look like a crudely drawn stick figure when she wore a sundress.

All three girls had their mother's coloring—fair skin and blue eyes with dark, nearly black hair. That, more than anything else, had children pegging them as weird from almost their first days of school. Making friends hadn't been easy for any of them, and they'd all found their outlets to deal with it—Ellie in her art, Becca in rebellion, and Charlotte in risk-taking and a heavy preoccupation with anything occult. Her current occupation as a ghost hunter had probably chased her husband away more than the witchcraft.

"Tony doesn't like much of anything, does he?" Charlotte came into the room and tossed her backpack onto the counter before she spooned some spaghetti into a bowl and sat across from Becca. "You tell him that if he hangs up on me one more time he's going to have a serious problem."

"When did he hang up on you?" Becca asked in between bites.

"This afternoon. He wouldn't even tell me if you were home or not." Charlotte shook her head, her hair brushing across her shoulders. "I swear, Becca, I have no idea what you see in that guy. You wouldn't think it would be a problem for him to give you a message if you were out."

"I worked this afternoon. I wasn't at home." Becca sounded confused. Ellie thought she saw the first sparks of doubt in her sister's eyes, and she silently cheered. But when she spoke again, she continued to defend the jerk. "He got a job at the grocery store in Randall, and he's been working the overnight shift stocking shelves. You probably woke him up."

"He's working?" Ellie and Charlotte asked at the same time.

"Well, yeah," Becca answered like they should have expected it. "Did you think he was going to sit around on the couch forever?"

Actually, Ellie had. And it would have made things a whole lot easier. She'd find a way to get Becca away from Tony, even if she had to resort to calling in muscle like Royce and Marco for help.

"Are you seeing Royce tonight?" Becca asked, obviously looking to change the subject.

"No."

"Are you getting tired of him yet?" Charlotte chimed in. "Because I'd be glad to take him off your hands for a little while."

"He's way too old for you, kiddo."

Charlotte laughed. "He's way too old for you, too. That doesn't stop you from seeing him."

The subject didn't come up often with them, but they knew that Royce and his family were vampires. Marco had been their grandmother's neighbor when they were kids, and it was kind of hard not to notice how he hadn't aged in twenty years.

Charlotte and Becca had been too young to understand it then, but Ellie had noticed right away that he was different. In her mind, he'd taken over the role of a big brother, or the father figure she'd never really had since her own had taken off a month after Becca was born. She'd learned to love painting through Marco, and that had given her a career as well as an outlet for her frustrations. He'd never mentioned the vampire thing, but she'd always had her suspicions. By the time she turned seventeen and he'd gotten the guts to confess, she'd already known for three years.

Charlotte's voice broke into her thoughts, and Ellie turned her focus back to the conversation. "Of course it's romantic. Spending an eternity with the man you love, having amazing sex, living most of your life at night—"

"And drinking blood?" Becca wrinkled her nose in disgust. "*Eww.*"

"Well, you've got to make some sacrifices for love. Right, Ellie?"

"Yeah, sure." She left the two of them to debate the supposedly romantic side of vampirism while she concentrated on cleaning up after dinner.

Somehow, she just couldn't imagine that Royce's life was all that romantic.

Chapter 3

The next day, Ellie prepared herself for time at her easel. The air conditioner in the studio window started with a *thump*, followed by a low whine. Almost time for a new one, if she could fit it into her budget. It promised to be another scorching summer, and Ellie didn't foresee the ancient unit lasting through the end of June. She could probably scrape together the cash, as soon as she convinced Charlotte to find a steady job with a regular paycheck and start to chip in some money for household expenses. The woman was twenty-five, a little too old to be expecting a free ride.

She placed two candles—rosemary for mental clarity, and pine for protection—on glass dishes on top of a small round table in the corner of the room and lit them before setting up her painting supplies and settling in on a stool in front of her easel. She clipped a picture she'd taken a few days ago of the rocky shoreline to a small stand on her supply table and went to work. Normally she preferred to work from live subjects as opposed to photographs, but in this weather, spending time outside wasn't high on her list.

"Do you always leave your door unlocked?"

She jumped a mile when she heard the deep, smooth voice behind her. Her hand flying to cover her heart—the paintbrush clasped tightly in it smearing blue paint along her jaw line—and spun to face the unexpected visitor.

Eric Malcolm.

He stood in the open doorway, his shoulder propped against the doorframe and his arms crossed over his chest. The hard look in his eyes and the grim set of his jaw unnerved her. She swallowed hard even as something in her sparked to life at the sight of him. What was he doing here? She'd invited him to view her work in the gallery, not come over to her home studio. The fact that he'd been able to find her with apparent ease made her stomach clench into a knot, anxiety and arousal in equal parts mixing within her.

She understood the anxiety. The man was a stranger, a *dark* stranger who probably had quite a few dark secrets. But the arousal mystified her. She'd never been this attracted to someone she didn't know before, especially not a man who scared her nearly as much as he fascinated her. She took a moment to compose herself before she spoke, not willing to give him a hint at her inner confusion.

"I live out in the middle of nowhere. I'm not usually disturbed when I'm working." She let out a frustrated breath, not sure whether she was more annoyed with his presence, or her exaggerated reaction. "Besides, the decent thing would be to call before you visit someone."

"I tried. No one answered."

"You called?" she parroted, surprised at his answer.

He nodded, a humorous smile playing across his lips. "And I knocked on your front door. No one answered there, either. Then your grandmother came out of her apartment and told me where to find you."

She nearly groaned. If Carol had gotten to him, Ellie would never hear the end of it.

"How did you know where I live?"

He shrugged. "Telephone book. There's only one listing for A. Holmes, and I took a chance that it would be you."

She blinked. "It was that easy, huh?"

She hadn't been hiding, but she hadn't expected anyone to actually look up her address and seek her out, either. It hadn't helped that she'd blurted out her full name when he'd flustered her in the park. Most people weren't even aware that the nickname "Ellie" came from her middle name, and not her first.

His expression bordered on predatory for a second before his gentleman mask slipped back into place. He shrugged elegantly, his gaze mild, and she began to wonder if she was imagining the whole mysterious aura about him. "It was easy, yes, but I would have found you anyway. I needed to see you again."

"Oh." Shocked speechless by his declaration, it took her a full minute to find her voice. She turned back to her canvas. "Well...it's not very nice to sneak up on people."

He was silent for so long she thought he'd left. When she felt him right behind her, she gasped. He reached his hand up and brushed his fingers over her jaw, sending ripples of sensation through her nerves. She shivered and a glint of humor sparkled in his eyes.

"Paint," he said softly as he pulled his hand away, his fingertips blue.

She nodded, still recovering from her reaction to his brief touch. When she spoke, her voice was barely above a whisper. "I'll get it off later."

He grabbed a rag off her supply table and brought it to her face, rubbing the paint spot gently. The circular motion of the rough cloth in his hands sent tiny quivers down her spine, like little bolts of lightning. She held her breath, her gaze locked with his, while he attempted to remove the paint from her skin.

Why did her heart have to beat so hard when he was around? The worst part was she knew he could hear it. He could probably *feel* it from all the way across the room. But she couldn't control the intense reaction to having him stand so close, touching her in a way that shouldn't feel so familiar, but did. "If...if you don't mind, I have work to do."

One corner of his mouth lifted mockingly. "No time for a little conversation while you work?"

"I don't even know you." And conversation would be a very bad idea, since when he got within twenty feet of her, her brain refused to function.

He cocked his head to the side and furrowed his brow. "I told you who I am."

"Telling me your name doesn't constitute getting to know you." She reached up to brush away the hand still caressing her skin, but he grabbed her wrist and turned it, bringing her palm up to his lips and kissing the center. *Oh, goddess.* She sighed, her insides melting at the warmth of his lips against her sensitive skin. The gesture was shockingly intimate coming from a virtual stranger, but it felt *right*.

That idea was almost unsettling enough for her to get over her schoolgirl crush. *Almost.* She tried her best for cool and aloof, thinking she'd pulled it off until he laughed. "What's so funny?"

"Why are you so afraid of me?"

"It's the twenty-first century. It isn't safe to trust strangers."

"I agree." He smiled and arousal hit her hard and fast. "I'd like to get to know you. Do you have time for a break, at least?"

She shook her head, but felt her resistance slipping a little more.

"One quick cup of coffee? I promise I don't mean you any harm. You can trust me."

The expression on his face seemed sincere. On the surface, he looked like a nice, calm man. But deep in his eyes, there was something dark and foreboding. That was what set her on edge—the unknown of what this man could be. She wondered if the perfect gentleman act was just that—*an act*. Did she really want him to stick around long enough to find out?

"I really don't think that's such a great idea." She set her brush down and got up from the stool, walking out the wide-open studio door. Despite the air conditioner, the tension-filled air clogged her lungs and burned in her chest. The outside air wasn't much better, but at least she didn't feel stifled in a confined space with a man who radiated enough electricity to power an entire neighborhood. He followed, and she turned to face him, her hands on her hips. "You need to leave now. I don't have time for this, whatever *this* is. I have a family that needs me."

"Children?" He looked surprised.

"They might as well be." She grimaced at the thought. "My sisters. They're both adults, they just don't always act like it. And Carol, my grandmother. But you've already met her."

"Oh." He looked decidedly relieved. "I'm sure they can fend for themselves for a little while, and I'm sure it wouldn't hurt for you to take some time to yourself."

She blinked and turned away, his words hitting too close to home. She rounded the corner of the garage studio and stopped when she saw her grandmother's white insulated carafe and a couple of mugs in the patio table.

"What is this?" she yelled over her shoulder. He didn't answer, just kept walking until he was inches away. He'd stopped before their bodies touched, but he was still too close. She felt the heat radiate from his body and his breath on the back of her neck. Her heart skidded to a stop before it thumped loudly in her chest. Her pulse raced and she drew a deep, shaky breath, clutching onto the table so she didn't fall down.

She'd *never* reacted like this to a man before. What was her problem now?

"Just one cup of coffee. That's all." He spoke in a slow, measured whisper that she could only describe as seductive. "I promise. Your grandmother went to all this trouble, told me to make sure you took a break. You wouldn't want to disappoint her, would you?"

His words played along her senses, making every nerve in her body feel raw and exposed. "No. I wouldn't."

'Then do you think you could spare five minutes of your time?"

"It's too hot for coffee," she protested weakly.

"Your grandmother thought this would make you happy. Can you just sit and talk with me for a little while? I promise I won't bite."

She wasn't too sure of that, but it didn't matter. At this point in time, with him so close and her body screaming for him to get closer, she'd give him just about anything he wanted.

"Outside? Won't being out in the sun bother you?"

She heard the confusion in his tone when he answered. "No. Why would it?"

Not the reaction she'd expected. Very strange. "Okay. Fine. I'll have coffee with you." She couldn't see him, but she was pretty sure he was smiling. She added hastily, more for her benefit than his, "Just one cup. That's all."

"I wouldn't expect anything more." The humor and triumph were evident in his voice.

She flopped down into one of the cushioned outdoor chairs, too embarrassed by her apparent willingness to bend to his will to speak. What was wrong with her? If she didn't know any better, she'd think his voice alone had the power to hypnotize her into agreement. She closed her eyes and breathed deeply, the scent of roses and tulips heavy in the air. He poured her coffee before filling his own mug, then slid the small pitcher of milk across the table to her and took a seat.

"No sugar?" she asked, pouring milk into the steaming coffee—not what she'd usually drink on a hot day, but Carol had gone to the trouble of making it so she'd deal.

"You don't take sugar in your coffee."

"How would you know that?" she asked, but then realized Carol had most likely told him. She'd have to remind her grandmother of the dangers of talking to strangers.

"Ellie," he said softly, as if testing the sound of her name on his lips. "Tell me something about yourself, Ellie."

She liked the way he said it, heck, she liked the way he said *anything*. As long as he kept talking, she'd sit here all day.

"There isn't much to tell." She sipped her coffee, the brew so strong it tasted like it had been laced with lemon juice. It amazed her that Carol could work any spell given to her, yet hadn't managed in her eighty-odd years to master the coffee maker. "I've lived here most of my life. As you've obviously seen, I set up a studio in my garage for my painting. My mother moved to Georgia with my stepfather a few years ago, leaving my two younger sisters in my care. My grandmother just moved into the apartment above my garage a short while ago."

His expression was interested, and concerned. "It sounds like you take care of everyone."

He didn't even know the half of it. "I do okay."

"Why don't you tell me something about you? Your family sounds interesting, but that's not why I'm here."

She found herself watching his lips move when he spoke, and wondering what it would be like to kiss him. She was having a harder and harder time keeping up her end of the conversation. "I'm not a very interesting person. I work at home, keep to myself most of the time, and I have only a few close friends in town."

He nodded slowly. "That's a start. What about your hopes? Your dreams?"

She scoffed at that. "I'm living my dream."

"Taking care of everyone? Having no time for yourself?" He shook his head and leaned across the table, his eyes dark. "What kind of dreams are those?"

"They're *my* dreams. I have a nice home, a wonderful family, and my painting, which I love. What more could I ask for?" She squinted at him through the bright sunlight, looking for humor in his expression. She found none.

"You're a talented artist, Ellie. Before I came to find you today, I took a look at the paintings in the gallery."

A wave of anxiety washed over her at his words. "If you say so."

"You aren't making getting to know you very easy."

"It shouldn't be." She smiled in triumph, finally getting some of her footing back. "Now how about you tell me about you?"

"I don't have many living family members. Just one younger sister. I travel whenever I get the chance."

"What do you do for a living?" She sipped her coffee while she waited for his answer.

"This and that. I own a couple of small companies."

His eyes met hers, and she knew he'd lied to her. For some reason, he seemed to want her to call him on it. So she didn't. "That must keep you busy."

"It does. But like I said, I enjoy traveling whenever my schedule permits."

Yeah, right. Why was he lying to her, and why didn't she feel threatened by it? For some reason, she was warming to him, even knowing he wasn't being entirely truthful.

He set his mug down on the table, his fingers brushing hers in the process, something she thought wasn't an accident.

She drained the last of her coffee, needing to be away from him before she begged him to strip her and take her right there in the middle of the yard. "I have to get back to work now."

"Are you interested in having dinner with me?"

"I don't think that's a good idea."

"Why not? You do eat, don't you?"

She set her mug on the table with a thump. "Of course. I just don't date men I don't know." *Especially men who don't eat.*

Eric was a vampire. She couldn't let herself forget that.

She didn't expect him to give up easily, and he didn't disappoint. "How will you get to know me if you don't take a chance?"

She hesitated just a moment. "I'm…kind of seeing someone." It wasn't exactly a lie. Well, maybe it was now that she and Royce had called it quits. But the excuse protected her from her intense reaction to Eric. If he thought she was seeing someone else, especially a man as big and powerful as Royce, he'd leave her alone.

Yeah, sure he would. Eric wasn't as tall or as big as Royce, but he had a commanding presence around him. His strength seemed to come from somewhere inside as well as the physical. She had a feeling he could hold his own with even someone like Royce or Marco.

A shadow passed over his eyes and his hands clenched tight around his mug. "Is it serious?"

She started to say yes, but she couldn't. She couldn't lie about that. "No."

He smiled, his teeth flashing white. "Then I see no harm in a simple dinner."

Simple didn't seem to fit the situation, or anything having to do with Eric. He was complex, unnerving, and entirely too sure of himself for her comfort. But she couldn't deny the fact that she was curious, and attracted, and maybe one dinner wouldn't be so bad. "Okay. Only dinner, though. I don't want you to expect anything more."

"Can I pick you up tonight at seven?"

"I'll meet you downtown, at the front entrance of the park, at seven."

She waited for him to protest, and he looked like he might, but in the end he agreed to her terms. "Good. I'll let you get back to your work now. I'll see you tonight."

He stood and walked away, leaving her at the table wondering how she would get through an entire meal when she could barely make it through a cup of coffee with her willpower remaining intact.

Chapter 4

"You have another date? Isn't that two or three this week? I think this is a record for you." Charlotte stood in the door, munching on a bowl of popcorn while she watched Ellie get ready for her dinner with Eric. "Is it with Royce, or someone different?"

Ellie sighed, but didn't bother to correct her sister's assumption. No sense confessing she was pretty much a failure when it came to relationships. "I'm allowed to date, Charlotte."

"It's about time you figured that one out." Charlotte laughed and tossed a piece of popcorn at Ellie. "Wear your hair down. It looks sexier that way."

Ellie paused, her hair half-piled on her head. "Really?" She let her hair drop, fluffing it as it fell past her shoulders. "You don't think it looks too…boring?"

Charlotte just rolled her eyes and ignored the question. "Are you going to sleep with him?"

"No." *Not tonight.* With the way things sparked between them, she couldn't make any guarantees beyond that. She was definitely attracted, and she wouldn't mind pursuing something further, provided he wasn't some kind of depraved psychopath. Or worse.

Married.

"I think you should." Charlotte smiled. "Is he as hot as Royce?"

Ellie swiped some red lip-gloss over her lips to match her red dress. "That's enough. You don't need to know any of this." She wasn't going to talk about Eric until she knew more about him. She knew his name, and that was about it. But she wanted to get to know him, despite her earlier promise to herself to not get involved with anyone right now.

"Grandma said some man named Eric came around looking for you. She said he was really nice, and pretty easy to look at, too." Charlotte smiled at Ellie through the mirror and helped her adjust the thin straps of the dress. "Is that the guy?"

Ellie sighed. Leave it to Carol, the one-woman grapevine. "Yes. Now shoo. I need to finish getting ready."

Charlotte walked into the bedroom and pulled a pair of four-inch spiked heels out of Ellie's closet, ones Ellie had worn one time to a costume party where she'd nearly broken her ankle walking up the front steps. "Wear these. They'll make your legs look incredible."

And they'd make it impossible to make a quick escape, if necessary. "I don't think so. I'm tall enough without them. I don't want to look like some kind of giant freak." She grabbed a pair of tan leather sandals instead, slipping them on before she walked out of the room.

Charlotte followed her downstairs and into the kitchen, still talking while Ellie grabbed her purse and keys. "I still can't believe you're meeting him downtown. I would have made my date drive out here and get me."

Just as she got to the front door, Ellie turned to her sister. "If I want to meet my date instead of having him pick me up, I can. If I want to pay for the meal, I can do that, too. Why don't you give Doug a call and try to work out your marriage and let me have a moment to breathe here."

Charlotte sulked, her mood turning stormy. "Doug's an idiot. Just go out and have fun, okay. Don't worry about my marriage, Ellie. I can take care of myself."

She slammed the bowl of popcorn on the counter and stalked out of the room without another word. Ellie watched her walk down the hall, her hands clenched into fists at her sides, and realized she should leave the subject of the failed marriage alone, at least for a little while. Maybe Royce was right—she needed to start concentrating on her own life and let everyone else live theirs.

She drove downtown instead of walking the mile, because she wanted an easy out in case Eric turned out to be a major creep. Her grandmother would call her a fool for even seeing him with the doubts she had, but she needed to do it. She had to find out more about him before she made her judgments.

Eric was already there, leaning against a fence post, when she pulled up in front of the park. He rested one hand on a fence post with the other in the front pocket of his dark slacks, his stance casual. Before she got out of the car, she took a deep breath, gathering her courage and calming her nerves. When she finally felt ready, she stepped out of the car and walked over to where he waited. The light gray shirt he wore brought out a metallic quality in his eyes, almost liquid, that she hadn't noticed before. In the muted lighting of the fading sun, they looked like strands of glittering gold in the clear emerald of his eyes.

"Hi." She smiled nervously, fidgeting from foot to foot. She hadn't had an actual date in years, not since before her marriage. What she'd been doing with Royce couldn't exactly be called dating—not that it would be much better with Eric. Going out to dinner with a vampire didn't hold a lot of appeal. But spending a few hours with a man who fascinated her did. Her curiosity had forced her to accept his offer, even when her commonsense had called her a fool.

He didn't say anything—he didn't have to. His gaze roamed over her with excruciating slowness, heating her whole body to the boiling point. She struggled to draw a breath, sure her skin must be close to the color of the dress by now. Why had she chosen to wear the little sundress tonight? She would have been much more comfortable in her navy blue short set, or even a pair of jeans. Maybe then she wouldn't have the distinct impression that he was undressing her with his eyes.

His gaze stopped at her neckline and his brow furrowed. "Interesting necklace."

Her hand flew to her neck and her fingers clutched the totem. "It was a gift from my grandmother for my eighth birthday."

"You've had it for that long?"

She nodded, her hands starting to shake. A faint electrical smell hung in the air, promising a summer thunderstorm.

"A panther is a strange choice for a little girl."

"Not really. Ever since I was little, it's been my favorite animal." Not a lie, exactly, but he didn't need to know the real reason her grandmother had bought her the totem. "Are you ready to go?"

Eric hesitated before he answered, his brow furrowed and his gaze challenging. "Yeah, sure. Lead the way."

They walked to a little restaurant down the street, one Ellie frequented with her sisters. The food was good, the atmosphere quiet, and the dining area open enough that she had plenty of choices for escape routes if needed.

Eric surprised her by ordering, and eating, a big meal. She blinked at his clean plate, when she still had half her food left. "Hungry?"

He narrowed his eyes for a second before he smiled, leaning forward in the chair. "Starved."

She gulped, suddenly struck with the idea that he wasn't talking about food. "Oh."

His smile widened, only making him appear more predatory. "Why do you seem so surprised that I've eaten?"

"I would have thought your preferred meal would come from a blood bank." She paused and shook her head. "No, you don't look much like the bagged type. I think you'd rather have it fresh, straight from the source. Am I right?"

"Bagged type?" He looked confused for a moment, and then he burst out laughing. "What exactly do you think I am?"

Did he really think he was fooling her? "A vampire." She raised her eyebrows, daring him to deny what was so obvious.

Or at least what *had been*, before she watched him down an entire steak and baked potato in the time it took her to eat two bites of chicken.

His expression turned stormy. "A vampire? Oh God, no. Don't insult me like that."

His tone was light, humorous even, but she suspected her statement had truly offended him. That made no sense. She couldn't be wrong about this, it just wasn't possible. If he wasn't a vampire, what else could he be?

"What are you?" she asked before she could stop herself. As soon as the words were out of her mouth, she wanted to take them back. It didn't matter what he was. The man was obviously a complete lunatic, or a very impressive liar. There was something about him that just screamed "supernatural being" and "vampire" seemed to fit.

"What makes you think I'm any different than you?" He bit off a large chunk of bread and popped it into his mouth. She waited for him to finish chewing before he continued. "I'm just a regular guy, Ellie."

Right. "You know, even if you are a vampire, I wouldn't care. I have a few vampire friends, and it honestly doesn't bother me."

"Oh, yeah?" An amused half-smile lit his face. "Well, I'm sorry to disappoint you, but feeding on blood isn't an integral part of my survival." He leaned even closer across the table, so close that his breath feathered across her skin. He smiled knowingly, as if he was about to share a secret, and spoke in hushed tones that went straight to her clit. "But I might bite, if you're really, really good."

In her head, she knew letting him talk to her that way on a first date was a *very* bad idea. But her body disagreed, arching toward him almost of its own volition. She snapped herself back, leaning into the chair to separate herself from whatever it was about him that caused her brain cells to go into sleep mode.

"Don't trust me yet?" He sat back and took a big sip of his water, his gaze following her every move.

He seemed to find her dilemma amusing, and she fought the urge to wipe the smug smile off his handsome face. "Why should I trust you? You just threatened to bite me." She crossed her arms over her chest to hide the most blatant evidence of her arousal.

She *should not* react to his candor in this way. That wasn't what nice girls like her did. She should slap him and take herself home before she let this go any further.

She gulped as she realized he was looking at *her* as if she was his next meal. That knocked a smidgen of sense into her, considering she wasn't entirely convinced that the man *wasn't* a vampire. "Well, vampire or not, I'm not into feeding for kicks. It doesn't do anything for me."

"I take it you've had experience?"

"By necessity only. It's not like I go around looking for someone to drink my blood." Just the thought turned her stomach.

His grin widened. "Who said anything about becoming my *meal*? Perhaps I'm interested in something else entirely."

"And what would that be?" She was having a difficult time keeping up the false bravado when her body wanted to melt into a puddle in her seat. Maybe she shouldn't fight it so hard. Maybe if she just let him touch her, kiss her even, she'd get over whatever this was and be capable of normalcy again. She'd find out that he really was just an ordinary man, no more capable of arousing her than any of the men she'd ever dated.

Ha! Ordinary wasn't a fitting description, and she knew deep inside that he was *nothing* like any of the men she'd dated. Her mouth went dry at the thought.

"Do you even have to ask what I want from you?" he asked, his voice barely above a whisper. His eyes narrowed and the darkness she'd glimpsed in them before was now front-and-center. "If you don't, then I guess I'm getting a little rusty."

She blinked. He didn't even try to hide it. It was the first time he'd let her see him as anything less than a perfect gentleman. She liked it. A lot. Her panties were damp just being this close to him, listening to him talk to her so frankly. She wondered how much of a gentleman he'd be when he wasn't trying to impress a woman—how much of a gentleman he'd be in bed.

Just as quickly as it had appeared, the darkness vanished. He took her hand in his and kissed the top of it. Then he turned it over and kissed the underside of her wrist. A shiver ran down her arm, followed by an electrical spark of pain and pleasure when he nipped lightly at her sensitive skin. She tried to pull her hand away, glancing around the restaurant to make sure no one was watching, but the other diners were all too engrossed in their own conversations to notice.

Time to slow this down a bit. He was a stranger. She'd been out with him once, twice if she counted twenty minutes in her backyard as a date. She knew practically nothing about him, and vampire or not, he wasn't safe. As a general rule, she didn't indulge in one-night stands, and she'd learned from her time with Royce that she really wasn't cut out for even casual flings. She needed serious, steady commitment, and she highly doubted a man like Eric would be willing for that kind of a relationship. He was too intense, too…dark to be truly interested in what she had to offer.

Still, she was definitely attracted to him, and to the air of danger about him. She could pretend and deny it all she wanted, but there was definitely something there between them. She'd never felt that kind of connection before. Someone up there had a sick sense of humor—she would have preferred the man who finally stirred her to at least be of the mortal race.

"You need time to think about this," he said, bringing her out of her thoughts. "Why is it that you can accept that you think I'm a vampire—which you *are* wrong about, by the way— but you can't accept that there's chemistry between us?"

There *was* that, in spades. But every time she thought about getting deeply involved, Todd's face formed in her mind. She wanted the closeness, the intimacy of an exclusive relationship, but she just didn't know if she had the emotional strength to handle the bad that came along with the good. "It just isn't what I'm looking for. I'm not able to commit to any kind of a relationship right now, so no matter what you are, you can stop wasting your time." *You are such a liar, Ann Elizabeth!*

"Sometimes you go looking for one thing, but find something entirely different. Would you give up something that has so much potential, just because you weren't looking for it?"

"What are you talking about? I've known you for two days." Her denial sounded weak, even to her own ears. He knew she was lying, she could see it in his eyes. But she couldn't seem to stop. This went against everything inside her, everything she'd been raised to believe in, but she didn't know how much longer she'd be able to fight against what she really wanted.

When he spoke, his voice was low and husky. "Ellie, I've had a thousand years to decide what I do, and *don't* look for in a woman. I want to get to know you better. *Much* better."

A strong breeze could have blown her out of her chair at that moment. "A thousand years?" she repeated, her voice dangerously close to a squeak. "What are you?"

"Yes, Ellie. A thousand years. Does that bother you?" He asked, completely ignoring her second question.

If he'd lived for a thousand years, but he wasn't a vampire, what did that make him? She probably should have done more reading in the occult books Charlotte had kept around when they were kids. She swallowed hard, truly afraid of the answer. "I don't know. I think it does. You can't just casually dump something like that on me. It's a little hard to take."

"Thank you for being honest. Will you please give me a little time to convince you?"

"I don't even know what you are," she said softly, knowing that even as she denied him her answer she slowly lost the battle between her mind and body. Even her instincts, usually impeccable, warred with each other. Half of her knew she should run far away and never look back, while the other half wanted to give herself over to whatever he wanted. The battle raging inside her mind confused her. As a rule, she prided herself on her clear thinking, but it seemed around him she wasn't capable.

"We'll talk about it when it's time," Eric said softly, his voice unbearably gentle. "I don't want to scare you."

She sucked in a shaky breath, wiping her sweaty palms on her thighs and willing her heart rate to return to a more normal level. "You just did."

"I'll never hurt you. Ever."

He stared at her for a long time, his gaze dark and sensual and...very convincing. She had a feeling he was doing something to her to make her accept him, but she'd let him get away with it. For now. "Okay, but I'm warning you. I'm really not interested." She squeezed her thighs together, since the sound of his voice alone was now enough to drive her to the brink.

"You don't need to be." He said one thing, but his gaze told her something entirely different.

He *knew*. He knew how aroused she was, and he was having a great time playing with her. For a moment, she got the impression that this was all some kind of a game—like a cat toying with a mouse before he ate it for dinner. A whimper escaped her before she could stop it, and she covered her anxiety with a glare.

She had to get control of herself before she turned into some quivering idiot. She pulled herself away from the situation mentally, forcing her mind into a tranquil place. Her thoughts cleared, but it took a great deal of effort to slam that mental door. When she spoke, she sounded more like herself than she had all evening. "This conversation is heading in a direction I'm not comfortable with. Maybe we should talk about something else now."

An expression resembling annoyance passed over his face before he smiled. He raised an eyebrow, but didn't say anything to contradict her. *Smart man.*

For the rest of the meal, she kept the conversation trained on safe, but admittedly boring, topics. Tension hung thick in the air between them, but it couldn't be helped. She wouldn't allow what she *thought* she felt for the man to cloud her decisions. When she had time at home, alone, to think about it all, she'd be better equipped to decide what to do about him.

Eric paid for the meal, despite Ellie's insistence to pay for half, and walked her back to her car. The sun had set, and they had the quiet street mostly to themselves.

They stopped by her car and Eric opened the door for her. He was such an intriguing mix of old-school gentleman and wild man that she couldn't help but be curious of what lay beneath the surface. She had a feeling it would be more of the latter. "Thanks for dinner," she said as she turned toward her car.

"I'm glad you agreed, even if you don't feel entirely comfortable around me."

The tone of his voice made her pause and pivot back toward him. "I—"

"No lies, Ellie. I haven't lied to you. I don't expect you to lie to me."

The harshness in his words made her heart stutter. Illuminated by the old-fashioned street lamps that lined the park entrance, he stood with his feet wide and his shoulders squared, his chest heaving with each breath. At that moment, it struck her that he reminded her of the panther that hung around her neck—strong, dark, sleek, and ready to pounce. A shiver ran through her and she clasped the totem so tightly it bit into her palm.

He backed her to the side of her car, bracketing his feet on either side of hers. He cupped her face in his palm and leaned in, brushing his lips over her mouth. She ignited like a brush fire burning straight to her toes. She wrapped her arms around his neck and leaned back against her car. Her mind shut down completely, allowing her body to step up to the controls as he released her face and settled his palms on her waist. From there the kiss got quickly out of hand.

Eric slid his hands up her sides until he cupped her breasts in his palms. He delved his tongue into her mouth and nibbled on her lower lip with his teeth. As his thigh came up between her legs, she rested herself on him. He had to feel how wet she was, even through the layers of the fabric. That thought turned her on even more, and she reached a hand between them to brush her fingers over his cock. He was hard, and large, and she wanted him right there against the side of the car, in the backseat, or the hood. She wasn't in a position to be picky.

Well before she'd had enough, Eric broke the kiss and stepped away. "*My God.*"

"What's wrong?" Her mind was still cloudy from the intensity of the kiss, and she shook her head to free herself from the sensual fog.

He laughed bitterly, turning away. "Don't you know? You should go home. *Now.*"

"Why?" Why would he possibly want to stop? Didn't he feel the spark between them, threatening to ignite and burn out of control at the slightest provocation?

Was she out of her mind? She'd just met him a couple days ago.

"It shouldn't be this way," he continued, raking a hand through his hair. He shook his head vigorously, as if trying to shake some sense into himself.

"*What* shouldn't?" She let irritation creep into her voice, hoping it would goad him into explaining his cryptic comments.

The kiss had obviously left him shaken, even more so than her, and she wanted to know why.

He turned back to her, a look of desperation in his eyes. "This...us. I-I need to get back to my hotel. I have an early morning tomorrow."

She couldn't help the little whimper of disappointment that escaped her lips. The emotions he evoked in her were too strong, too powerful. She felt like he was consuming her, and, goddess help her, she wanted the feeling to continue as long as possible. "But I—"

"Have a safe drive home, Ellie," he interrupted with such finality she didn't bother to protest. She blinked at the hard look in his eyes, a twinge of fear returning, and got into her car. Not until she was safely on the road back home did she let out the breath she hadn't realized she'd been holding.

* * * * *

Ellie raced through the woods, the sensitive soles of her bare feet scraping against the rough leaves and twigs that covered the dirt floor. The scent of impending rain filled the humid air. The chilled night breeze rippled over her flesh, making her shiver. The moon, full and yellow, sat in the sky high above the tops of the trees, casting an eerie golden glow on the world around her.

She broke free of the woods and found herself in her back yard. She stopped, the breath heaving in and out of her lungs from the exertion. The sky opened and rain began to fall. Her hair hung heavy all around her as the water poured over her. Her white nightgown clung to her body, now sheer and useless. A growl nearby her caught her attention and she pivoted toward it. A black panther watched her from the edge of the trees, crouched low to the ground as if ready to pounce. She instinctively backed up a step, afraid of the fire in the animal's glowing gold and green eyes.

The panther stayed in its place at the edge of the woods, its gaze never leaving hers. She opened her mouth to speak, or maybe to cry out for help, but no sound came. She couldn't move, could barely breathe, as the cat took a step in her direction. This was different from her normal visions. The panther's eyes held a quality that was almost human.

Finally, she willed her legs to move and she turned to run. A low tree branch snagged the hem of her nightgown and pulled her back. The snapping of twigs behind her let her know the animal was close behind. A scream tore from her throat when she couldn't get her footing. She looked over her shoulder just as a large paw landed in the center of her back, knocking her to her knees. Her hands hit the scratchy carpet of leaves and sharp jolts of pain ran up her wrists. The breath whooshed out of her lungs and she coughed, struggling to pull out of its grasp. She tried to push herself back into a standing position, but the panther covered her with its body, leaving her unable to move.

"Don't fight me," a deep voice rasped in her ear—a familiar voice that made her body go limp.

"Eric?"

She glanced over her shoulder, surprised to find it was Eric, not a wild animal, holding her down. She looked around the woods, but saw no panther anywhere. "How did you get here?"

"It doesn't matter." He pulled at her nightgown as he spoke, tearing the fragile material to shreds with his fingers. Sharp claws dug into the flesh of her thighs. Teeth stung her neck and shoulders. Her blood boiled, every heartbeat working her closer to fevered arousal until she couldn't stand another second.

"Eric," she moaned, her voice barely above a whisper.

The wind took the fabric as Eric tore it from her body. She watched it sail away into the night, floating like gossamer ghosts in the sky. The night air fanned over her heated flesh and she shivered. The blood rushed in her ears, drowning out the sounds of the forest. He dipped his hand between her legs and stroked along her slit. Her cunt contracted as his rough fingertips skimmed the smooth, tender flesh. His hand wrapped in her hair and pulled until her back arched, exposing her sex like an offering. And then he was inside her. She hadn't expected the heavy thrust of his cock, and she gasped as he filled her in one complete, agonizing stroke. He stretched her to the point of pain, only adding to her growing arousal.

Her nipples beaded and her clit ached, the wind teasing her every nerve. She felt stripped bare—lust and mortification mixing equally within her. He slammed into her hard, rocking her body forward. The rough ground bit into her knees and palms, but she didn't want him to stop. She never wanted it to end.

All too soon, her body exploded in climax, her cunt clenching around his thrusting cock. She screamed her release, the sound echoing across the night. Starlight burst out all around her just before her world went black.

* * * * *

Ellie woke with a start, sweat coating her body. Her breathing was labored, her vision cloudy, and every muscle in her body tense. She blinked and glanced around, surprised to find herself alone in her bed. The dream had been so real. Her legs were tangled in the sheet, the blanket on the floor, and her panties soaked. Her cunt still pulsed with tremors from the powerful orgasm. What was happening to her? She'd had lucid dreams in the past, but nothing compared to what she'd just experienced.

It felt like she'd been there. She'd felt the cool breeze on her skin, the heated flesh of Eric against her back – the claws grazing her skin. Flipping on the lamp on the bedside table, she pulled the covers back to examine her legs. Nothing. She let out a sigh of relief. She'd been certain she would have found scratches left by...the panther? Eric? She didn't know. It didn't matter. The skin on her legs remained unmarred. It had been just a dream. A strange and disturbing dream, but it hadn't been real.

Frustrated with her sudden inability to distinguish between dreams and reality, she climbed out of bed and walked to the window. The clock on the dresser read 4:20. It was still dark outside, but it wouldn't be for long. Now would be a perfect time for a jog.

She ran her usual route, a giant circle around the back roads that took her a little over an hour to complete. The humidity that hung in the air made the run more difficult than usual, and by the time she turned the corner toward home, her legs felt full of cement and her lungs burned. But her mind had cleared, allowing her to step back and look at things calmly. She had a feeling she'd need that mental clarity in the days to come.

She heard the shrill ring of the phone as she walked through the front door. No one would call at this hour unless it was an emergency. She grabbed it and answered, still out of breath.

Amara's voice sounded strained. "Ellie, where have you been?"

"I went running. What's wrong?"

"There was a murder in town. The police found a body behind the Blue Moon Café late last night."

A chill ran down her spine. That was the restaurant where she and Eric had dinner. "What happened?"

"All I've learned from the news is that the victim was a young woman who died of blood loss."

Ellie's blood turned to ice in her veins. "*Blood loss?*"

"Yeah, lots. Like all of it." Amara went silent for a minute. "You know it wasn't any of us, right?"

Ellie had an idea of what her friend was thinking. She spoke without hesitation. "Of course. I know you would never hurt anyone."

"That means there's another vampire around, someone who isn't so polite."

Amara's voice held a distressed quality that made Ellie nervous. If Amara was worried, that meant the problem was serious.

Eric. The thought was out before she could stop it. She shook her head, refusing to believe he could have had anything to do with it. Eric wasn't a vampire. No matter what she'd thought she knew, a vampire wouldn't have been able to eat a full meal the way he did. But he wasn't human, either. He was...something else, something that had lived for a thousand years. Honestly, she didn't know what he was capable of.

"Maybe not. Maybe it's just some jerk playing vampire. Goddess knows it's happened before."

Amara sighed, her frustration clear in her voice when she spoke. "No. A vampire definitely committed this crime, Ellie. Someone I don't know. Someone who has to be found before he does it again."

"You said *he*. Couldn't it be a woman?"

"I really don't think so. The vibe I'm getting here is definitely male, but anything beyond that is fuzzy. Honestly, I don't know what to make of this situation."

Ellie shivered. She wished she had some way to contact Eric, but he hadn't given her a clue as to where he was staying. She supposed she could call the area hotels and ask around, but she decided against it. If she was going to confront him with anything, it would be in person, on her own terms. She didn't really believe he could have murdered anyone, but still she had to do what it took to keep her safe.

"Why so quiet?" Amara asked softly, suspicion lacing her tone. "Is there something you want to tell me?"

"No, of course not."

"Ellie, watch out. I don't want to see you get into any trouble."

The hair on the back of Ellie's neck rose and she got up to pace the room, taking the cordless phone with her. Amara was the one person who could tell, without fail, when someone lied. She normally despised deceit, but this time couldn't help it. Ellie *had* to lie, and she'd continue to lie until she knew without a doubt that Eric meant no harm.

The dream had concerned and shaken her, but could she really trust what she saw when she'd been sleeping? She didn't know. Until she was absolutely sure, she wasn't going to let Amara sic Marco and Royce on Eric. She wouldn't wish the two of them in a nasty mood on her worst enemy, and he wasn't her enemy.

At least she didn't think so.

"Okay." Amara sounded unconvinced, but she let the subject drop. "Just promise me you'll call if you need anything."

Ellie agreed and hung up the phone, glad to be done with the conversation. A sense of dread settled in the pit of her stomach, and she almost picked the phone up and called Amara back. She closed her eyes and breathed deeply, asking for guidance and *answers* to her problems. She was in over her head, and couldn't find any way to get out. The answer came to her with sickening clarity. *There was no way out.* It was already too late.

* * * * *

Eric walked through town, his senses, honed to near perfection in his years of existence, on full alert. He planned to put them to good use this morning. He had a job to do, and *nothing* would stop that. The threat must be found, and eliminated, before anyone else was hurt.

He'd followed the blood trail to Stone Harbor, where it had disappeared somewhere within the quaint little seaside village. He hadn't been able to find it again, but things had started to look promising. The murder proved without a doubt that he'd come to the right place. It was only a matter of time before things got worse.

Thoughts of Ellie filled his head, creating a distraction. He'd never before had a problem focusing on his work because of a woman, but she was different from most of the women he'd known. His sister would laugh at him and tell him he was getting soft. Was he? Possibly. Maybe the time had come to start thinking about retirement.

No. He knew he could do the job. He *would* do this job, just as he had all the others. Sam trusted him to get rid of the threat by whatever means necessary, and he refused to betray that trust for any reason. He'd just have to find a way to work around his growing fixation with Ellie.

When he'd first arrived, he'd been sure Royce Cardoso was the man he'd been tracking. Now he had his doubts. The man was unstable, possibly dangerous, but it just didn't fit. He didn't like Cardoso, didn't *trust* him, but that didn't mean he had the right to brand him a killer, either.

If Royce wasn't the killer, then he was in just as much danger as Eric. He'd been there too, that night so many years ago. There'd been five of them, and three were dead. The two remaining were both in the same town. Everything about the situation warned of a setup. Had this all been an elaborate ruse to get them in the same place at the same time? Of course. It had to be. He should have seen it sooner, but he'd been too bent on staying alive long enough to dispose of his friends' killer. Now that he realized the mistake he'd made in coming here, it was too late to turn back. If he walked away, more innocents would die. Ellie might be one of them.

Once he'd completed the job, he could focus on bashing in Royce Cardoso's skull. He'd never forgive the man for putting his hands on Ellie. He stopped by the stone steps that led down to one of the town's public beaches, breathing in the sea-scented air. He'd stood in the same spot a week ago, watching Ellie and Royce walk together along the water on a moonlit night. He'd had known her for all of two days, as she'd so eagerly pointed out, yet he couldn't help the pang of jealousy he felt every time he thought about her with another man. He would have been fine to walk away from any other woman, but he'd been around long enough to recognize what she was to him, especially after that out-of-control kiss.

Ellie was his mate.

That certainly complicated things. The strong urge to guard his territory filled him, working him into an aggressive state. He would do *anything* it took to make sure no other man ever touched her again. His mind spun with that single fact, the words jabbing at him like jagged glass. *His mate.* His to protect.

It couldn't be possible, nothing about it was logical, yet he knew without a doubt that it was true. How could this have happened? His life, as he'd known it for the past millennium, had just changed forever with this simple twist of fate.

In her heart, she recognized him, too. The panther she wore around her neck cemented that fact for him, but it would take some convincing to get her conscious mind to accept it. He didn't know if he was up for another challenge.

Heaving a sigh, he walked on, prodding his mind to focus on the task at hand. He forced himself to concentrate on his search for the rogue vampire. He was old, able to cloak himself thoroughly to avoid detection. If he'd been a fledgling, Eric would already have taken care of him as he had so many others. Seeking out the vamp and destroying him, would prove to be a lot harder than he'd originally hoped.

Too bad the only puzzle his mind found worth solving was how to get Ellie into bed and into his life. How would he convince her that she was what had been missing for so long? That would take time—being human, she'd be prone to look at matters of commitment with her heart first, and then her mind. His kind did neither, at least not when it came to finding one's true mate. *That* was done solely with the body, and the chemistry between the two people involved. His body fairly screamed that Ellie was the one.

How could it be possible for him to have a human mate?

The questions he had frustrated him. The unlikelihood of the situation didn't matter. He didn't choose his mate—fate did that for him. When she'd said he wasn't what she'd been looking for, he understood. He hadn't been looking for her, either, but he'd found her. And he'd be damned if he was going to lose her to a *vampire*.

Now he had two reasons for staying in town until everything was resolved. He just hoped he could accomplish both with minimal bloodshed. He had a feeling a human like Ellie would frown on the kind of mayhem his job involved. He laughed to himself at the thought. She'd better get used to it.

It would be bad enough when she found out what he did for a living. Despite her apparent ease at accepting the paranormal, she might not accept *him*. His kind made vampires look like innocent little schoolchildren. It was important that he make her understand, though, if he was going to spend the rest of his life...

With a *human*.

A mental image of her necklace again flashed through his mind. It had rattled him at first, when he'd seen it, but it had also made him wonder. It was just one of the many things he refused to call coincidence. He'd been brought here for a reason—that much he accepted as true. He turned away from the beach and made his way through the downtown streets. Her race didn't matter, not in the end.

If she'd been *Panthicenos*, she'd have been his since day one. Neither of them would have needed to declare anything. The bond between mates didn't need a license of any kind, or a ring-swapping ceremony. It was formed on the emotional plane just below the physical one, and strong enough to survive eternity. She would have known instinctively, as he had, that their meeting had been more than random. He just hoped he could convince her of her place in his life soon. As it was, he'd have to work hard to get her to accept him willingly. He didn't relish the thought of keeping her against her will, but he'd do *anything* it took. Knowing what he knew, he didn't have a choice.

Chapter 5

Could Eric really have killed that woman? Instinct told Ellie it wasn't possible. Something inside her told her to trust him—ridiculous considering she'd just met him days ago, and she knew almost nothing about him. Common sense, something she seemed to be lacking these days, told her to be careful, to wait and watch, and see if this time instinct failed her.

For the first time in as long as she could remember, she felt real fear. Murder didn't happen often in Stone Harbor. Crime of any kind was a rarity. The murder didn't seem premeditated, but it certainly hadn't been an accident. The bizarre method of killing most likely baffled the police, and put Amara, Marco, and Royce in danger. If they were discovered—*if* anyone around here besides her immediate family actually believed in vampires—terrible things could happen to them.

Or not. It wasn't the sixteen hundreds anymore, and the world had gotten pretty strange.

She took a quick shower and dressed before stepping outside to get the morning paper. When she opened the front door, she found a bouquet of flowers, tied with a white ribbon, resting on the porch. She picked them up and opened the attached card. The message, short and simple, read "Thinking of you", with Eric's name written in bold handwriting.

Ellie blinked in surprise. No man had ever given her flowers the morning after when she'd left him without satisfaction during the date. She allowed herself a small smile as she brought the bouquet into the kitchen, cut the stems, and put the flowers in water. Shaking off the feeling that something was wrong, she pushed all thoughts of her disturbing dream out of her mind. For now, at least, she'd allow herself a little time to enjoy her gift.

She'd just poured herself a second cup of coffee when Amara burst through the back door.

"You're a hard person to get a hold of lately," Amara complained as she sat at the table. "First you were out running this morning, and now this. I had to come out in the morning sunshine to find you, and believe me, that's not something I enjoy doing."

"What are you talking about?"

Amara sighed and shook her head. "There's a murderer out there, Ell, and I think you need to be a lot more careful. When I couldn't get in touch with you a little bit ago, I got nervous."

"I was in the shower." Ellie couldn't keep the irritation from her voice. Amara had genuine psychic abilities, but sometimes she got a little carried away. "I just spoke to you a few hours ago. Did something else happen?"

"No, nothing else happened, at least I don't think so, but you worried me. You need to lock your doors. It's not safe in town anymore." Amara drummed her nails on the tabletop, fidgeting like she always did when she got upset. "Where did you get these?" she asked, touching one of the flowers in the vase Ellie had set on the table. She wrinkled her nose and sniffed the air. "Did you get a cat?"

The dream forced its way into Ellie's mind, no matter how hard she tried to keep it out. Amara's questions only added to her anxiety. "I found them on the front porch this morning, and no, I didn't get a cat. Why do you ask?"

"I could have sworn I smelled a cat in here. It's faint, but it's definitely there. Never mind." Amara rubbed a petal in between her thumb and finger, a frown marring her features. "Do you have any clue as to who would send you flowers?"

Ellie shrugged one shoulder and ignored the question. She wasn't even close to ready to tell Amara the truth yet. "Why? What's the matter?"

"They just feel…weird." Amara's face took on a thoughtful expression. "I know they're just flowers, but they feel…malicious somehow."

Malicious flowers? "You've got to be kidding me."

"I wish." Amara plucked a petal off a large, blood-red rose and let it flutter to the table. She pushed it around the tabletop with the tip of her long fingernail before stabbing it through its center. "Someone's watching you."

"I don't think so." Ellie took a big gulp of her coffee, the hot liquid burning her throat on the way down. "Why would anyone bother with me? I mind my own business."

"Beats me. But it's what I see. You've always trusted me before."

In the year since Amara's husband, Marco, had accidentally turned her into a vampire, Amara had been working on her dormant psychic powers. They were getting strong, but what she saw was still random. She had no control over what she did and didn't see.

"Are you almost ready?" Marco walked into the house through the back door without bothering to knock first. Yes, it was definitely time to start locking those doors.

Ellie frowned. "You're lucky I like you. Otherwise I might have to hurt you for just barging in without even letting me know you're there."

"Yeah, I love you too, Ellie." Marco shook his head and turned to his wife. "Are you ready to go?"

"Ellie has a stalker." Amara blurted, her eyes impossibly wide.

"*A what?*" Ellie and Marco asked at the same time.

Amara pointed to the flowers. "She has a stalker. Someone's been watching her."

"Yeah, right." Ellie scoffed at the idea. Women like Amara, the former horror film queen, had stalkers. Women like Ellie, the quiet painter no one ever noticed, did not.

"I'm serious. I told you these things feel malicious." Amara wrinkled her nose again at the flowers. "I've been through a couple of these situations before. I know what you're dealing with, and it's nothing to take lightly."

The woman really didn't have any idea. As much as she trusted her friend's abilities, this time Amara was wrong. Eric was definitely not a stalker. But was he malicious? Not to her. "Amara, I'm fine. Stop overreacting."

Apparently, Marco didn't agree. "A stalker, huh? Are you going to be okay alone?"

"Are you both out of your minds?" she asked, shaking her head.

"Do you want to move in with us until this whole thing blows over?" he continued.

She'd rather eat dirt than move in with them—and Royce—and let them protect her from some imaginary threat. "There is no *thing* to blow over! I got *flowers*, not bloody body parts. You two are making a huge deal out of nothing."

They both stared at her for a full minute before Marco spoke. "Are you sure you're okay?" He articulated each word slowly and carefully, like he was speaking to a three- year-old or a small animal. She clenched her hands into fists to keep from hitting something.

A couple of deep breaths later, she had a decent handle on her burgeoning temper. "I. Am. Fine. What part of that are you having trouble understanding?" She sighed, her anger not as controlled as she'd hoped. "Is your English failing in your old age, Marco? Perhaps I should find you a translator?"

Amara spoke up before Marco had a chance to answer. "Calm down, Ellie. We're just concerned. What's going on with you? Why are you getting so defensive if everything is okay?"

"I'm sorry. I'm just not used to having someone question me so much." She managed a tight smile, despite the fact that she felt like her head might burst from the stress. "Now you'd better be going, because I have a lot to do today."

Marco knew her well enough to know it was time to quit, although the grim set of his jaw indicted he wasn't happy about it. "Yeah, okay. You know you can always call me if you need anything. I'm sure I still owe you a couple of favors."

She hadn't been keeping score, not really. She didn't mind doing favors for friends, unless they went off the deep end like Marco had briefly the year before.

At least his foray into insane criminal kidnapping had gone well, relatively speaking. He'd gotten himself a wife—and she hadn't even pressed charges. Now that he had Amara to take care of him, Ellie could worry less about him and more about her family. Her grandmother was getting old, whether she wanted to admit it or not, and Becca's predicament was never far from her mind. Charlotte...well, Charlotte was going through a phase of another kind, and it didn't worry Ellie any less. With the three of them all relying on her for something, she had her hands full.

She did *not* have time for stalkers or malicious flowers—or meddling vampires, for that matter.

"We'll talk later." Amara's unblinking gaze held Ellie's for a little too long as she spoke, making Ellie burst out laughing. Mind control had become something of a hobby of Amara's, a fact she had yet to share with her husband.

"Knock it off, Amara. There's nothing to tell."

Amara narrowed her eyes, her lips pursing in a comical pout. "Fine. Be that way." She turned just before she walked out the door. "I'll call you soon. We'll *talk* then."

Ellie shook her head as Marco shut the door behind them. She loved Marco and Amara dearly, but she was happy to see them leave. Sometimes Amara gave her the creeps.

* * * * *

The second the car was on the road, Amara turned to Marco. "What the hell is going on around here?"

"Are you talking about the situation you think is happening with Ellie, or something else?"

"Gee, I wonder. What do you think?"

"You're touchy this morning." He drummed his fingers on the wheel, which he knew damned well annoyed her beyond reason. She had the sudden urge to reach across the console and break his fingers, but she resisted. *Barely.* "Are you absolutely sure about this stalker issue? Trust me, you don't want to piss Ellie off with something like this unless you're serious. She might put a curse on you or something."

The slight hint of an accent in her husband's voice—a remnant from his childhood in Portugal—turned her insides to mush every time he spoke. She blew out a frustrated breath, determined not to let him distract her.

"Do you think I'm an *idiot*? Of course I'm serious. And you know damned well she wouldn't put a curse on anyone." Amara rolled her eyes and poked his arm with her fingernail. Why was it that he had such a hard time taking her seriously? "Look, Marco, someone is after her, and she needs protection. I don't care if you believe me or not. But if you don't do something about it, you'll be sleeping on the couch for the rest of your life. Take into consideration how long your life span is, and choose *wisely.*"

He stopped at a stop sign and glanced her way. The concern in his eyes took her by surprise. "I'm already planning something. When we get home I'll talk to Royce. He can—"

"Drive her to the brink of insanity in just a couple of hours? I don't know if that's such a good idea. I think they might need a little time apart."

"I don't know what else you want me to do. You can't be thinking about calling the police."

"Yeah, that would go over really well." Amara snorted. "I'm sure they'd be perfectly willing to listen to a psychic vampire. I was thinking something more along the lines of making her stay with us until this guy is caught. That's a little less conspicuous."

"Don't you think you're jumping the gun a little?" Marco asked, his tone heavy with aggravation. "She got flowers, babe. *Flowers*. There's absolutely nothing threatening about that."

"So now you're not even going to listen? I *know* what I feel. *You're* the one who's been telling me to trust my hunches. You've been pushing me to use these powers almost since day one. Why do you feel the need to doubt me now?" She crossed her arms over her chest and faced the window. "I hope you enjoy sleeping on the couch every day, and your legs don't get too cramped. It's not a very big couch, you know."

"No, it's not. And that's why Royce and I are going to have a talk when we get back. Ellie would be a lot less suspicious of him than she would of one of us, and I think he needs another push in her direction, anyway." She opened her mouth to protest, but he stopped her with a quick shake of his head. "Unless you know some other big, strong guy with too much free time on his hands, I suggest you keep your mouth shut. Right now, I want to get home and get out of the bright sun. If it's bothering me this much, I can just imagine how someone as newly turned as you must feel. If you stay outside too much longer, it will zap all your energy and make you sick. How about we shelve this discussion for later this evening and go home to bed?"

He had a point there. Something about the way he said "bed" made her want to tell him to speed up so they could get home faster. She wisely closed her mouth for a while, hoping Royce could handle this bit of a problem. She had some serious doubts that Royce could help, though, especially since there was a woman involved.

* * * * *

"It's about time you got back."

"Is there a problem?" Royce walked up the front steps and joined his brother on the porch.

"What happened to you last night and this morning? You never came home." Marco glanced at him, his expression worried.

"I have to check in with you now? Why would it matter where I spend my time?" Last minute details before his trip had kept him out of town for most of the night, and his day had been spent sleeping in a hotel room to rest up so he could drive back home that evening.

The worry on Marco's face only increased. "This is serious, Royce, not some game."

"Sorry. Talk to me. Tell me what I can do to help."

"This whole thing with that murder has Amara damned near hysterical, and it's driving me out of my mind. Now she thinks Ellie's got some stalker after her, and she won't let it go. She keeps telling me I have to do something about it, but what if she's wrong?"

With everything going on around here lately, Amara's revelations wouldn't surprise him in the least. "If she's wrong, you're going to have a couple of really pissed- off ladies around here."

"Don't I know it." Marco shook his head and let out a harsh breath. "I just don't know what to think about this. Ellie says nothing strange has been happening, but I don't believe her."

"Maybe she's got a reason for hiding things from you."

"And maybe she's just being her usual stubborn, independent self."

Royce glanced at his brother over the top of his sunglasses. "I think you're missing a big point here. You're not being up front with her, either."

"When did you become the morality police? I have my reasons. You know that." Marco looked away, his gaze following the line of the ocean a few hundred feet away. "I decided—we both decided—not to tell either of them about what's happening for their own protection. Amara has enough on her mind without dealing with an immortal killer. It's been bad enough that she sits on the couch all evening, glued to the TV, watching the news. If she knew...well, Eric Malcolm is a dangerous man. We've got to find a way to stop him before he hurts someone else."

Or before Amara found out what they'd been keeping from her and decided to take it upon herself to confront the man. "Before we try to stop him, we need clear evidence that he's the killer. He's too powerful to go after just for the hell of it. He could seriously injure one of us. We need to be absolutely sure here, or we'll just be wasting time."

Marco's head snapped up, his eyes narrowed. "You sound like you're not so sure it's Malcolm anymore."

Royce shrugged, not sure how to explain what he was feeling to his brother. Marco didn't know the guy, not like Royce did. Yeah, Eric was a killer, but this didn't seem like his style. "I'd love to string that guy up for *something*, but I don't want to take any chances. *Panthicenos* have a lot more power than we do. I wouldn't want to risk anything, not until we're sure."

"What if he's Ellie's stalker?" Marco asked. He stood up and paced the length of the porch, the old floorboards creaking under his weight. "I wish she'd at least listen to reason. This town has suddenly become a very dangerous place to live."

"Just what I need in my life. Another independent woman," Royce grumbled, glad he'd be leaving soon. He couldn't wait to get his life back to normal.

Marco stopped pacing and faced him, his head cocked to the side. "I thought you and Ellie got along."

"We do." Royce sighed and shook his head. He didn't have time for this, not now. "She and I...it's too complicated to explain. I've got a little more than a week before I leave for South Africa. I'll see what I can do about Ellie's situation before then, but after that you're on your own."

First, he had to deal with Eric Malcolm. There had to be a reason he was in town—men like Eric didn't just hang around a place like this for the fun of it. That meant Eric was probably working. The thought sent a shiver through Royce. He'd had Eric after him once, and the man was damned near relentless. Royce would be dead now, if he hadn't found a way to bargain with the man.

The *bargain* had cost more than he could ever reconcile. Just the thought of Eric courting Ellie made his blood run cold. Putting trust in Eric could be a huge mistake. Eric had taught him that painful lesson many years ago. Royce didn't want to see Ellie hurt. Ellie, with her sweet, nurturing ways, had no business getting involved with a murderer.

A surge of hot anger ran through him, and he fought the need to hurt something. Just because he couldn't give her what she needed didn't mean he'd stopped caring. He'd do whatever it took to keep Eric Malcolm away from Ellie, even if he had to kill to do it.

Chapter 6

After a very unproductive morning in the studio, Ellie packed up her paints and washed her brushes before she headed outside. She worked in her garden, hoping weeding and planting would help get her mind off her confusion with Eric.

Confusion, in this case, was an understatement.

She had no idea who he really was, or *what* he really was, and he seemed intent on keeping her in the dark on both counts. That made her angry, but intrigued her at the same time. Who was he? Was he one of the good guys, or not? She'd find out, even if she had to do some digging on her own. No matter how he affected her, she wasn't about to let him get away with hiding so much from her—not if he wanted anything to come out of what was growing between them.

She sighed and ran a hand over her face, not caring if she streaked her skin with dirt. He hadn't called, and maybe she should take that as a sign. He'd sent flowers, but that didn't mean anything. For all she knew it could be a brush-off. He hadn't exactly been clear with his intentions. Yes, he'd kissed her, but she'd been around long enough to know that it might not have meant the same for him as it did for her.

For her, his kiss had awakened something inside she'd tried to lock away after her divorce. She'd let herself go, given in to what he'd asked for with his actions, and she'd enjoyed every second. To Eric, it might have been just something to do to pass the time. She'd lived in the same small town for most of her life, done the same things. A woman like her couldn't possibly hold his interest for long.

"Ellie?"

She glanced up sharply, sure at first that she'd imagined his voice, that she'd been so engrossed in analyzing the situation that she was hearing things. But there he was, on the flagstone path, standing over her. In her crouched position, he towered over her, looming like a giant stone statue against the backdrop of the sun. A chill ran through her as her eyes took in his tense stance.

"What are you doing here?" she blurted, squinting to see him through the bright afternoon light.

"I think we need to talk." He spoke softly but confidently.

She bit back the urge to tell him to leave. "So talk." She waited as patiently as she could, almost certain the words that would come out of his mouth would be lies. She hadn't met a man yet who didn't lie to her. Even Marco, who told her the lies were "for her own protection", occasionally had a problem with the truth. She wouldn't let Eric get away with it. She wanted honesty from everyone in her life, especially a man who'd had his tongue down her throat in a public parking lot!

When he spoke, his answer surprised her. "I got called away on business. I would have called to let you know, but it was a sudden trip, and I didn't think you'd even notice I was gone. I'm sorry if I upset you, but I had to go."

She frowned at what sounded like the truth mixed in with excuses. "It would have taken just a minute to make a phone call."

"Yeah, but once I got you on the phone I would have wanted to see you, and that wasn't possible at the time." He sighed heavily and shifted his stance.

Her mouth went dry at the sight of his powerful thigh muscles flexing under the fabric of his tight black jeans.

"Ellie?"

She blinked up at him, just realizing he'd said something else. "Yes?"

"Carol says you should probably get out of the sun before you get sunstroke. You've been out here all afternoon and she's worried about you."

"You talked to Carol again?" Did he really have to be so friendly with her family? It was one thing for her to put herself in possible danger, but she wasn't comfortable with him spending time with her grandmother.

"When you didn't answer the door, she came outside and told me you were out here." He paused and shoved his hands into his pockets, pulling the fabric taut across the front placket.

Oh, boy. She looked him over, her gaze tracing every line and angle of his body. His shirt fit snugly, outlining his muscled torso and narrow hips and...parts of his body she really shouldn't be thinking about when she still didn't know if he was some kind of psychotic killer. She cleared her throat and spoke, hoping to find the strength to send him away before she did something really stupid. "You seem to have escaped her relatively unscathed."

He laughed. "You think so? She held me hostage in her kitchen for twenty minutes. I didn't think she was ever going to let me come find you. I probably know more now about your family history than you do."

That was an unsettling thought. If he knew as much as he thought he did, why wasn't he running in the other direction? "What can I do for you?" she asked, turning her attention back to her weeding. "If you just came here to check up on me, you're wasting my time. I have a lot to do."

"Ellie?" This time his tone bordered on angry. Good. Let him be mad. He deserved it for what he'd been putting her through with his secrecy.

"Yes?" She kept her gaze glued to the flowers, not allowing herself to look up at him again. If she'd stared for another second she would have begged him to strip her naked and take her in the middle of the flowerbed. Not a good thing for a woman trying to assert her independence.

"Can you look at me for a minute?"

She didn't even glance up, just continued to pull at the weeds. She yanked a particularly tough one hard and it popped out of the ground, a clump of dirt smacking her in the face. She sighed in annoyance. "Why would I want to look at you? I have better things to do with my time. I want to get this weeding finished while the weather is still good. New England weather's not exactly stable."

"Are you afraid to look at me?"

He didn't know how close he was to the truth. What scared her, really, was that if she looked, she might just give in and believe everything he said. His gaze held enough power that it could make her forget her reservations. That was a dangerous thing. "Of course not. Why would I be afraid of you?"

"You shouldn't be, but you are." Frustration hung heavy in his tone. "I know we haven't known each other long, but I would have thought you'd know by now that you can trust me. I would never hurt you. I'd never hurt your grandmother either, and I think deep down inside you know that."

She set her trowel down and looked up at him. "I never thought that."

"Yes, you did."

"How could you know that? Are you reading my mind or something?" Her jaw dropped at the look in his eyes, the one that told her exactly what he'd been doing. "Oh, God. Have you been able to do that the whole time?"

"Do what?" He shrugged, his shoulders moving up and down in a deceptively casual motion. He took a step closer and she rocked back on her heels, ready to run if it came to that.

"Read my mind. Please tell me you haven't been." Her heart stopped while she waited for his answer. With the thoughts she'd been having about him, she'd never be able to look him in the eye again.

"Not exactly. I don't read minds. It's more like reading emotions." He shook his head and knelt down next to her, so close her heart sped up and a thin layer of sweat broke out over her forehead. She blamed it on the heat wave, because there was no way she could be reacting to Eric this strongly. It had absolutely *nothing* to do with the fact that, from this position, she had a clear view of the way his pants stretched tightly over his impressive erection. She was supposed to be *mad* at him.

She had to take a deep breath before she could speak again, and even then her voice wavered. She felt weak and detached, like she might pass out. "What do you mean?"

Eric leaned closer and tucked a strand of her hair behind her ear. "You have a little dirt here." He brushed his thumb across her cheek.

She shivered and bit down hard on her lower lip, and at his touch, her senses went wild. Her body was morphing into a big bundle of nerves and it took every ounce of concentration she had to keep from melting into the ground. "Please answer my question." She sucked in a sharp breath when his teeth grazed her earlobe.

That did it. She pushed up into a standing position and walked a few steps away to put some distance between them. She knew his actions were to distract her from her questions, and it was working better than she'd ever tell him. "Are you going to answer me, or do you want me to guess?"

He stood and snagged her wrist, pulling her back to him and laughing softly. "We should talk about this. Why don't we walk for a while? I can explain things as we go."

A *walk*? Here she was trembling with aggravation and arousal, and he wanted to *walk*? "Are you serious?"

"Well, yeah. I thought maybe we could walk through the woods and get away from your grandmother's prying eyes for a few minutes." He gestured toward Carol's apartment, and sure enough, the woman watched them intently through partially drawn curtains.

"Okay. Fine. A walk." She pulled away from him and wiped her hands on her shorts. She'd take a walk with him, but she wasn't going to stop asking questions.

She checked to make sure her cell phone still hung from her waistband—just in case—and turned to face him. "Let's go." She took off toward the path that led into the woods behind the house, not waiting to see if he followed.

She walked ten feet down the path, just out of Carol's line of vision, before she spun on him, her hands on her hips. The confrontation to come would be so much easier without an audience. "Okay, Eric. No more lies. I want the truth, and I want it right now. Why are you really here?"

"I told you. I wanted to see you."

"Sure you did." He told the truth, she could see it in his eyes, but why? He'd disappeared off the face of the earth for the day, and now the urge to *visit* suddenly struck him? She nearly laughed at the thought. He didn't seem like the type to make casual visits. He was up to something. She just wished she knew what.

She walked a few more steps down the path, watching out for roots and other objects on the ground that might trip her. The trees were thick and someone could get lost if they weren't familiar with the area. She knew the place well, but Eric didn't. He'd have to stick pretty close to her.

Or she could lose him, and let him find his own way back. She smiled to herself at the appealing thought. It would serve him right for the way he'd treated her.

"You wouldn't dare." He grabbed her arm and hauled her back against him, gazing down at her and shaking his head slowly from side to side.

His response caught her off-guard. "How do you know? Maybe that's exactly what I'd do."

"Then I'll just have to keep you close to make sure you won't leave me." He loosened his grip on her arm, massaging the inside of her elbow with his thumb and sending a tingling sensation down to her wrist. "Now you can't get away."

She nearly bolted at that thought. Was she an idiot for walking through the woods, alone, with a man she barely knew? Probably, but she had her phone with her and Carol knew where she was, so she'd most likely be fine. She had to put at least a little trust in the protection spell she'd cast the night before.

They walked silently for a few minutes before Eric spoke. "Carol told me you work too hard. She thinks you need to get out and date more often."

She shuddered at what else Carol might have said to him. "Right. Carol is trying to marry me off. She's old and getting senile. Don't pay any attention to her." She stole a glance at him and saw the curious expression on his face. "Don't worry. I'm not looking for a husband. I've been there before, and I'm not planning on going back. Ever."

He smiled. "I'm sure she means well."

"Of course she does. She just has a little trouble understanding why I'd prefer to remain single."

Eric stopped, his grip tightening on her arm. "Just out of curiosity, why is that?"

She shrugged. "It's not worth the trouble, I guess. I do better on my own."

"Does it have something to do with your ex-husband?"

She closed her eyes momentarily and let out a frustrated breath. "Did Carol tell you about that, too?" When she let her eyelids flutter open, she caught a worried look pass over his face.

"Yeah. She mentioned that he didn't accept you for yourself and you deserve someone a lot better."

Leave it to the woman to butt into every aspect of her personal life. "My ex- husband was a lying, cheating, dirtbag. Most men are. Happy now?"

"Not all men are like that," he said so softly she had to strain to hear. "Sometimes you have to go with what you know inside, and forget what you've been taught."

"I wish it were that easy. This is the real world, not some fantasy in my mind. My actions, and the actions of others, can have some pretty bad consequences."

"Sometimes." He regarded her with a mix of longing and curiosity, his gaze sliding over every inch of her. "Tell me something, Ellie. Why are you suddenly so uneasy around me?"

She didn't want to talk about the murder. She wanted to forget, to pretend it had never happened. She wanted to go on playing make-believe, convincing herself that, no matter what, she'd be safe. But she couldn't. She had to confront this now, once and for all, and let fate take its course.

She took a good look at Eric, trying hard to read the expression in his eyes. Did he kill that woman? A voice in her head said no, but she couldn't tell if it was his voice, or hers. Was he inside her head, thinking her thoughts as well as reading them? A chill ran through her as she thought that was exactly what he was doing.

"I didn't kill that woman," he said softly, hypnotically. "I know you doubt me right now and probably with good reason, but I swear it wasn't me."

"I know," she answered automatically, good old Ann Elizabeth always trying to avoid a fight.

"No, you don't. Not yet. But you will. I'll show you somehow."

His gaze held hers, his eyes burning with intensity. She shivered at just the eye contact, remembering how soft and warm, then hard and demanding, his mouth had been against hers. She begged her legs to run, to get her far away from whatever danger she saw behind his gaze. But she didn't move. Curiosity overrode nerves. She needed to stay, to find out exactly what he was and why he was in Stone Harbor, and how it involved her.

Most of all, she wanted to find out why he affected her so strongly, when not even her ex-husband had been able to do that during their marriage. Not for the first time since they'd met, she wondered if his skin would smolder if she ran her hands over his chest. Would his breathing hitch? Would he groan?

Would he touch her the way he had that first night, with an intimate familiarity that shook her to her toes? Just the thought of that kiss sent shivers down her spine. She licked her lips, almost an involuntary reaction as she remembered how quickly the kiss had gotten out of control.

His expression darkened considerably and he drew a deep, slow breath. "Unless you want me to kiss you, I suggest you keep your lusty expressions to yourself."

She sucked in a breath as her body cried for his kiss. She secretly reveled in her ability to invoke such strong desire in a man, even if said desire had her entire psyche tied in double knots. "I don't know what I want."

That was a lie. She knew exactly what she wanted. She wanted Eric, in her bed, naked, all night. But at the same time, it was too soon. She hadn't known him nearly long enough. Confusion reigned inside her, warring thoughts telling her to run, and to stay and find out what he really meant to her. She felt him in her mind again, teetering on the edge of her consciousness and making her doubt if any of her thoughts were actually her own. She threw her hands up in frustration, letting out a sigh of irritation. "*Stop it.*"

"Stop what, Ellie?"

"Get out of my head," she ground out, glaring at him. "I can't think straight with you messing with my thoughts."

"I know the feeling." He sounded…annoyed, which caught her by surprise. "It works both ways, Ellie, even if you don't know how to control it yet."

"That can't be." She shook her head furiously, wondering if this was some kind of a dream. Vampires she could handle, but ambiguous supernatural beings who forced their way into her thoughts and wormed their way into her grandmother's good graces without *her* permission were a little too much to take. She covered her face with her hands, hoping she'd wake up in her bed, back in the life she once thought boring.

He stepped closer and ran his finger along her temple, back and forth. "I've heard it could be this way, but I never believed it." He sounded like he was speaking to himself more than her. "Not until I met you in the park, and all my priorities changed."

His words gave her pause. She took her hands off her face and looked at him uncertainly. "Excuse me? And don't give me any of that 'the one' crap because I've heard it all before and I don't buy into any of it."

He smiled. "I wouldn't dream of it." He leaned in and brushed his lips over hers.

The feather-light kiss lasted only seconds, but it set off warning bells all over her body. The jolt that passed from his lips to hers made her forget everything she wanted to say, everything she needed to ask. The man was a master of distraction, and she grudgingly admired that in him.

He pulled back and closed his eyes. When he opened them, his gaze was wild, and too intense to take. He begged her with his gaze to open up to him, to let him into her trust and her bed. The sensual promise in those eyes made her weak. Her body shut down the sensibilities of her mind, not giving her the chance to back away.

"Do you want me to walk you back home?" he asked, his brows rising in offering. His stance shifted in an obvious attempt to look unthreatening as a grin broke out over his face. He had her, and he knew it.

She shook her head in resignation, frowning at him. "Not yet. But don't think I won't walk away from you if you don't behave yourself."

With Todd, she'd made the mistake of not trusting her instincts. They'd told her to forget him—that he wasn't worth her time and would only hurt her in the end. But she'd been young and stupidly in love and had ignored what her mind told her, with disastrous results.

With Eric, her instincts told her the opposite. He'd never hurt her, at least not intentionally, and she could put her trust in him. It would all work out in the end, one way or another. At least she hoped it would. She still didn't know if the instincts were real, or manufactured by the man in front of her.

For the first time in a long time, she decided to let fate take her where it would. If she'd learned anything from Amara and her psychic abilities, it was that it was nearly impossible to change the future. She'd been raised to believe she could control her own destiny, yet time and again it slipped away from her, into the hands of some unseen power. If she couldn't change what would happen, she might as well enjoy the present before it was gone. She wrapped a hand around the back of his neck, pulling him down for another kiss.

His mouth covered hers, much more intimately this time. He thrust his tongue between her parted lips, darting in and out of her mouth in a move that blatantly mimicked the sex act she so desperately craved. He backed her up a few steps into the trunk of a large tree and cupped her chin in one of his hands, tilting her head up to deepen the kiss. He swallowed her moan when the back of his other hand brushed across her nipples, covered only in a thin cotton T-shirt. Her nipples instantly puckered against his gentle touch and she dug her fingers into his shoulders to pull him even closer.

His mouth left hers to trail hot, wet kisses along her throat. He licked and sucked and nibbled, unerringly finding all of the places that made her weak-kneed and wanton. With a harsh groan, he pulled his mouth off her throat and nuzzled into her hair.

"You taste incredible, Ellie."

She moaned in response as he lightly flicked her nipple.

"I want you so bad. *So damned bad.*" His voice was a harsh growl that echoed through the stillness of the woods around them. "Are you wet for me?"

She felt every detail of his lips as they moved against her ear. "Yes." Her body cried out for his touch. She ached for him, needing to feel him between her legs. She shifted, pressing her pelvis against him. He took the hint, moving his hand lower until he cupped her mound through her shorts.

"I bet you'll be so tight when I sink my cock into your sweet pussy." He growled against her ear. "But you'd take me all the way, wouldn't you?"

She moaned again, which surprised her since he was barely touching her. Goddess, the things he said aroused her unbearably. He knew it. He drove her to the brink, made her nearly mindless with need until she forgot everything but the feel of him against her. She pulled at the neckline of his shirt, wanting to rip the soft material away from his skin. She recalled the strange dream, remembering how turned-on she'd been when she'd woken up. That was nothing compared to how she felt now. She felt drugged, needy, and desperate.

His breath skimmed her neck as he spoke. "You're so turned-on right now. I love seeing you like this. You have no idea how hard you're making me."

She ground her hips shamelessly against his hand. He used his body to press her more tightly against the tree trunk, stopping any further movement. The rough bark bit into her back and she cried out. Eric swallowed her cry with a deep kiss.

"Do you know what I want to do to you?" he asked when he pulled his mouth away.

She shook her head, eager to hear what dirty thoughts ran through his mind. She was sopping wet now, and they were both still fully dressed.

"I want to strip off all your clothes and lay you down on the leaves." He ran his tongue over her throat and she shivered with delight. "Then I would spread your legs and kneel between them, and lift your body up to my mouth. I'd lick you until you came, and then I'd thrust my tongue inside you to feel your muscles clenching around me."

She very nearly came right then and there. Her legs buckled and she clung to him for support. She whimpered, wishing he'd do just what he professed to want. "*Please*."

He shook his head. "Listen to me. I'm not finished yet."

Neither was she, but with any luck she would be soon. If he'd just shut up and strip her, they could both walk away very happy.

"I want to pound my cock into you and make you come again. Would you like that, Ellie?"

Yes! She didn't care how or where, she just knew she had to have that cock inside her soon, before she exploded from sensory overload.

Eric leaned down and closed his mouth over one of her nipples, his tongue dampening the fabric of her shirt. He had her moaning and begging for more in seconds. He unzipped her shorts and slid his hand inside, his fingers stroking the sensitive folds of her sex. As he pushed one finger inside her, she dug her nails into his upper arms, trying to hold herself upright.

His mouth left her breast and he brought it to her neck, his teeth sharp as they scraped along her skin. Her resulting shiver was almost violent. She didn't usually like sex rough, but she had a feeling it would be different with Eric. She could let herself go, enjoy everything, and trust him to take care of her. He ran his tongue from her collarbone to her jaw and back again, punctuating the rough satin touch with the gentle nip of his teeth.

At the same time, he slid his finger in and out of her cunt and brushed his thumb over her clit. She whimpered, trying to control the urge to scream a primal yell she was sure would drive him over the edge of gentle into something wild. How did he do this to her—make her forget that he was keeping secrets, and make her care more about climaxing than her own life?

All of her resolve to take things slowly, not to let him get to her too soon, vanished. She wanted more. Her greedy body absorbed and relished all his attention. She tried to hold back and cling to the moment of ecstasy with everything she had, but her body exploded in a starburst of light and she came hard, sagging against him. He held her up, kissing her softly until reality returned and she realized she was up against a tree, in the middle of the woods — in the middle of the *afternoon* — with a man she'd known for a couple of days. *Not very smart.*

She didn't care. She hadn't been in control of her normal thought processes at the time. It had been worth every second.

She reached for him, but he stepped away, shaking his head. "I'm sorry. I didn't expect it to go that far." Gently he pulled his fingers from her wet folds.

Neither had she, but she wasn't complaining. Or apologizing. "Forgive me if I don't understand what the problem is here."

He sighed and paused, his muscles taut. When he spoke, she heard the tension in his voice. "I only wanted to kiss you. I tried to tell myself that one kiss would be enough, but obviously, I was wrong. I want more, but now is not the time." He looked at her, his gaze so intense and hot it was scary. The lust she saw there conflicted with his next words. "I really didn't want to rush things with you."

Her body screamed, "Please rush things", but her mind thanked him as it slowly took back control.

"You're not the only one who's confused, Ellie," he said softly, his gaze boring into hers. He lifted her chin with his thumb and kissed her forehead. "This thing between us is tearing me apart, too."

She wasn't sure if she wanted to know what he meant by that.

Chapter 7

"You got the flowers," Eric said as they walked into her kitchen a few minutes later.

"Yes, and I would have thanked you for them, if I'd been able to *find* you."

He frowned. "I told you I had to go out of town for a little while."

His expression told her he wasn't used to having to answer to anyone. He didn't look upset, just confused.

"I suppose you should have a way to get a hold of me. I'm staying at the Harbor Inn, but I'm not there often. Let me give you my cell phone number. I can't promise I'll answer it, but I'll try my best."

He tore a sheet of notepaper off the pad on the counter and scrawled two numbers on it. "The top one is my cell number. The bottom one is just in case of emergencies."

Emergencies? She gulped at the thought. Given the situation, that word took on a whole new meaning. "What kind of emergencies do you expect?"

He sighed and ran a hand through his hair, obviously uncomfortable with the question. "Look, I'm not always able to answer my phone, and if I'm not close to you I won't be in touch with your emotions. It's too much to explain right now. But if anything ever happens and you can't get in touch with me, call that other number. Sam always answers, and he's willing to help."

She looked at the paper in her hand, waiting for it to burst into flames or something equally ominous. She didn't like the sudden shift in Eric's behavior, or the direction of the conversation. "Who's Sam?"

"My boss."

"You're boss, huh? Where do you work?" Now was the perfect time to ask the questions she'd been holding for the last couple of days. "What exactly do you do for a living?"

He paused a little too long before he answered, guilt flashing in his eyes. "You don't want to know."

"Actually, I think I do. I need to know." Something told her not to ask—that she wouldn't like his answer—but she had to find out. "Please, Eric. Nothing you can say will shock me."

He laughed, his tone tinged with bitterness. "Oh, I think you're wrong about that. You'd be surprised at the things I could tell you. You'd probably have nightmares for weeks."

"You obviously haven't told me the truth about your occupation, or much else. If you want me to trust you, you're going to have to start being honest with me." *Please, trust in me enough to be honest with me. I really need that from you.*

He glanced at the ground, scuffing the toe of his shoe on the linoleum. "I guess you could say I'm a bounty hunter, of sorts."

"A bounty hunter? Like a bail-bond recovery agent?" That wasn't such a bad job, was it?

He didn't speak, just shook his head slowly, his gaze making it clear to her that the questions needed to stop. "Suffice it to say that I take care of some of the evil in the world, and I'm very good at my job. Don't ask any more questions about it. That's really all I can tell you without scaring you off, and believe me, that's not my intention."

She turned away, unsure of what to do next. His closeness set her on edge.

He came up behind her and hugged his arms around her, resting his chin on her head. "I won't ever hurt you, Ellie. I can promise you that. I'll take care of you."

She'd known this guy for less than a week. "Don't make a promise you can't keep. You never know what's going to happen."

She felt his nod against her hair. His hand came up to her rib cage, stopping just short of her breast, and an unsettling thought hit her.

"How many women have there been in your life? How many have you promised the same things to?" She braced herself for the answer, knowing she wouldn't like his response.

"That's another question you'd be better off not asking."

She gulped even as her body warmed to his touch. "A lot?"

He sighed and brushed a kiss across her hair. "There are three hundred and sixty- five days in every year, Ellie, and I've lived through roughly a thousand of them. Keep that in mind as you go fishing for information. There's a lot about me you're better off not knowing."

She swallowed hard, ready to press on with her questions even though she knew his answers might hurt her. "So that's what, *hundreds* of women you've promised to take care of and protect? And that's supposed to make me feel *special*?" She did *not* want this kind of information, yet she couldn't stop herself from asking.

Eric held her closer when she tried to break out of the circle of his arms. "Actually, I've *never* promised to care for and protect another woman, not unless I'd been paid for it as part of a job. I've never *wanted* to. You're the first. The *only*."

Some of her anger deflated, replaced with confusion. "Oh."

"Yeah. *Oh*." He laughed. "And before you read too much into this, keep in mind that I don't come with the same emotional baggage you humans do. When I meet a woman, I know right away if there's a future for us. I don't bother with any of that ridiculous courting stuff. At least I hadn't, until now." He gestured to the flowers on the table.

She opened her mouth to speak, but no sound came out. Did he just admit to courting her? Is that what this was all about? What did he mean about emotional baggage?

What did he mean by "you humans"?

She remembered Amara's passing comment about cats. Ellie hadn't thought much about it at the time, but now it seemed to fit the situation. "You wouldn't happen to have a cat, would you?"

She felt him stiffen behind her. When he spoke, his voice sounded tight. "No, why?"

"Just curious." She took a deep breath, steadying herself for what was to come. "So should I assume you're some kind of lycanthrope?"

He barked a laugh, but she felt his arms tighten around her and his breathing change. "Where did that come from?"

"I figured if you didn't have a cat, you must *be* a cat. It's pretty simple, really."

He let go of her and turned her around, his eyes burning. "What do you know about lycanthropes?"

"Not much. Don't look so worried. I don't shock easily. A couple of my close friends are vampires." So was a former lover, but she'd keep that little bit to herself for now. "But I didn't think it was possible for a lycanthrope to live thousands of years."

"I'm not a lycanthrope of any kind, Ellie."

Her breath caught in her throat and dread settled in her stomach like a ball of ice, chilling her through. "Then I suggest you start explaining the truth to me. Right now."

He leaned on the counter, his arms crossed over his chest. He looked uncertain, distrustful, and a little angry. She had a feeling she was in for some sort of long and drawn-out explanation. She was wrong.

"My kind is called *Panthicenos*. 'Cat' is a pretty apt description, though I have no idea how you reached that conclusion." His eyes drifted to her panther totem and he shook his head. "I can shift, but not because of some form of lycanthropy. I'm not a were-animal of any sort. I'm not governed by the moons, or by temper. I can shift at will."

"*Panthicenos?*" That was a word she'd never heard before. It made her think of some kind of Greek god. Her mind refused to wrap around what he told her, rejecting his words as too bizarre to believe. She felt like she'd fallen down the rabbit hole. That dream she'd had about the panther...her hand flew to the totem and she gasped as it warmed in her hand. Were the animal in her dream and the man standing before her one in the same? "So you're, um..." She let her voice trail off, not sure if she really wanted to know exactly what *Panthicenos* meant. Considering the fact that her mind was currently threatening to shut down, Eric's next suggestion was more than welcome.

"Okay, I think it's time we change the subject."

"Great idea." She attempted a smile, but only managed a grimace. Why couldn't she just have a normal life?

"Tell me, Ann Elizabeth, how many sexual partners have you had?"

"*What?*" *This* was his idea of a safer subject? "Not something I want to talk about with you, thanks. Please pick something else."

"I don't think so. You started this. Now I get to ask you a few questions," he said. "I think I have a right to know."

"Fine. Enough that I know what I'm doing," she answered. "But not enough to populate a small country, unlike some people."

"Don't get huffy. You asked. I was just being truthful."

Of course he was. It was her own fault if she didn't like the results of her curiosity. It shouldn't matter to her, anyway. They lived very different lives. "Sorry."

"Don't be. It was an honest question."

Yeah, she was just full of them that afternoon. She breathed in and out slowly, anchoring herself back into reality. "I have one more, if you don't mind."

"What's that?"

"How come so many? Are you that bad of a lover that none of them want to stick around long?"

He didn't say anything for a minute, but then suddenly burst out laughing. "Maybe you'd like to find out before you go making wild accusations."

"*I'm* not the one who's wild." She tried to be angry, but he'd worked his way into her defenses and she couldn't be upset with him for long. She just hoped her budding trust wouldn't get her into serious trouble later on down the road.

He smiled in a way that affected her right down to her toes. "I could make you wild, if you—" His phone rang before he could finish his sentence. "Hold on," he said as he took the small cell phone out of his shirt pocket and answered.

He glanced at her when he finished the conversation. "I hate to do this to you, but I have to leave."

"Where are you going?"

"Unfortunately, I have to go to work. I'll call as soon as I'm free." His expression softened. "I don't want to go. Believe me, if I could stay, I would."

"You're trying to stop the killer, aren't you?"

He closed his eyes for a moment before he nodded. "Yeah, I suppose I am. But don't concern yourself with that. I'll call soon."

"Fine, but we are so *not done* with this conversation, Eric."

He kissed her hard and fast before he smiled down at her. "I had a feeling you were going to say that."

With that he was gone, and leaving her alone and confused.

* * * * *

It was just after sunset, and the streets were quiet. No one dared to venture out after dark anymore, not after the murder in their safe little town. These people had no idea what they were dealing with. The danger was real, and more terrifying than anyone could have guessed.

Tony fisted his hands at his sides, fighting for control of his mind. In a way, he wished they'd succeeded in killing him. But *she'd* saved him, the woman who had systematically taken his life apart piece by piece since that terrible night. He hadn't realized it at first. She'd told him she only wanted to help. He hadn't recognized her manipulative, evil intentions until it was much too late.

Eric had tried to warn him, but he'd been a fool—and so in love he hadn't listened. If he had, she wouldn't have gotten the chance to worm her way into his consciousness.

He'd hidden for so long, sometimes it seemed to him that he wasn't alive. Aiala had done a number on him, starting with that night, and he hadn't been the same since. Part of her was still there, lurking in the depths of his psyche. He felt her sometimes, late at night when he was all alone with his thoughts and Becca was sleeping quietly beside him. Aiala had twisted an integral part of him. There was little left resembling the man he used to be. He was like a broken vase that had been put back together wrong—not all the pieces lined up correctly. They were all there; they just didn't fit the way the used to.

A seagull circled above him, its mournful cries filling the humid air. When he stepped back and took a look at himself, he saw that what he was doing was wrong. But he couldn't help it. It's what *she* did to him. Her vendetta against those who had wronged her had become his burden to carry. He'd become no more than an energy source for a wounded demon, no better than a farmer's cow. She'd been sucking the life out of him for hundreds of years, and he was powerless to stop her.

His mind flashed back to that night, still vivid even after all this time. She'd promised him the world, plied him with sex until he was mindless putty for her to mold. And molded him she had. She'd turned him against his friends, the men who had trusted him with their lives. They'd come after Aiala that night to destroy her. Royce had nearly killed him for helping her, but in the end the man had let him live. That had been a very big mistake. Now Aiala wanted revenge on those who'd tried to take her life, and she used Tony as the instrument to exact her punishment. Three were dead. Eric and Royce were the only two left of his former friends. What would happen when he'd done her bidding and killed them as well?

She'd kill *him*. There'd be no reason to keep him around once he'd overstayed his welcome in her life. She'd get another source of energy.

He wanted to find Eric and Royce to warn them, but he didn't dare. Too many innocent lives were at stake. Aiala's demonic presence called to him, pulling him in all directions until he felt torn apart at the seams. Sometimes he fooled himself into thinking he was in control. But it was a lie. As long as she lived, he belonged to Aiala.

She wanted Eric Malcolm and Royce Cardoso dead, and she would make him do it. She'd given him powers he never dreamed of, and in return she wanted undying loyalty and service. The trade hadn't seemed unfair until she'd taken control and forced him to kill his friends.

He stepped into the shadows, able after years of practice to hide himself well. He was stronger than even Eric now. That thought frightened him more than he wanted to admit. He didn't *want* to harm anyone, but he couldn't find a way to stop it, either.

"You're late."

He closed his eyes and drew in a sharp breath at the sound of her voice. "I'm sorry, Aiala. I got held up."

"No excuses, Antonio. You serve me and only me. That little girlfriend of yours means nothing." He heard the click of her heels against the pavement behind him. "Turn around, Antonio, and look at your Master."

He pivoted slowly until he faced Aiala. Her beauty struck him as it always did, even though he now knew it to be tainted with evil. Her white-blond hair hung to her waist in soft waves. Her alabaster skin contrasted sharply with her midnight-blue eyes, and her full lips were designed to make men think illicit thoughts. Small and frail in appearance, no one would ever guess when they met her that they were in the presence of a very powerful demon. He saw the malevolence clearly in her now. How had he not seen it when they'd first met?

She ran a long, sharp fingernail across his cheek, pressing hard enough that he knew he'd be left with a welt. "You have not done as I've asked."

He hung his head, knowing she'd hurt him if he disobeyed. Worse, she could force him to hurt Becca. He pictured her face in his mind, so young and innocent. She didn't deserve him, but Aiala had insisted on the union. She'd said it would get him one step closer to Royce Cardoso, since the families were close.

"I haven't yet had the chance."

"Liar!" With a swoop of her hand, she sent a bolt of electricity through the air. It smacked him square in the chest and he stumbled back into an old brick building. "You need to remember your place. I've given you ultimate power, slave, and I expect your obedience in return."

His head began to pound and he fought to keep her out. Even as he did, she planted ideas in his mind. Hatred filled him, emotions that weren't his own. He could only push her away for so long before she wormed her way inside, and that's when the killings happened. There hadn't been many here, not yet, but that was sure to change in the near future.

"There is a new pawn on the board, slave," Aiala continued. "Your girlfriend's sister. She's the key to getting Malcolm to come to you. Use her."

"Ellie? I can't do that." He expended a lot of effort staying away from her. That woman was very astute—surely she'd know almost immediately what he really was. If he wanted to make Aiala happy, he couldn't let Ellie find out him out and run to Eric or Royce.

"You must. If you don't, Rebecca will suffer."

He let out a breath, defeated. He wouldn't let Aiala hurt Becca, no matter what happened. "Fine. I will do as you've asked. But I need time."

"Your time is running out, slave." Aiala smiled coldly, a deadly expression in her eyes. "Soon I won't be able to wait. Do it quickly before I lose my temper again."

He shuddered at the thought. The last time she'd truly lost her temper with him, his body had taken sixty years to recover. "I will do it."

"See that you do. If you do as I ask, I might be inclined to reward you." She laughed at that, apparently amused with herself. "Once this task is complete, I will welcome you back into my bed. I'm sure you would like that, after having your little human for so long."

Once, bedding Aiala had been the only thing on his mind. Now that he knew her true nature, it only made him sick.

She approached and kissed him, hard and long, full on the lips. He felt none of the desire he used to feel. Now there was only repulsion.

"Go. Feed," she ordered when she broke the kiss. "I will be in touch."

With that, she disappeared into the night, leaving him alone and desolate. Soon the obsession built in him. He needed blood, and he needed human energy. It was her obsession, her drive forcing him to do these things. He bent to her will, fearing nothing would ever be the same again.

He left to find his meal, knowing his feeding would sustain Aiala as well as himself. Not for the first time, he thought about ending it all. But if he did...Becca would suffer. He'd given his soul to a black sorceress, a demon with unspeakable powers, and she'd turned him into something he couldn't even explain. Sometimes the hunger got to be too much. He *had* to feed or he'd die. If he died now, before Aiala's goals were accomplished—he hated to think of what would happen to Becca then.

He shook his head to clear his thoughts. He needed sustenance—his concentration should be only on that. Unfortunately, he had yet to find a suitable donor.

He turned the corner off the main road onto a quiet side street and he saw the ideal woman. Young and healthy, she'd be perfect. Her skin glowed with a pinkish tint when she walked under the streetlight. Something inside him snapped, the mental gates he used to keep Aiala out most of the time collapsing under her psychic weight. His head pounded, and he stumbled a few steps before regaining his footing, the demon now in control. Tony heard everything she made his body do and say, but he had no power to stop what was about to happen. He followed the woman, staying silently a few steps behind to avoid detection.

When she paused by a car on the side of the road, he knew he'd lose her if he didn't act. "Excuse me?"

She jumped and turned, her hand on her heart. "Do you need something?"

He felt her nervousness, and it only fueled his hunger—*Aiala's* hunger. "My car broke down a couple of blocks back. Do you have a cell phone so I can call a tow truck?"

He planted the idea in her head that she was safe. She nodded and handed him a phone as she pulled it out of her pocket. "Sure. Here you go."

He snagged her wrist and pulled her up against him. In the past, he'd have been more careful, done something to make her forget what happened, but it no longer mattered. She wouldn't be alive in the morning to tell her story. His demonic jailor wouldn't allow it. He sank his fangs deep into the woman's neck, trying to ignore her scream as it cut right through him.

This was only the beginning.

Chapter 8

Eric sat in the dark on his hotel room balcony, listening to the sounds of the night. The waves breaking against the shore mingled with the crickets chirping and the wind rustling the leaves of the trees. A night like this should calm his frayed nerves, but too much had happened to allow him to relax.

His mind drifted to Ellie. What was she doing right now? He thought about her at home, tucked safely into bed, and wished he could be there with her. The connection he felt between them wasn't imagined — she'd felt it as much as he had. She accepted him so easily — *too* easily. But she still had no idea what he was. He'd skirted the truth, overwhelmed her with sensual distractions to avoid her uncomfortable questions — questions better left unanswered. If he hadn't been called away to help Sam tie up the loose ends of another job, she would have pressed harder for the answers she'd been looking for.

The ones he'd been unable to give.

Would she want to see him again when she learned the truth? He doubted it. No human woman would willingly spend time with one of his kind. But he wished she'd be different. She responded to him in a way no woman had before. She'd been wild in his arms. He'd been shaken when she'd come so hard around his fingers. Hell, he was *still* shaking — which was a good part of the reason he'd been hesitate to call since he'd left her yesterday afternoon. He didn't like feeling so out of control.

The fact that she seemed to trust him, even with all her questions, made him think all would work itself out. He'd meant everything he said. He wouldn't allow her to get hurt, and he'd do everything in his power to keep her safe and protected. But even as he vowed it, he understood that all he could do might not be enough.

There had been another murder.

A body had been found in an alley a block away from the first one early that morning, apparently the victim of an overnight attack. It bothered him to be so off his game. Any other case and the murderer would have already been destroyed. But this one was different. He wondered if they were dealing with an ordinary vampire — or something else entirely.

He shivered at the thought. A few names came to mind when he thought about the kind of creature they were dealing with, and none of them would be easy to kill. But the name that brought a rush of fear and adrenaline, despite the many years of his life, was the one he suspected to be behind the killings.

Aiala.

The daughter of a powerful demon, the woman had a masochistic streak a mile wide. She kept slaves, human and non-human alike, to do her dirty work. This kind of killing fit her pattern perfectly.

If Aiala was behind this, she'd want to possess someone and make him do her bidding. But vamps weren't easily possessed. Whoever he was, he would fight her. Eventually his control would slip enough to remove her shields, and that's how Eric would find him. Aiala was too smart to leave any kind of a track. Seeking out the killer would be nearly impossible with her psychic defense mechanisms in place.

A knock on the door brought him out of his thoughts. He went back into the room and opened the door, thinking he knew who would be there. He'd been waiting for this visit since the night he arrived in Stone Harbor, and frankly was a little surprised it had taken the man so long.

"I was wondering when you'd find me," he said to Royce Cardoso as he opened the door. "I have to admit, it took you a lot longer than I expected. I'm disappointed. You used to be so much better than that."

Royce answered with a humorless laugh. "Oh, yeah. You made it so easy for me. Why are you here? Is this some kind of torment you have planned?"

"Don't flatter yourself. You're not that significant."

To think there was a time in his life he'd actually considered the man a friend. That was saying a lot, considering the natural disdain the *Panthicenos* had for vampires. Royce Cardoso had been a very young vampire when he'd come to work for Sam Kincaid. He'd been good at the job, too, until that night they had tried to destroy Aiala. They'd failed, and it had caused a rift between Royce and the others. In almost four hundred years, it had never been repaired. Now it was too late.

"Leave Ellie alone." Royce pushed past him and walked into the room, slamming the door behind him. "She doesn't belong to you."

"Not yet." He widened his smile, intent on making the man suffer a little longer. "But she will. I have no doubts of that." His words had the desired effect. Royce's eyes narrowed and he took a step toward Eric, his hands clenched into fists. Strangely, Eric didn't enjoy the reaction as much as he'd thought he would. The urge to distress the man had faded with time and distance.

"She doesn't belong to anyone. You can't just take whatever you want, Eric. The world doesn't work that way anymore."

He kept his tone acidic, partly to cover up the fact that he genuinely cared for Ellie. "The world works however I want it to. You've warned me to stay away from your woman. You may leave now."

Royce relaxed his stance, shoving his hands into his pants pockets. Defeat took root in his expression. "Believe it or not, that's not why I'm here."

"Would you care to elaborate on that?"

"I want to talk to you about the murders."

Realization dawned. He should have seen this sooner. "And you think I've had something to do with this."

"It wasn't me, or Marco or Amara. That leaves you." Royce paused, letting the information sink in. "And I've got to tell you, with your history I wouldn't put it past you."

Eric stalked to the balcony and looked out through the doors. "I wouldn't kill a woman for the sake of a meal. Vampires do that sort of thing. I'm far less barbaric. I don't kill humans, at least not often. And that's only if they deserve it. Deep down, I think you know that."

"It seems to me that you'd do just about anything if the mood struck." Royce leaned against the wall, not moving more than a few feet away from the door. "You weren't exactly discriminating before. Why change now, after so many years?"

Eric reined in the urge to haul off and punch the man. Royce truly didn't understand, even after all these years, the importance of Eric's job. Royce didn't approve of the killing aspect, but sometimes it was necessary. If someone didn't take care of the rogues, the planet would be overrun by vampires, werewolves, and similar creatures. Such egos running rampant would destroy the planet in a matter of months. The balance had to be kept, in whatever way was required. Sometimes, it took the death of a few to protect the masses.

"I haven't killed humans, or any other being, without good reason in a thousand years, no matter what you *think* you believe. You should go now, before I decide to kill for fun, starting with you."

The corners of Royce's mouth curled in a sneer, but he looked like he as fighting a genuine smile. "You wouldn't dare."

"And why not? According to you, I live for killing. What's one more vampire to me?"

"Okay. Enough. This has gone too far, for too long." Royce shook his head, his expression turning weary. "This may surprise you, but I'm sick of the hostility. It's time to move on. You're going to hurt Ellie. I'm going to tell you this right now. I'll do anything to prevent that from happening. She means a lot to me, and to my brother and his wife. Hurting her would be a big mistake."

"If I didn't know you better, I'd think you were jealous." Eric raised his eyebrows and waited for the reaction.

Royce crossed his arms over his chest, his gaze unwavering. "Ellie's a friend. I don't suppose you'd understand that, since you don't have any. But I care about her, and I refuse to stand by and watch you tear her apart. That's my only warning. Now tell me what you know about these murders. Prove to me that you're not involved."

Eric nearly rolled his eyes. He'd never had to *prove* himself so often in his life. He took a deep breath, not sure how much he should tell the man—one who'd shunned his kind of lifestyle so many years ago. "I think Aiala's involved."

Royce laughed, but Eric didn't miss the apprehension that flashed across his face. "Aiala wouldn't sully herself killing ordinary humans in a place like this."

"It isn't about the humans. It's about us." He paused. "Christopher, Bryant, and Edward are dead." He paused again to let the implications of his words sink in. Royce's gaze grew incredulous, then suspicious.

"And that couldn't be a coincidence, considering the lives they led? They weren't exactly saints."

"It's not a coincidence. I've been tracking the same vampire for months. I tracked him here, and then the trail vanished. He didn't leave, but I can't find him. And now the bodies are starting to appear."

Royce rubbed the bridge of his nose between his index finger and thumb. "That sounds just like a game Aiala would love to play—Cat and Mouse of the highest order. Does Ellie know any of this? Does she know what you are?"

Eric shook his head. If she knew, she'd never speak to him again. "She knows the name. I didn't explain it."

"You'd better, before she finds another source of information—one that might be misleading. You wouldn't want her getting the wrong idea."

He was right, of course, but Eric would cut out his tongue with a plastic knife before he admitted it. "I'll think about it. She doesn't need that much information."

Royce snorted. "It sounds more like you don't want her to know, because you're afraid she'll walk away from you if she finds out. Trust me on this, Malcolm. Ellie is one lady who doesn't like being kept in the dark. If you want even a chance with her, you've got to tell her."

"Thanks for the advice," Eric said, but he still planned to do nothing just yet. If she really wanted to know, she had a name she could reference at the library. He'd rolled, and now he just had to wait and see where the dice landed—at least on the personal front. The professional front still troubled him. That was where he needed to focus. "Have you noticed anything unusual around town recently?"

"Not since I've been here. What about you?"

"I'm not even close on this one. Honestly, I don't know where to turn next." It killed him to admit that. For Eric, failure of any kind was not acceptable. Royce knew that, and Eric had no doubt he'd exploit that weakness. He didn't, which baffled Eric.

Royce nodded slowly, his gaze fixed on the window across the room. "Let me talk to my brother and see if we can come up with something. I'll get back to you soon." He walked to the door and turned back to face Eric. "If you hurt Ellie, I'll kill you. If you get out of line once, I'll rip your head off."

Without waiting for a response, he left the room, slamming the door behind him. Eric sank onto the bed and turned on the TV with the remote on the nightstand. He should feel better after that visit, but he only felt worse. He had to find the vampire before it destroyed him. He found the eleven o'clock news and watched the anchor talk about the latest murder, which only added to his melancholy.

"The woman's body was found half dressed in an alley behind a restaurant. Her identity has yet to be confirmed. The police aren't yet revealing any other details about the crime."

He sighed heavily. He didn't need to hear the cause of death to know what had happened—severe loss of blood. He had to find a way to bring Aiala and her lackey out into the open before someone else died, possibly someone he'd grown fond of in his time in the little town.

* * * * *

Ellie couldn't concentrate on anything the next day. That seemed to be a common occurrence since Eric had started hanging around. Even the hour she usually spent meditating in her quiet place—a dark corner of her studio—hadn't helped. She sat out on her patio, her laptop on the table in front of her. A damp chill hung in the air, promising a summer storm.

She wrapped her arms around herself and shivered, thinking about what those poor women must have gone through. For a vampire to kill during a feeding, it would take an amazingly long time and a great deal of strength. The woman would have squirmed at first, maybe fought violently when she realized what was happening to her. To hold her down for that long would never be an accident, unless the vampire was a fledgling with no understanding of what they were doing.

Amara would have easily detected a fledgling.

So the killings had to be deliberate murders. Not accidents caused by someone young and out-of-control. The thought left her blood cold. There were *never* murders in Stone Harbor. She liked it here because she felt safe, all the time. It had been the perfect place to live.

But not anymore.

Two women were dead, most likely victims of vampire attacks, and she had a feeling it wasn't over yet.

Her nerves were shot and her hands shaky. She *needed* to talk to Eric, see if he could make sense of any of this. The way they'd left things the last time they spoke bothered her. She wanted his explanation of what he'd told her, but so far he hadn't been available. She'd been afraid of the questions she had, and more afraid of the answers, but now she didn't care.

She had to know.

She logged online through her cell phone and typed the name he'd given her into the search engine. It took a few tries to get the spelling right, but once she did she found a wealth of information. *Disturbing* information. Her throat went dry and she almost fell out of her chair. He hadn't been lying when he'd told her he was neither a vampire nor a lycanthrope. He wasn't any of those things—wasn't even close. She now realized why she'd never heard of *Panthicenos* before she'd met him. This wasn't the kind of thing a person readily disclosed.

She shook her head, her hands shaking so much she could barely scroll through the pages. She didn't believe in absolute evil of any kind—not hell, or Satan, or anything of the sort. Her mother and grandmother had raised her in that tradition and she'd accepted it blindly, until now. If the information she found proved to be true, then some of what she'd accepted as fact all her life was a lie. It wasn't possible, but at the same time she knew what she read had to be true, and now her life would never be the same.

Eric was a demon.

Chapter 9

Ellie stared at the screen in mute distress, not knowing what to think. According to her family, demons didn't exist, but Eric was definitely not a figment of her imagination. So who was she to believe—the family she'd trusted all her life or a couple of Internet websites? There had to be some other explanation.

"*Panthicenos* are demons with the ability to shift into several forms, including that of a large cat similar to a panther and a human form." She took a deep breath before she continued reading, not certain she really wanted any more information than she already had. "The true *Panthicenos* form has been depicted as a large feline with black fur, red eyes, enormous teeth, and a row of spiked scales along the length of the spine." She ran her fingers over a black-and-white drawing of the *Panthicenos* on the screen.

She shivered at the thought, unable to accept that she could very well be reading a description of Eric.

"What are you looking at? Anything interesting?"

Ellie whirled at the sound of Eric's voice behind her. "Why are you here?" She glared at him to cover the fact that her heart threatened to pound right out of her chest. She'd never known fear like she did at this moment, faced with something that could have come from childhood nightmares, but she couldn't let him see how frightened she was. "What do you want from me?"

He leaned against the side of the house, remaining a few feet away, and shrugged. "That depends. How much do you know?"

He shook his head when she must have looked ready to pass out. A smile broke over his face—out of place with everything she'd just read. "Sorry. Bad joke. I suppose, by the look on your face, I should assume that you've taken it upon yourself to do some research?"

She pursed her lips and nodded, looking for a way to get away from him—and *not* have him follow. How could he joke with her at a time like this? Confusion had replaced any sensibilities she'd had, and she couldn't think straight.

"You don't have to worry, Ellie. I didn't lie when I said I wouldn't hurt you. In fact, lately I've been thinking more and more about protecting you."

Amara's words about a stalker came back to her then. Had she been right? She'd been so sure she could trust him. She rubbed her totem, asking for clarity. She remembered the disturbing dream as the panther heated again under her touch. With jerky movements she unclasped the silver chain and set the necklace roughly down on the table surface, the connection she felt with the animal severed. In one afternoon, one minute, she'd gone from having absolute trust in her faith to doubting *everything*. She turned slowly to face him, a knot of fear twisting her gut.

His gaze begged her to believe in him, but she couldn't, not yet. Her world had just fallen down around her and she needed some time to pick up the pieces.

"Ellie, say something. I can't stand the silence." His voice held so much sadness she felt a sharp urge to go to him, to wrap her arms around him and comfort him. Instead, she just sat there, unable to convince her body to move.

"I don't believe in you."

"What?" Confusion etched his features as he shook his head.

She let out a heavy breath before she answered, choosing her words carefully. "My family has been practicing witchcraft for generations. It's a big part of who I am. Witches don't believe in evil. I've always been told that demons are figments of imagination, horrible stories parents invented to scare misbehaving children. So either my family lied to me, or you did."

"I haven't lied to you. I'm willing to talk now, if you still want to." His words, and the sincerity in his gaze, gave her pause. How could she even entertain the idea that this man could be evil? She knew in her heart at that moment, as the clarity she'd been begging for calmed her rampant emotions, that there was more to the situation that what she'd read.

"Will you answer my questions now? All of them?"

He quickly nodded. The simple act, coupled with the hope that flared in his eyes, made her believe that anything was possible. Maybe this would work out fine in the end.

"Are you a demon, Eric?"

His stance shifted and he seemed to shrink away from her. At the same time, she felt him in her mind, not controlling or reading, but comforting—just *there*. He begged her to understand, to accept him for what he was. "Yes."

Now she couldn't pretend anymore. She couldn't call her fears the work of an overactive imagination, or the result of an article full of mistruths. This was all very real, and it was her life. She'd allowed him to get close, and allowed herself to care about him, and now she'd have to live with the consequences.

He took one step closer, then another. "The word 'demon' by definition doesn't have an evil connotation. There are good demons in the world as well as evil ones. Unfortunately, the general populace only cares about the evil ones."

A question from an old movie popped into her head. *Are you a good witch or a bad witch?* The absurdity of the situation made a hysterical laugh bubble in her throat. "So then, you're a...good demon?"

"Not exactly."

She pushed out of her chair and stalked away from the table, hugging her arms around her to ward off the sudden chill. "Excuse me if I find this conversation more confusing than enlightening."

"This situation isn't black and white. It's so hard to explain this to someone who hasn't lived the life I do. We all have our urges—anyone is capable of killing if the circumstances are right. You know me well enough to know what kind of a man I am." He walked over to her and toyed with a strand of her hair. She jerked her head back and stepped away, and his expression darkened.

"I hardly know you at all," she whispered, just learning how truthful that statement was.

"You might not know me with your mind," he paused, brushing one finger over her head. When he spoke again, he did so in a whispered tone. "But you know me with your body, and with your heart." He settled his finger over her wildly thumping heart. "It's been like that from the beginning, for both of us."

"I don't think..." Her words trailed off when she realized he was right. Something in her recognized him in a very primal way, and she knew he felt the same. But it didn't make trusting him any easier, not with this new information.

"Can we talk for a little while?" he asked when she didn't say anything.

She hesitated. The news of the murders had shaken the entire town—her especially. The more she heard about them, the more she assumed it was a vampire killing. But what if demons were the problem instead?

He read her suspicions before she could voice them. "I know you don't trust me. I understand. I don't blame you for being angry, and scared, but I thought if you didn't know..." He sighed when she raised an eyebrow at him. "Okay. I was being selfish. I thought if you knew what I was, you would think of me differently."

"Gee, ya think?" She couldn't keep the sarcasm out of her voice. "This is not the sort of thing that happens every day, you know."

"I realize that. It's not something that's ever happened to me before, either, so this is new for both of us. I thought if I told you the truth, you'd never want to see me again. I couldn't take that. Haven't you ever been rejected because of something other people found different about you?"

She opened her mouth to berate him again, but snapped it shut when his words sank in. She thought back to her marriage, and how poorly Todd had reacted to the idea of her being a witch. Even during grade school, she hadn't fit in. She'd been the creepy girl from the weird family, the girl who wore a pentacle around her neck when the other children wore crosses. She'd hated it then, the way they'd judged her without really taking the time to know her, the way they'd made her feel she had to hide her true self in order to be accepted. Wasn't she doing the same thing to Eric?

He took her hand in his and brought it to his lips, kissing the center of her palm. "You know me, Ellie. I can feel it inside you. Don't give up what we could have because you think you know something about me."

She shook her head, but at the same time his words hit a chord inside her. When she thought of demons, she pictured the typical storybook image—horns and claws and fangs and fire, the smell of brimstone in the air. She'd certainly never pictured a man who looked like an ordinary human. It just didn't fit. She glanced at him and saw his expression filled with apprehension and remorse. Maybe she *was* judging him unfairly. Didn't he deserve a chance to relay his side of the story before she made snap judgments? "Tell me about yourself, Eric. I need to hear it from you, not from some website."

A small smile broke over his face, and it warmed her inside. "*Panthicenos* are keepers of the peace. It's been that way since ancient times. Not much has changed since then. By nature, we can't be described as either good or evil, because we're both. As far as demons go, we're as neutral as you can get."

He reached his hand up and stroked his finger along her jaw line, sending a ripple of sensation through her. She gasped and backed up a step, confused at how she could still respond so strongly to him, knowing what he was.

His hands gripped her arms and stopped her retreat. He smiled hesitantly as he leaned in and kissed her softly, his lips barely brushing over hers before he pulled back. The little kiss was all it took for her insides to melt. "I worry about you, you know."

Her response came automatically after years of taking care of everyone else. She waved a hand in the air and shook her head, brushing off his concern. "You don't need to. I've got it covered."

"I know. I *want* to."

That had to be one of the nicest things anyone had ever said to her. How long had it been since a man had really cared about her? Had a man *ever* really cared about her enough to say such things to her? She couldn't remember. It figured. The one guy who finally treated her right just happened to be a demon.

"Do you forgive me?" he asked, his gaze questioning. "I would have told you, if I hadn't thought it would push you away."

"I'll think about it." That was probably *all* she would do, for weeks. He'd given her a lot to contemplate.

"Think fast," he grumbled, turning away. "I can't deal with another stress in my life right now."

"Well, excuse me. Forgive me if I don't want to blow this off like it's nothing. Because it's most definitely *something*." She frowned at him, letting him know how upset she still was at his deception. "This changes my whole life, you know. Nothing is ever going to be the same again."

"That's not always a bad thing."

Her frown melted away at the sensual look in his eyes. She planted her hands on her hips and glared at him, still trying to be furious. But she just didn't have the heart to keep up the emotions. Sure, he'd kept the truth—a pretty *important* truth— from her for too long, and he'd dodged most of her questions until she'd done some research on her own, but she couldn't judge him as bad just because of what he was. She hadn't done that to Marco, or Amara or Royce, and she couldn't do it to Eric, either. She couldn't respect people who prejudged others before getting to know them, and she wasn't going to stoop to that level.

She reached deep inside herself for answers, and was surprised at what she found. She lifted her necklace from the table and secured the chain around her neck. The connection she'd had all her life with the panther hadn't been broken. It was stronger now than it had ever been, filling her with trust and strength.

"Do you want to come in for coffee or something?" she asked, finally giving in to what she really wanted — to end the disagreements and get on with her life. So the guy was a demon. As long as he wasn't into ritualistic killing, she supposed she could deal with it.

An amused, yet hesitant, expression crossed his face. "I'd like to come in for a while, but only if you're sure."

Sure? She wasn't sure about anything. But to be honest, her life had been on pause since her divorce, and it was about time she started living again. Maybe getting involved with Eric was a little extreme, but she couldn't help it now. She was in too deep, and it was too late to turn back now.

"Yes, I'm sure." She smiled at him before she turned and walked away across the yard.

She entered the house through the kitchen door. Eric followed, but he stayed a few feet behind. She paused by the sink and turned to him. "Do you want coffee or tea?"

"No."

No? "Well, okay. How about water?"

"No." He shook his head slowly, his gaze spearing hers.

The hot intensity in his eyes went straight to her stomach, settling like a ball of fire. She gulped and drew in a sharp breath, suddenly nervous. For the first time, he gave her a glimpse of his power, and it excited and scared her at the same time. For just a few seconds she saw him as the forceful man in her dreams instead of the man she thought she knew. Clenching her hands into fists at her sides, she tried her best to appear calm and collected. She knew she failed when her question came out as a squeak. "Can I get you anything at all?"

He shook his head. "Are you still scared of me?"

She was scared of what this could become. There were so many reasons why she shouldn't get involved with Eric, and she'd been thinking about them nonstop since they'd met. If she took him upstairs to her bedroom, there wouldn't be any going back. She'd be involved, and there wouldn't be any denying it. She didn't know how long it would last, but she had a feeling it would be a wild ride.

"I'm not scared of you," she answered as honestly as she could. "It's this thing between us that scares me."

"It's chemistry, Ellie, nothing to be afraid of. I know what I want from you. Now you need to decide what you want from me." He spread his hands out in front of him as he spoke. "Whatever happens has to be your decision."

And what exactly was it that he wanted from her? She was afraid to ask.

He continued when she didn't answer. "Will you give me a chance to show you what I want to do to you?"

His expression took on a wicked gleam and her heart skipped a beat. Whatever things confused her about this man, the sexual attraction she felt for him wasn't one of them. She knew, without a doubt, that sex with him would be fabulous. What she didn't know was if she could have sex with him, and not want more. He shook her more than anyone ever had, and she didn't know if she'd be able to get past that, but as far as she could tell they had no chance at a future together.

"I can give you whatever you want," he said. "Anything at all. What is it you want from me, Ellie? I don't know, so you're going to have to tell me."

"What exactly are you offering?"

"Anything. Everything."

She shoved the implications of those words out of her mind, deciding to concentrate on the physical. She took a deep breath, her decision made. Demon or not, she wanted him. However weird it might sound, this could be a once-in-a-lifetime opportunity. "I want you. For now, I want to forget about the rest of it, forget what you are. I just want to be with you right now. Is that even possible?" She dropped her gaze to the ground, embarrassed at her cluelessness.

He laughed softly. "Honey, it's more than possible. I think it's inevitable."

"But how can we...if you're not...?"

"Trust me, Ellie. We're very compatible. In this form, I'm just like any other man."

Somehow, she doubted that. A smile spread over her face. "Prove it."

Chapter 10

"Prove it?"

Eric's eyes darkened, turning a deep shade of forest green. The gold flecks stood out even more with the change, making his eyes appear inhuman—predatory in the basest sense of the word. The heat in his gaze snagged her, pinning her to the spot where she stood on the kitchen floor as effectively as if he'd shackled her. She drew a deep breath, her body shaking, as she waited for his response.

Several seconds passed. His gaze held her prisoner and she felt the conflicting need to run into his arms, and run away. Something in him had altered, become more...animalistic. It stunned her with both fear and excitement. He walked across the kitchen as if in slow motion. She gasped and gripped the counter behind her for support as he stepped closer, his long limbs moving with a grace that belied his strength.

He stopped in front of her and placed his hands on the counter, one on each side of her body. Now physically trapped, she shuddered at what he could do to her. She'd had a small sampling of his touch, and it only whet her appetite for more. Would he give her what she wanted—what her body so desperately craved—or would he distance himself like he had before?

She reached her hand up to his chest, but he shook his head as her fingers brushed his shirt. "Hold still." His raspy command drew her gaze back up to his eyes, and she wet her lips with the tip of her tongue.

She opened her mouth to answer, but he shook his head again. The faintest of smiles played on his lips. "Don't speak."

"What—?"

He brushed his lips over hers, silencing her question. "Trust yourself." His tongue traced the seam of her lips. "Trust *us*."

She took a deep breath to steady herself, the beginnings of arousal stirring low in her belly. She let the air out slowly and completely, willing her body to remain still—not an easy task as Eric's teeth grazed the sensitive skin just below her ear. She shivered and gripped the counter more tightly, a small moan escaping her lips.

"You like that." His warm breath whispered across her skin as he spoke. She nodded in agreement. Even though only his mouth made contact with her body, she felt his touch on every inch of her.

He nudged her chin with his lips and she let her head drop back as he ran his tongue along the pulse beating fiercely in her neck. He nipped gently. Unable—and unwilling—to hide her state of arousal from him, she reveled in it instead. She allowed her body to take over, overriding concern and logic and anything else that got in the way.

Finally, he pressed fully against her, trapping her between the hard wall of his chest and groin, and the counter. Heat radiated from him and she arched into it, greedily absorbing it into her body until she was liquid fire. Her sex ached with a need so great it nearly brought her to her knees. She leaned into the counter, her grip iron and her legs no longer able to support her weight.

He kissed her then, hard and demanding. His tongue delved into the heat of her mouth as he rocked his hips gently against hers. She moaned and clung to the counter—her position prohibiting any further movement. If he continued with this torture, she might just die on the spot. Eric made her feel so needy that she responded wildly.

She didn't hear the front door open or the footsteps in the hall until Charlotte spoke from the kitchen doorway. "Ellie, did you see that—? Oh, I'm sorry. I didn't mean to interrupt."

Eric rested his forehead against Ellie's for a moment, breathing heavily, before he released her. She sagged against the counter, her legs still not willing to hold her. "What's wrong, Charlotte?"

Charlotte looked from Ellie to Eric, and back to Ellie again. A smile spread across her face. "Oh, nothing important. Go on with whatever you're doing. I won't bother you again."

She grabbed a can of soda from the fridge and walked out of the room. Ellie didn't speak until she heard the sounds of the TV set in the living room.

"I'm so sorry, Eric. I didn't know she planned to be home today."

He raised an eyebrow and shot a glance in the direction of the living room. "Where's your bedroom?"

Ellie's eyes widened in shock. "We can't now. She'll know what we're doing."

"She already knows. She's an adult. I'm sure she'll understand." He snagged her wrist and drew her up against him, dipping his mouth to hers for a kiss that left her breathless and wanting all over again. "I think it'll be okay."

"Upstairs. My bedroom is upstairs. But we have to be quiet."

"Absolutely." Something in his eyes told her he didn't mean it, but she took his hand anyway and led him up the stairs.

When the reached the first landing, Eric pushed her against the wall and kissed her hard. He lifted one of her legs up over his hip and rocked his pelvis against hers. His hard cock ground against her mound, sending a jolt through her despite the layers of fabric between them. She put her palms on the wall behind her to keep her balance, afraid of falling down the stairs.

He worked his hands under the hem of her shirt, his fingers skimming along her skin until they brushed the undersides of her breasts. He started to lift the shirt over her head, but a smidgen of common sense kicked in, and she put her hands over his to stop him.

"Hold up, Romeo. Why don't we take this into the bedroom?" She pulled her shirt back down and walked the rest of the way up the stairs, batting at his hands when he grabbed for her.

Eric sighed dramatically. "Do we have to? I was having so much fun."

"Yes, we do." By the time she shut the bedroom door behind them, the intensity was back in his gaze.

"Eric?" she asked, suddenly uncertain. Charlotte's interruption had shaken her, brought back so much of the logic she'd tried to bury.

He didn't answer, didn't speak at all, as he gripped her waist and pulled her toward the bed. He let himself fall back when his legs hit the mattress, taking her with him. In seconds, he had her rolled over onto her back, pinned under him on the mattress.

She cleared her throat, not wanting to bring up an uncomfortable situation but knowing it needed to be done before thing went too far. "Um, I don't have any protection. Do you, maybe...?"

He looked down at her, his face a mask of frustration. "We don't need any. This isn't something a guy usually admits to a woman he's about to make love to, but I can't get you pregnant."

"You can't? Are you sure?"

"You're human." He kissed the tip of her nose. "If you were a cat, it might happen, but with a human, it's not even a possibility."

She let out a sigh of relief. "That's good to know."

He smiled in answer before he leaned in and kissed her long and deep. His knee wedged between her legs, moving them further apart until he settled himself between them. He felt so hard, *everywhere,* and so good against her that she moaned into his mouth. She could barely hold back for wanting him so badly.

It had never been like this. With Eric, everything was different. He had the skill to touch her in just the right place—just the right *way*—and she felt like her body melted and dissolved, replaced by thousands of points of light. She ground her hips shamelessly against him, relishing in the pressure of his cock against her throbbing sex. She tore at his shirt, desperate to feel his bare skin against hers.

He didn't stop her this time. He showered her face and neck with kisses while she worked the buttons, finally freeing the last one and tugging the shirt out of the waistband of his pants. Her hands splayed on his bare chest, her fingers moving through the dark hair sprinkled across his skin. He let out a soft groan when she flicked his flat nipples with her fingernails.

He slid off her when she grasped the zipper of his pants. "Not yet." He sat on the edge of the bed and unzipped her shorts, sliding them down her legs.

She sat up halfway to let him remove her shirt, and before she had a chance to react, he'd flipped her onto her stomach. He skimmed her panties down her legs. The satin rubbed against her sensitive skin, and she squirmed.

He ran his hands down her back, kissing her spine just above her ass. When his touch left her, she tried to turn over to reach for him, but he nudged her back against the mattress. He took her leg in his hands and used his thumbs to massage the tender skin of her sole. The soft pressure tickled and aroused at the same time and she found herself unable to hold still. She'd expected him to be inside her already, not to be playing with her foot.

As new and different as it was, it felt good. His touch scorched her wherever he touched—the fact that he touched such a usually unsexy place didn't matter. She relaxed against the mattress and let him do what he wanted.

Seeming to sense her need, he slid a finger along her slit, finally pressing the very tip into her cunt. She arched into the touch, trying to get more of him inside her. With slow deliberation, he inched his finger deeper. Every time she wriggled, he stopped moving until she finally gave up and stilled. He placed a kiss in the center of the sole of her foot.

"*Eric*," she pleaded. He didn't understand her struggle to hold still while he tortured her. The vibrations of his answering laugh traveled a path from the sole of her foot straight to her clit, making her inner muscles contract and tremble. She fisted her hands in the comforter, fighting desperately for control. In another second, she was going to come, with or without his help.

He thrust his finger deep inside her at the same time as his thumb pressed down on her clit. Her body bowed and her orgasm took her with a force that exploded all the way to her toes. She cried out, bucking against his hand as much as her position would allow.

Not giving her much time to recover, he rolled her to her back and settled himself next to her on the bed. He splayed his palm over her stomach and kissed the side of her neck. "Feel better now?"

She could barely move, barely speak, but she managed a slight nod before she let her head flop to the side on the pillow. Eric laughed. "Should I take that as a no?"

"I'm fine." She struggled to smile, yet her muscles refused to obey even that simple command. Sated, she let her eyelids flutter closed.

"Ellie?"

She opened an eye at his command.

"We're not finished yet."

She let her gaze wander down the length of his body. His cock jutted out, the tip brushing against the side of her leg. Smiling sleepily, she reached for him. "Well, I hope not."

His laugh bordered on pained as she stroked him, catching the drop of pre-come with her thumb and spreading it around the head. He held out for only a few minutes before he removed her hand. "Do you want the top or the bottom?"

He had to be kidding. She could barely keep her eyes open. There was no way she'd be able to hold herself upright. "Bottom."

He draped her leg over his hip and pulled her toward him so they faced each other, side by side. "How about we compromise?"

He slid into her slowly, fully impaling her with one long, torturously slow stroke. The fire she'd thought extinguished returned as he pushed inside, burning low in her belly and spreading to her cunt. He filled her completely, moving in and out with measured precision. His hand caressed the sweat-slicked skin of her back in time with his strokes, his touch sending tiny jolts of sensation through her. She sighed quietly and wrapped her leg tighter around his hip to pull him closer.

This was it. He was the one she'd been waiting for. The thought almost made her laugh, though, since all her life she'd believed she made her own destiny. This time, fate had snuck up on her, smacking her with a seemingly impossible truth before she even realized it.

His gaze snagged hers, mirroring the lust she felt inside, and she couldn't look away. She threaded her fingers in the hair at the nape of his neck, pulling him to her for a kiss. She felt him holding back—for her sake, most likely, but she didn't want him to think he had to. She was a lot tougher than she looked, and she could handle most anything he could do to her. She *wanted* him rough. She didn't want him to be gentle—it wasn't what she was looking for. She wanted *Eric*, and whatever else went along with that.

She deepened the kiss and cupped his ass in her hand, squeezing gently. His response to her silent demand came immediately, harshly. He groaned and thrust harder, increasing the tempo of his strokes. She pulled him closer with her heel, but it wasn't close enough. Her lethargy had all but faded, leaving her with a renewed sense of wanton desire that baffled her.

He seemed to sense how she felt, and rolled her onto her back. His strokes grew quicker—short, stabbing thrusts that pushed him deeply inside her. The vibrations of his deep thrusts spiraled within her, pushing her into another earth-shattering climax. She dug her fingers into his biceps and hung on as her whole body convulsed. When she finally relaxed under him he took his release, a primal groan escaping his lips as he stiffened and shuddered over her.

Eric kissed her forehead before he withdrew and lay down by her side. He rested his head on her stomach, his damp hair brushing across her breasts. His lips tickled her when he kissed her navel, and then traced the thin blue lines of her veins, just visible beneath the skin, with his tongue. She quivered and he laughed. "How are you feeling?"

"Fine. What about you?" She stroked his now damp hair, absently twisting the strands around her fingers.

"I don't know." He laughed again. "I think you're trying to kill me. I don't know how I held out that long without..."

His voice trailed off, but she'd known what he was going to say. "You wouldn't have hurt me."

He rested his chin on her stomach and looked up at her. "I might have. I tried to be careful, but it's difficult. You're so delicate. I don't know what I was thinking. I never should have let that happen."

He scooted up in the bed and tried to roll away, but she wrapped her arms around his neck and pulled him back to her. "Don't start. I'm fine. I'm not as fragile as I look. You're not going to break me by touching me."

He stared at her for a long time, as if judging her sincerity. He closed his eyes and took a deep breath. When he opened them, the golden tone had intensified even more, and it gave her a slight shiver. "I had to struggle to keep myself in check. It wasn't easy, Ellie."

"You promised to never hurt me, and I believe you. Don't worry about it. I trust you."

He raised an eyebrow at her confession, surprise lighting his features. "You do?"

"Of course I do." She rolled her eyes. "Do you think I would have invited you into my bed if I didn't?"

He laughed, the sound rumbling in his chest and vibrating against her skin. The vibrant colors of the sunset flooded the room, washing the white bed linens in pastel pinks and oranges. Eric's skin appeared even more bronze in the soft light, and she was surprised to find he didn't have a single tan line. She liked the contrast of his dark skin against the paleness of her own. He had a few scars on his back, arms, and chest, but it only made him seem more real to her.

She stroked his back lightly with her fingers, delighting in the tremor that ran through him. One corner of his mouth raised in a lopsided smile. "You scare me, you know."

She frowned, his statement being the last thing she expected. "How do *I* scare *you*?"

He took a deep breath and let it out slowly before he answered. "My mother died many years ago, leaving me to care for my sister alone. I was young, but Merida wasn't much more than a baby. It was hard, too hard for a couple of kids. I had trouble finding food and shelter in bad weather."

Her heart broke for him, knowing he'd been born into a time when there were no shelters, no places for him to go. "Have you always lived…? I don't even know what to ask here."

"*Panthicenos* are earthbound demons. We can't leave, couldn't survive life on the demonic plane. We have to live basically the same as humans, eating and sleeping, buying or finding what we need, unlike some demonic races we can't just conjure up whatever we want." He sighed heavily and settled his head down on the mattress. "Like I told you before, our original purpose was to maintain the status quo. So yes, I've lived on this plane for my entire life. Sam took in Merida and me, put me to work, and helped me raise my sister. I…I went through a lot before he found me, Ellie, and I've seen a lot since. I don't trust easily. I just wanted you to know that."

His confession sounded suspiciously like a warning. "You don't trust me?"

He barked a laugh, his hand patting her ass. "The thing is, I do trust you. I've told you that I'd had other lovers. But I never felt the urge to lounge around and talk afterwards, and I never told any of them about my family and my childhood—or any other part of my life."

"You haven't?"

He shook his head, his chin moving back and forth across her shoulder. "I won't say I've never been in love before, because I have. In a thousand years, you're bound to meet a few people you're drawn to. But there are so many things I'm telling you that I've never told anyone before. This is different."

"How so?"

He didn't answer. Instead he shook his head again, nipped her earlobe, and rested his cheek against her skin. She felt him sigh and knew the conversation was over.

For now.

If he thought that he was going to dump a confession like that on her and expect her to ignore it, he was sadly mistaken. He'd just about told her he loved her, and she wasn't going to let him get away with such a casual statement. Just like she wasn't going to let him get away with keeping secrets from her either. He'd pay for the whole demon thing, too, but later when the afterglow had subsided and she didn't feel so sated. Right now she needed time to recover, and at least a few days to sort through all the information.

* * * * *

Ellie accepted the glass of iced tea from her grandmother and sat in one of the plastic chairs on the porch. Eric had stayed with her for a few hours before he'd gotten up and dressed, saying he needed to get to work. Something about his tone had worried her. There was still so much about him that she didn't know, but with any luck she'd have plenty of time to ask questions later.

The man was a demon, not entirely good, but not entirely evil. A man who spent his life "taking care of" the bad guys, in the worst sense of the word—those thoughts settled a knot in the pit of her stomach and filled her with apprehension. She hadn't wanted him to leave, but maybe it had been for the best. A little separation might do her some good.

"You've been very busy lately." Carol sat down across from her, breaking into her thoughts. "I haven't seen you much. Is it because of your painting, or is it something more personal?"

Ellie shrugged. In all honesty, she'd done hardly any painting since she'd met Eric. Her concentration, and her drive, just hadn't been there. "Personal, I guess."

"Eric seems very nice."

Oh, yeah. About as nice as you could get for a demon. She bit back a bubble of hysterical laughter. When had her life turned into some kind of supernatural soap opera?

"Tell me about him," Carol continued, leaning forward on the table. The interrogation was about to start.

Ellie shook her head. "There's not much to tell."

"What does he do for a living?"

I don't think so. "Oh, this and that."

"He's unemployed."

"No, he's not unemployed. It's complicated, okay?" She felt bad for snapping, but she wished her family would just butt out of her business for once. It was bad enough that she was becoming attached to the man—Carol would definitely not approve, she'd liked Royce fine as long as he stayed away from her granddaughter—but she had a feeling there was a lot more to his job than being a simple bounty hunter.

"You're very touchy today. Maybe you need to get more sleep."

"Yeah, that must be it." Ellie took a long sip of iced tea through the straw. She'd been decidedly crabby lately, and most of it could be attributed to the murderer still on the loose. She wasn't usually extremely intuitive, but she had a feeling this was going to last for a while, or at least until the murderer was stopped.

"Make sure you don't go out alone, especially after dark," Ellie said to Carol. "It's not safe for anyone right now."

Carol nodded. "I know. I had a talk with Charlotte about it, but I'm concerned about you, too. Sometimes those friends of yours make me a little nervous."

"They're vampires, Nana, not serial killers. I'm safer with them than Charlotte is with those ghost investigator guys she hangs out with." Ellie set her glass down on the table. "I'll be fine. I have plenty of people watching out for me."

"I'm glad to hear that. You worry me, you know that?"

That was a change. "I do?"

"Of course. You've always been too independent for your own good. So headstrong, and you take too many chances. I think it's getting to be about time that you settle down with a nice man and give me a couple of great-grandchildren."

Ellie laughed. "Oh, I don't think so."

"Why not? Just as long as the nice young man is a *human* one, I'll approve."

Lovely. Ellie made a mental note to keep the woman away from Eric. If she ever found out that he was something worse than the vampires, Ellie would never hear the end of it. "I'm not ready to settle down yet. When I change my mind, you'll be the first to know."

Carol sighed. "It would just be nice to know that you've got a man around the house to take care of you. I hope you've done a protection spell, with all that's going on around here."

"Of course I have." She'd also done one for Becca, who refused to do her own. With that shady boyfriend, Becca probably needed it much more than Ellie did. She finished her iced tea and stood up. "I've got to get going now. I promised to meet Amara in the park. There's something she wanted to talk to me about."

"I swear, Ann Elizabeth. Don't you have any human friends?"

Ellie sighed. She was getting sick of having to explain this to the woman. "They *are* human, Nana, just not the same as we are." Well, at least that was close enough to the truth.

Carol had known about vampires for years. It had been twenty years ago, in this town, that she'd first met Marco. The big brother Ellie had never had, he'd inspired her to take up painting. She'd known right away that Marco was different — sometimes children saw things differently than adults — and by the time he saw fit to confess to her when she was seventeen, she'd already known his secret for two years. It had taken her mother and grandmother a long time to get used to the idea, but Ellie had warmed up to it easily.

Sometimes her family still struggled with it, even after Marco helped Ellie's mom get rid of some particularly hostile neighbors. That was part of the reason she was being so hesitant with Eric. She wanted a normal life, not one she'd seen her friends live. If she'd ever met a human man like him, it would be a miracle. He was just what she'd been looking for.

Unfortunately, he was also many things she'd rather not have in her life. He was dangerous, and part of her knew that. She didn't want to give him up just yet, but she knew eventually she'd have to. Last time she'd checked, there weren't a heck of many stable human-demon marriages.

She thanked her grandmother for the visit and drove downtown. When she got to the park, Amara was already there, sitting under a tree with sunglasses on her face and a large brimmed straw hat covering her dark hair. "I don't know why we couldn't have met somewhere inside," she complained, looking up as Ellie approached. "This sunlight is a killer."

Ellie checked her watch. "Wimp. It's not so bad this time of day. Besides, I'm getting sick of going into restaurants and being the only one to ever order anything."

Amara smiled. "I could turn you if you want. Then you won't feel left out." Her smile widened and she cackled dramatically. "Better yet, let Royce do it. I'm sure he wouldn't mind."

Royce. Had he not gotten around to telling his brother and sister-in-law that he'd dumped her a couple days ago? Ellie shook her head. "I'm all set. Believe me, I prefer to live my life as a human."

"That's too bad. I hate to think I'm going to lose you soon." Amara stopped at her own words and gulped audibly. "I didn't mean… You know, I just… Oh, hell. You've got me so worried I can't even talk straight. All I meant was that the human life span is so short compared to the vampire's."

Ellie fixed Amara with a glare. Her friend had something to say, but for some reason insisted on avoiding the truth. "Tell me."

"Tell you what?" Amara feigned innocence, but she'd never been very good at that particular ploy.

"Tell me why you'd make a comment like that, and then refuse to explain it." Ellie swallowed convulsively. What had Amara seen that would cause her to get so upset? "What do you know?"

Amara wet her lips and looked away, wringing her hands in her lap—a sight which set off warning bells in Ellie's head. Amara wasn't the type of person to fidget unless it was serious. A lump formed in her throat.

"Amara?" she prodded when she got no answer from her friend.

"You're in a lot of danger," Amara blurted, reminding Ellie of her reaction to the flowers.

"That's crazy. You said that before, and you were wrong."

"No, I wasn't. Something terrible is going to happen. You really should listen to me." She paused, looking out across the pond. "You should let Royce move in with you."

Ellie couldn't hold back the snort of disbelief. "That would never happen."

"Did you two have a fight? You seemed so happy before."

"Happy? Are you kidding?" Ellie sighed. "If you want to know something, just ask."

Amara was silent for a long time. "It worries me that you've been pushing him away. This other guy, the one who has your attention, he's dangerous. He's not what he seems."

"How do you know there's someone else?"

Amara rolled her eyes. "I may be new at this whole psychic stuff, but I've got a better handle on it than I used to. Someone has your heart, and it's not Royce."

"There's someone, but it's too soon to say anything."

Amara scowled. "Okay, Ell, for now I'll buy that. But don't make me send Marco and Royce after this guy. If he ever hurts you, you know they'll kill him. Hell, *I'll* kill him."

That wasn't going to be a problem. "Amara, I can take care of him, not that I expect him to do anything."

"Humans are one thing, Ell, but you're messing with an entity better left alone. You might feel things for him, but make sure he feels something back, and that it's real. His kind are not play toys, Ell. If you get involved with someone like Eric Malcolm, you'd better be sure you're serious."

Ellie's gaze snapped back to Amara's. "How did you know?"

Amara shrugged. "His presence is all over you. I met him last year, before Marco and I moved here from L.A. He came to talk to Marco about something, him and some big guy with scars on his face. To be honest with you, they both kind of gave me the creeps. I won't mention it to Marco—yet—because I trust your judgment. As long as you're sure he isn't pressuring you into anything."

Ellie didn't even hesitate. "No, he's not."

"When are you seeing him again?" Amara asked, her tone laced with suspicion.

Ellie shrugged. "I'm not sure."

"Okay, have it your way. Be all secretive with me. But you know you can trust me, right?"

Normally she'd say yes, but she didn't know if she could trust Amara to keep the secret from her husband. Marco and Eric would not be a good combination.

Whatever she thought, it didn't seem to matter. She was drawn to Eric, and she couldn't have stayed away from him if she wanted to. Instead of answering, she chose to change the subject. "So what was it you wanted to talk to me about? You sounded upset over the phone."

Amara frowned, her expression growing serious. "There's something going on with Marco. He's been so secretive lately. He thinks I don't notice, but how can I not when every little thing makes him jump?"

"What do you think the problem is?" Ellie asked, hoping Amara didn't think he was being unfaithful. He might be a little impulsive, but she'd seen him with Amara and knew he'd never do anything like that to her.

"This is probably going to sound crazy, but I think he's chasing this killer."

Amara's statement floored Ellie. "Why would you think that?"

"He and Royce are sneaking out at all hours of the night, acting ridiculous. I don't know exactly what it is, but I think they know something they don't want me to find out."

That kind of behavior seemed pretty common lately. "What are you going to do about it?"

Amara shrugged. "Nothing, right now. But I might need your help later if I change my mind."

Ellie smiled, knowing Amara wouldn't wait long before she decided to crack some heads. If Marco was indeed hiding something from her, she pitied him. Despite her small stature, Amara was ruthless. "If you need me, let me know. I think I'd enjoy watching the two of them squirm."

Chapter 11

"You're late," Royce said as Eric approached.

Eric narrowed his eyes at the other man. "Something came up. It couldn't be avoided. What have you learned?"

Royce nodded to a dilapidated three-story apartment house on the corner of the quiet street. "Watch. I think you'll enjoy this."

Eric took a seat on the stone wall next to Royce and settled his gaze on the building. A few minutes later, a man walked out the door and jogged down the road in the opposite direction. Eric's senses prickled. He'd caught a glimpse of the man's face before he'd turned his back to them, and he didn't like what he'd seen. "That can't be Antonio."

Royce scoffed. "That's what I thought at first, but it is."

"*Shit.*" Eric let out a sigh as he watched Antonio's form fade into the darkness of the night. "We're in a lot of trouble here."

"Gee, really?" Royce lowered himself off the stone wall and walked a few feet down the road, but he didn't follow Antonio. "If we go after him now, Aiala will kill us. Or *he* will."

Eric couldn't agree more. "That's exactly what she wants us to do. She expects us to tail him so he can lead us right to her."

"Yeah, but it gets worse," Royce confirmed, pointing toward the house Antonio had just exited. "Do you know who lives with him?"

"No."

"Ellie's sister, Becca."

Eric's mouth went dry and his heart rate tripled. If anything ever happened to Ellie's sister, she'd never forgive him. Hell, he'd never forgive himself. "What do we do now? We can't touch him, or Becca might end up dead."

"Yeah. I know. I wish I had the answers, but I'm at a total loss." Royce raked his hand through his long blond hair and turned back to Eric. "We've got to get her away from him. I hate to admit this, but I think we're going to need Sam's help with this one."

"I'll see what I can do." Eric pulled out his cell phone and started to dial Sam's number, but changed his mind and dialed another one instead. After three rings, he heard the sound of Liam's deep, raspy voice on the other end.

"Yeah?"

"Liam, it's Eric."

"Hey, Eric. Hold on." Eric heard faint rustling in the background, accompanied by a woman's muffled complaints.

"Sorry about that. What's up?" Liam asked when he came back on the phone.

"Did I catch you at a bad time?"

"No. Debbie was just leaving," Liam confirmed. "Ouch! Sorry. I meant Maggie. *Relax.* Okay, Eric, what do you need?"

Eric resisted the urge to laugh. Liam was young—very young as far as cats went—but completely capable of what Eric needed him to do. "Can you get away for a couple of days? I need you to watch someone for me."

"Yeah, no problem."

Eric gave him the particulars and hung up the phone, satisfied that he'd gotten at least one task accomplished. Now he had to tackle the rest of them. "All set," he confirmed to Royce. "I've got someone coming to watch over Becca until we can get Antonio straightened out."

"What about Ellie?"

A spike of white-hot anger tore through Eric as Royce mentioned her name. "Don't worry about her. *I'll* take care of her."

Royce held his hands on front of him in mock-surrender. "Okay. Fine. You do that." He turned away, shaking his head. When he looked back, Eric thought he caught a glimpse of sadness in the man's eyes. He brushed it away, not sure Royce was capable of such emotions.

"How's that sister of yours?" Royce asked, taking Eric by surprise. "I haven't seen her in a few hundred years. Is she still as cute now as she was then?"

Again, Eric had to fight the urge to tear Royce apart. White-hot anger swelled in him until he felt like he might burst. "You leave my sister alone."

Royce stared at him for a long time, his gaze boring into Eric's. "Now you know how I feel about Ellie. I think of her as family, and I just don't want to see her hurt."

Eric glared at Royce. "I'll keep that in mind."

* * * * *

A draft blew across Ellie's face, waking her from a deep sleep. She sat up in bed and looked around the room, searching for the source of the disturbance. The French doors leading to her small balcony were wide open, the sheer white curtains billowing in the breeze. Fear knifed through her. She reached for the phone on the bedside table, but a cold hand clamped over hers before she could lift the receiver. She looked up into the *inhuman* glowing eyes of a gigantic man dressed in black.

She opened her mouth to scream, but his free hand covered her mouth. "Shut up. You. Come with me." His voice sounded oddly stilted, like he didn't speak English well—but he had no discernible accent.

She grabbed his wrist and jerked his hand off her mouth and pushed at the man's chest, but he didn't budge. He encircled her wrists in his hands, and without any effort, lifted her from the bed. She didn't even bother to fight yet, it would be useless. A man this big could overpower her easily.

Unless she caught him off-guard.

He was strong, but he didn't appear to be an astrophysicist. If she could distract him and gain the upper hand, which shouldn't be too hard considering his apparent lack of usable brain matter, she might be okay.

Her gaze fell on a vase on her dresser that her mother had given her for a birthday present last year. She'd always hated the thing anyway, so it would make the perfect distraction. She kicked it over, sending it to the floor with a crash. When he turned to investigate the noise, she ducked out from under his grasp. He was quicker than she'd first assumed, grabbing her around the waist before she could get very far. She picked up a chair from near the closet and swung it at his head. It connected with a smack and she heard the sound of snapping bones.

"Bitch!" He charged at her, but she ducked again. Another blow with the chair momentarily stunned him. He stood a few feet away from her, close to the open French doors, his breath heaving in and out of his lungs as if he'd just run a marathon. Before she could decide on her next move, the bedroom door burst open and Charlotte ran in, a cast iron frying pan in her hand. "What's going on in here? I heard a crash."

Ellie gestured to the advancing thug. "He got in through the balcony."

Charlotte snorted. "Oh, easy." Without giving Ellie a chance to speak, she flung the frying pan at the man. It hit him in the shoulder, and while he stumbled from the blow Charlotte took care of him with a quick side-kick to the chest. He staggered backwards and flipped over the balcony railing. They listened as his scream ended abruptly in a thud.

"Oh, shit," Charlotte said, blinking hard. "Do you think I killed him?"

Ellie ran to the balcony and peered over the edge. The man lay motionless on the grass two stories below, his head bent at an odd angle. "Um, yeah. I'm pretty sure he's dead."

She pulled on a sweatshirt and a pair of sweatpants over her nightshirt and slipped a pair of canvas sneakers on her feet.

She ran through the house with Charlotte right behind her, throwing open the front door and sprinting into the yard. The moonlit night made it easy to find the body on the ground. A quick check of his wrist confirmed that he had no pulse. "Charlotte, you'd better hope we can find some way to fix this."

Charlotte shrugged, but Ellie saw the nervousness in her sister's stance. "What do you want me to do? I can't bring him back to life. Hey, it was self-defense, right?"

Ellie shook her head and started walking back toward the house. "I'm going to call Amara. Maybe she'll know what to do. You stay here and watch him."

Charlotte's comment reached her as she got to the front door. "Why? He's not *going* anywhere."

A few minutes later Ellie heard a car pull into the driveway. She said a quick prayer that it would be Amara—and that she'd come alone.

"Ellie? What's going on? I'll have you know that Marco isn't too happy about you dragging me away for some emergency." Amara walked around the corner of the house, her hair a mess and her shirt buttoned wrong. "Why are the two of you out here in the middle of the night, whispering like a couple of teenagers? I'm sure there are better places to hold a conversation than— Oh, my God. There's a body in your yard!"

"Well, now that we're all clear on that, would you both mind giving me a hand?" Ellie gave his arms a hard yank, but only succeeded in tearing his jacket. "This isn't going to work if you don't help me."

Amara recovered quickly, dismissing her shock with a quick nod. "I had a feeling that something was going to happen. I guess I was right." She bent down to lift the man's ankles. Ellie and Charlotte each took an arm, and they were finally able to lift him off the ground.

"Geez. This guy must be three hundred pounds. I'm going to get a hernia," Charlotte complained.

"Shut up. The last thing we need is for Nana to wake up," Ellie scolded her as they half-dragged half-carried the body across the yard.

"Ellie? Charlotte?"

All three of them dropped the body when they heard Carol's whispered voice.

"What are you doing here?" Ellie asked, standing up and wiping her hands on her sweats. Could this night possibly get any worse? "Go back to bed."

Carol shook her head. "Not until you explain to me what you're doing trying to drag an unconscious man around the yard."

"He's not unconscious. He's *dead*," Charlotte chimed in, sounding a little too proud of herself.

"Dead?" Even in the moonlight, Ellie could see Carol's face pale. "Dead?"

"Yes, dead," Charlotte confirmed, looking annoyed. "I hate to sound like a cliché here, but it was either him, or Ellie and me. Will somebody grab his legs so we can get this guy out of here?"

Carol shook her head. "He can't be dead."

"Well, he is." Charlotte leaned down and grabbed his arms again, tugging hard enough to rip the sleeve of his shirt. "Do you see the way his head is crooked on his shoulders? That's not supposed to happen. The feet, Ellie."

Someone coughed in the background. All four women turned toward the corner of the house, where Royce was standing. "Girl talk over a dead body? That's a new one."

None of them spoke a word, so he continued. "Which one of you lovely ladies is responsible for his current condition? Or was it a group effort?"

"That would be me," Charlotte admitted. "He attacked Ellie, and he would have attacked me. It was self-defense."

Royce crossed his arms over his chest. "And exactly what were you planning to do with the body?"

"Dump it in the ocean," Charlotte answered as if it should have been obvious.

"Wouldn't have done you any good. He'd just have come back to life as soon as his neck healed." A new voice came from the shadows.

Ellie's jaw dropped when she heard Eric speak. He walked around the side of the house and came to stand next to the body.

"Worthless piece of demon garbage." He kicked the man with the toe of his shoe. "He deserved to die anyway. You have to watch out for those demon slaves. They have nasty tempers to make up for their stupidity."

"*Demon?*" Carol asked, looking ready to faint.

Eric nodded to her before focusing all his attention on Ellie. "Why didn't you call me? Weren't you going to tell me what was going on?"

"I wasn't thinking clearly. Calling Amara was the first thing that came into my head." She reached down to try to move the body again, but Eric nudged her out of the way.

"Stand away from this jerk for a second, will you?"

"What are you going to do?"

He stared down at her, his eyes hard and cold. "I'll take care of the body in a way that's not going to leave any evidence or allow him to reanimate. And then the two of us are going to have a nice, long talk."

Ellie moved away from the body, going to stand by the house where everyone else had migrated. She watched Eric curiously, wondering just how he planned to get rid of it all by himself.

He raised one hand in the air, pointing it in the direction of the body. It exploded in a puff of smoke and light, leaving no trace on the lawn where it had been. Eric turned, his mouth set in a grim line, and faced the group of them. "Everybody, go home."

Amara, Charlotte, and Carol started to protest, but Eric stopped them with a wave of his hand. "Goodnight, ladies." They scattered, going their separate ways without another word.

"Eric, I—" Ellie started, but he didn't let her finish.

"You, get your cute little ass inside. I have to talk to Royce for a minute, and then I'll be right in."

"You know Royce?"

He shrugged. "Yeah. I used to work with him."

He walked away from her, not giving her a chance to respond to his revelation. In a huff, she went into the house and flopped into a chair at the kitchen table. That was when it hit. The adrenaline rush had subsided, and she realized the gravity of what had happened. A—what had he called it?—demon slave had come after her tonight, no doubt to kill her. He might have succeeded if Charlotte hadn't come in and helped her.

She rested her arms on the table, burying her face in them, and drew deep, shuddering breaths. Her life was so out of control that she didn't know if anything would ever be back to normal. Amara might have been right, after all. She was no longer even safe in her own home. Something had to be done, before she or one of her family got hurt.

Five minutes later, Eric walked in through the back door and held his arms out to her. She stood up and ran to him, letting the warmth of his embrace comfort her. Small sobs shook her body as he patted her hair and kissed the top of her head. "Are you going to be okay?"

She looked up at him through the tears shining in her eyes and answered as honestly as she could. "I don't know."

"I'm here. I'm not going anywhere now. I promise."

She let him hold her for what seemed like an eternity before she broke away from his embrace. Grabbing a cup from the sink, she filled it with water from the tap and took a gulp, her shaky hands barely able to hold onto it.

"How did you do make him disappear like that?" she asked.

"It's just something I do. All part of my job."

Ellie swallowed hard. She didn't need to hear that. He made it sound so easy, so cold. "Well, thanks. I think I'm going to be okay now. I'll see you tomorrow?"

"Damn right you will," Eric answered, his voice hard. "Because I'm not leaving tonight."

"I just want to be alone right now. You can't stay," she said, her mind stuck on the idea that a demon had tried to kill her. A demon, like Eric? She knew Eric wasn't the same as the demon slave who'd attacked her, but her mind wouldn't let her forget that the man she cared about so much was, technically, a monster.

"The hell I can't! Next time you have a problem, I want you to call me right away. Don't chance getting hurt." He shook his head, his gaze angry and hurt. "Better yet, you won't need to call. I'm moving in."

"Oh, I don't think so. You can go right back to your hotel room. I don't need you here."

"You want to bet on that?" He stalked into the living room and sat down on the couch.

Ellie followed, still hoping to kick him out before he got too comfortable. Confusion and distress filled her, and she needed time to think things through. Having Eric hanging around wasn't exactly conducive to clear thinking. It would be nice to have someone here to watch over her, but she didn't want it to be Eric. "I don't want to bet on anything. I just want you to go back to the Middle Ages where you came from. Women don't get treated like possessions anymore, in case you hadn't noticed."

"I don't believe this. I'm trying to keep you from getting killed. Is this all a big joke to you?"

She sighed, tears threatening again. She fought to hold them back, knowing they'd only push him to stay. "No, it's not a joke. But I don't think it's as serious as you're making it, either."

"That's a lie, and we both know it." He grabbed her wrist and pulled her down on the couch beside him. "You could have been hurt."

"I wasn't." She yanked her hand away and shifted her body as far away from him as she could get, hoping he didn't know how much of a mess she was on the inside.

"You could have been *killed*." He brushed a stray lock of hair off her face, tucking it behind her ear.

She knocked his hand away even as she wanted to lean into him. "*But. I. Wasn't.* What do you care, anyway?"

"I care. Believe me, Ellie, I care." She saw the intent in his eyes and tried to duck away, but he was too quick. He wrapped his hand around the back of her head and pulled her close, brushing his lips over hers.

It took her two seconds to come to her senses and move away from the kiss. She saw the hurt in his eyes from her actions, but she couldn't do anything to make it better. She hurt, too, but she couldn't let herself cling to him for support.

"I'm sorry, Eric. I just need some time."

She just hoped time and space would be enough. She didn't want to lose him, but she didn't know what to do to hang on to him, either. Instead of deciding, she stood up and beckoned to him. "I have a small guest room upstairs. You can stay there tonight, since you insist on hanging around."

"Guest room? There's no way in hell you're going to stick me in some guest room when I've already shared your bed."

She faced him, her hands on her hips and her jaw set. She'd like nothing more than to let him share her room tonight, but she couldn't bring herself to do it. Too many things had happened, and she needed to sort them out in her mind so she could make a decision. If that meant he had to wait, well, that was his problem. If he couldn't handle her requests now, that didn't bode well for their future.

If they even had one. After tonight, she wasn't so certain.

Chapter 12

Eric sat slumped in a chair in Ellie's studio, his hands clasped over his chest. His eyes kept trying to close and he had to force himself to stay awake after the sleepless night he'd spent on the twin bed in the tiny guest room. His back hurt, his legs kept cramping up, and he'd done something funny to his neck. Irritation rose in him as he thought about Ellie, sleeping in her queen-sized bed with soft covers and comfortable pillows. Why had she banished him like some servant to a room no bigger than a closet?

The sun streamed in through the floor-to-ceiling windows that covered one wall of the converted garage, which only served to irritate his tired eyes. He supposed she needed as much natural light as possible to work, but at this point he didn't care. The fact that she'd barely spoken a word to him since getting up this morning increased his agitation.

"You're distant today. Do you want to talk about it?" he asked her, not really expecting an answer. The silent treatment would only get worse when he told her she had to leave Stone Harbor indefinitely. *That* was something he wasn't looking forward to.

She stopped her hand in midair, the paintbrush a few inches from the canvas. Her eyes darted his way, briefly, before turning back to her work. "I... You know what? It's nothing."

"Come on, Ellie. Tell me what's on your mind."

"I was thinking about my sister, Becca."

"She's the youngest?" he asked, trying to keep his tone even. He didn't want to alert her quite yet to the trouble Becca could be in. The girl was safe—Liam would make sure of it— and telling Ellie would only make her worry more.

She nodded. "Yeah, and she's got this jerk of a boyfriend. I don't know what to do about him."

"What's wrong with him?"

"He doesn't want her spending any time with her family, and he's been living off of her salary until recently when he finally got some overnight job at a grocery store. He treats her like dirt, and she lets him." She went back to focusing her attention on her painting in an obvious attempt to tune him out.

Well, that wouldn't be happening this morning. She'd pushed him away last night—for the *last* time. Now she was going to face her problems. He let his eyes drift closed and sighed deeply. "Do you want me to have a talk with him?"

She shook her head. "Not yet. Maybe later."

There wouldn't be a later, because none of them would be around. Eric had talked to Carol last night and asked her to make arrangements for all of them to visit Ellie's mother in Georgia until the town was safe again. He hesitated to tell Ellie, since she was already mad enough at him without throwing another problem into the mix.

"You know I'm here whenever you want to talk." He closed his eyes and drifted off to sleep.

* * * * *

Shaking her head, Ellie looked over to the corner of the room where Eric sat. It figured. How could he possibly sleep in the middle of the morning, in a room filled with bright sunlight? Surely *he'd* been able to get some sleep last night. A demon hadn't tried to kill *him*.

She'd wanted him to stop asking questions, but now that he'd fallen asleep she was angry. It made no sense. If she no longer wanted him to pry into her personal life, why did she suddenly feel the overwhelming need to talk?

She huffed as she went about cleaning up after herself. Today, for the first time in a long time, she'd been able to spend a decent amount of time with her work. But when she looked back at the canvas, the sight that greeted her disturbed her. The sunset she'd been wanting for weeks to paint took on a sinister look in tones of bright red and dark purple. The gray clouds looked angry. *Menacing.* The trees appeared to have grown human-like limbs with large, sharp claws ready to grab an unsuspecting person that walked by. Shuddering at the vision her mind had painted, she covered the canvas and walked away, set to the leave the studio for the day.

"Ellie?" Eric's voice was softly pleading as she reached the door. "I know what you're trying to do, but please, just stop now."

"Stop what? I don't know what you're talking about."

"Stop trying to put distance between us. I know there are many unknowns for you right now, and I know this whole thing makes you uncertain, but please let's just see where this goes before we throw it away. It could be the best thing that's ever happened to either of us."

Bull. The man had lived for over a thousand years. He'd probably had naps better than...whatever this was they were doing. She didn't want to endanger her entire family for a few nights of incredible sex—which was undoubtedly the only thing he truly wanted from her. "I'm going up into the house now. Feel free to sleep out here as long as you want. It won't bother me. I'll talk to you later."

To her surprise, he jumped up from the chair and pushed the door closed when she tried to open it. She watched him carefully, waiting for him to lunge at her. He didn't. Instead he pulled her into his arms and kissed her lovingly, almost reverently. Once she'd started kissing him back, he deepened the kiss until he'd turned it around and she was clinging to him. By the time he broke away, they were both panting.

"It's been a bad couple of months," he told her, a look of desolation in his eyes. "I think I brought this danger on you, at least part of it. The killer I'm tracking murdered three of my friends, and I might be next." He ran a hand through his hair and glanced around the studio. "Me, and Royce too. Please don't push me away now. I couldn't take it."

Her heart gave a little tug. How could she walk out on him, when he'd admitted to needing her so much? Still she couldn't help but feel he was sweeping their problems under the rug.

"I won't. Come into the house with me. We'll talk."

She felt his relief wash through her like it was her own. He kissed her quickly before pulling away to smile down at her. "I have a better idea."

He took her hand and led her to the worn armchair where he'd been resting. He stripped her clothes off slowly, kissing almost every inch of her body before he settled her into the chair. The faded denim fabric abraded her sensitized skin. She knew she should at least try to make a token protest, but her mouth refused to make any sounds other than soft moaning ones.

"Close your eyes," he told her, his tone commanding. Reluctantly, she leaned her head back against the chair and did as he asked. She listened to him rummage around in cabinets and drawers, and then she heard the sound of running water. What was he doing? She wasn't any closer to answers when he came back to her. She let her eyelids flutter open as he knelt on the floor in front of the chair, but she closed them immediately with the sharp shake of his head. He nudged her thighs apart and the cool air hit her swollen sex. She shivered, both cold and aroused. She felt so exposed that her body flushed with embarrassment.

"What's wrong, Ellie?" he asked, his tone no longer as gentle. He trailed his fingers up the insides of her thighs before sliding them through her folds. "You can't tell me you're not turned on. You're far too wet for that." He spread her moisture along her inner thighs, drawing small circles on her skin.

She started to open her eyes again, and this time he got serious. "I asked you to keep them closed. Now I guess I'll have to do it for you." He tied a clean white rag around her eyes before settling her back against the chair. The faint scent of paint mingled with the scent of laundry detergent on the rag tickled her senses as she drew in a deep breath.

"Do you know what I see when I look at you, Ellie?"

She shook her head, very aware of the room around her — the fragrance of her acrylics, the feel of the rough fabric against her back, Eric's subtle movements as he continued to touch her.

"I see a beautiful, sexy, intelligent woman. One I wouldn't mind spending all my free time with." He pushed one finger into her, then another. "But right now, I see the woman who's got me so hard that I can't even think straight. All night I thought about what I wanted to do to you when I got you alone, but you pushed me away. Now that I have you all to myself, I can't wait."

She felt something soft and wet trail up her leg. A paintbrush. She whimpered as Eric brought the soft bristles between her legs, circling her aching clit.

"What do you feel?" he asked.

"I feel..." Her voice dropped off as he dipped the brush into her cunt and then twirled the bristles over her engorged nipples, dousing them with her own fluids. "*Oh.*"

"You're beautiful."

His thumb brushed lightly over her clit, a soft teasing touch not designed to bring her to orgasm, but instead to drive her insane.

"Show me," she whispered.

"Not yet. Not until I'm finished."

He increased the pressure on her clit, the brush clattering on the ground as it fell from his hand. She pushed against him as a jolt of pleasure ran through her. She couldn't take much more before she burst, from both the intense pleasure and the...love she felt for the man giving it. She smiled to herself, just now realizing how true it was. She loved him. They still had miles to go before they worked out their differences, but she could wait for as long as it took.

He spread her legs even further and leaned down to put his mouth against her sex. She whimpered, so aroused now that it was nearly painful. His tongue skimmed over her clit, edging her to the brink or ecstasy. A quick thrust of his fingers inside her pushed her over, sending her into an orgasm increased in intensity by the makeshift blindfold.

He nuzzled his face into her pubic hair before he removed the blindfold. "You came too soon. I wanted to eat you for so much longer."

Another quiver ran through her cunt. "Oh," she whispered, not able to say much more.

He laughed softly against her neck. "All night I've been waiting to fuck you. All damned night, Ellie. I'm going to, right now."

A full-blown spasm shook her inner muscles.

"Do you want me to fuck you, Ellie?"

She closed her eyes and nodded, in the middle of a mini orgasm.

He slipped his fingers out of her and lightly slapped her thigh. "Look at me."

She snapped her eyes open and met his. His gaze was so hot and intense that it shook her to the very core. She glanced down at the floor and spied the paintbrush, an idea forming in her head.

"Strip for me, Eric."

"What?"

"Take off your clothes." She stood up from the chair and walked across the room to the cabinets and pulled a clean brush out of a drawer. She dampened it with warm water from the sink and turned around, putting her hands on her hips when she saw he was still fully dressed. "What are you doing?"

"I should be asking you that question." He shook his head, looking at her as if he thought she was nuts. "Put that down and get over here."

"No way." She walked over to him and pulled him down for a kiss, rubbing her body over him. Her fingers closed around his denim-covered cock, stroking him through his jeans. He groaned and stepped away, but she wasn't letting him get away that easily. "Undress, or I'm going to put my clothes back on and walk out of here."

He stared at her for a few seconds before he shook his head and, unceremoniously, stripped out of his clothes. "Happy now."

"Um-hmm." She smiled slowly, reveling in her sudden power, before she gazed pointedly at his jutting cock. "It looks like you are, too."

She shoved him back and he fell into the chair, looking dumbfounded. Good. It was about time she got to be the one to have a little fun. She knelt in front of him, as he'd done to her just a little while ago, and stroked his cock lightly with the tips of her fingers. His hips convulsed and he groaned. "God, Ellie. Don't tease me like that. I'm right on the edge."

She couldn't stop the wicked laugh that escaped her lips. "Why should I stop? I'm having so much fun."

She ran the paintbrush lightly down the length of his cock before bringing it back up again to swirl over the head. He hissed out a breath as she played the soft bristles against the slit. She continued teasing him there with the brush while she wrapped her free hand around his cock and stroked. She found, when she tightened her grip just a little his entire body shook. After only a couple minutes of play, he growled incoherently and yanked her off the floor to straddle his lap. The chair was confining and she wriggled her legs to get comfortable, eliciting a moan from Eric.

His gaze held hers while he lifted her up and fit the head of his cock inside her cunt. He thrust up hard as he pulled her down on him. It was so intense, so perfectly right, that she tried to close her eyes against the overwhelming emotions flooding her.

"Watch, Ellie." He tilted her body back a little, supporting her weight with one of his hands on the small of her back.

Her gaze dropped to where they joined. From this angle, she had an arousing view of his cock disappearing into her cunt. She licked her lips. It couldn't get any better than this. She took over the thrusts, riding him, enjoying the way she could see and feel him fill her to the hilt. He shifted in the chair, angling his hips up as she came down, allowing him to slide all the way inside her. His cock throbbed within her and her muscles contracted around it, her cunt trying to suck him back in whenever she rose up.

"Do you like this?" he asked harshly, his breathing jagged. She nodded, not able to say anything more.

"Touch yourself."

She stilled at his command. "You want me to…?"

"Yes. I want to feel you come around me, and I want to watch you rub your sweet clit while you do it. Show me what you like, Ellie." When she hesitated, he insisted. "Do it, Ellie. Touch yourself for me."

Embarrassed, she had trouble obeying his command. He grasped her hand in his and brought it to her mound, pressing her fingers against her clit. A few strokes and she took over, her embarrassment fading to almost nothing as the jolting, pleasurable sensations shot through her. He felt so good inside her, and her body enjoyed this so much, she couldn't do anything but follow his instructions. She lifted her gaze to his and saw the effect of her compliance in his eyes. He nodded slowly, the heat in his gaze filling her as she brought herself higher.

She came with a soft cry, bucking over him. She would have fallen if he hadn't held her in place with his hands on her back. He paused as she came back down, and when her breathing had regulated, he stroked into her harder than ever. Amazingly, she convulsed again as he came, still trembling as he pulled her against his chest.

"You're amazing." His whispered breath tickled her neck.

She shook her head as much as her weak muscles would allow. "Trust me. It's not me. It's you."

She'd never had sex like this before. Her entire adult life she'd had what she *thought* was good sex. But she was wrong. Eric had proved to her how little she really knew on the subject. Now that he'd shown her what she was missing, there wouldn't be any going back.

"Is this some kind of demon thing?" she asked softly.

"What?" His voice took on a wary tone as he shifted her so she sat across his lap. His arm came around her shoulder and he held her, making her feel warm and fuzzy inside.

"This amazing, incredible feeling. I didn't know it could be *this* good." She nuzzled her face against his chest, taking comfort in the sound of his heartbeat.

He sighed heavily. "It's *us*. It's this chemistry between us that makes it so good. You wouldn't get it from any other cat, not this good, so don't get any ideas."

"So I guess asking for an introduction to your friends is out of the question?"

"Ann Elizabeth…" he warned, his tone a low growl. His fingers dug into her shoulder.

She laughed and playfully bit his nipple. He drew in a sharp breath. "Don't do that unless you mean it. Otherwise you're going to end up in trouble."

She paused midway into her second bite. "What's that supposed to mean?"

"If you continue to play rough, I might ask you to do things you're not ready for."

"Like what?" She couldn't imagine what he was talking about.

"Like bite harder."

"Oh." She couldn't think of a single answer for that. Before she could reply, he spoke again.

"I want more from you, but I can't ask you yet. And I'm not talking just about sex here, Ellie, so if you don't want it all, keep your teeth to yourself."

It all? What could that possibly mean? "Eric, what—?"

"Don't. I can't. I don't want to get rough with you. I could end up really hurting you." He paused, breathing slowly in and out. "We'll talk more about the future when you're ready, okay?"

"Can I…?"

"Can you, what? Can you become like me?" He shook his head. "Not under normal circumstances, no. Supposedly there's a way, but I can't do it. It takes an ancient who knows a special rite, and I've never practiced rituals. We'd have to work something else out if…if you decided you wanted to stay with me. Maybe Royce could—"

"Don't even go there." What was this fascination with Royce turning her? "I do not want to live the rest of my life as a vampire."

He stared at her for a minute. "That's the only way I can think of that can keep us together, Ellie. I couldn't stand the thought of losing you after only fifty or sixty years."

Now he sounded like Amara. Why did they all have to keep reminding her of her mortality?

Maybe it was time to go out and find some normal friends. "Okay. Fine. Whatever. We'll talk about this later, okay?"

"I tried to warn you."

Yes, he had, but she'd had to keep pushing until she'd driven another wedge between them. Still, she'd done what she had to do. She could never live her life as a vampire. There had to be some other way.

Instead of continuing the conversation—like she knew he wanted—she cuddled closer and closed her eyes, willing herself to sleep.

Chapter 13

Ellie dozed off and on, waking up a short time later tangled with a hard, male body. *Eric*. She snuggled closer, absorbing his warmth through her skin. The man had the most amazing energy. He filled her in a way entirely new to her. Despite herself, she loved every minute of it.

After last night, she'd made an important choice. The demon attack had shown her that Amara had been right about the danger, and that Eric's life could be a hazard to her if she chose to live it with him. But she knew, deep in her heart, that she could never walk away. It didn't matter what he did, or what he was. The only thing that mattered was how she felt when he held her, and loved her. The fact that he was...well, a demon didn't bother her like it used to. She'd learned vampires weren't as evil as the world made them out to be—or at least most of them weren't—maybe the demon's reputation was stretched a little, too.

She snuggled closer, trying selfishly to get some more of his warmth. He groaned softly. "Hi, beautiful."

"Hi, yourself."

His hand moved up her ribcage until he cupped her breast in his palm. "Why don't we fool around for a little while? Just for a few more hours."

She laughed. "Even you couldn't last that long."

"Wanna bet on that?" he seemed to take personal offense to her comment.

"Maybe later. We should probably get up and get something to eat first."

He opened his mouth to protest, but his stomach growled in the silence. "Damn. I guess you're right."

She got up and pulled on her clothes, and Eric followed suit. "I'll go get some coffee ready. You take a shower and I'll meet you in the kitchen in a little while."

They walked into the house together and Eric gave her a quick kiss before he went up the stairs toward the bathroom. When Ellie got to the kitchen, Charlotte was sitting at the table. A fresh pot of coffee sat on a trivet on the tabletop.

"I thought you might need it after last night," Charlotte explained as she gestured to the carafe.

"Thanks." Ellie poured some into her favorite mug and took a sip, not even caring that any other day the coffee would be utterly undrinkable. Charlotte and pretty much any kitchen appliance didn't mix. They sat in silence for a few minutes while Ellie let the caffeine take effect on her overstressed body.

"How are you doing?" she asked her sister after a little while.

Charlotte shrugged off the question. "He was just a demon, right? Who cares if there's one less in the world? How are *you*? You're the one he tried to kill."

"I'm fine. You know better than anyone that I can handle anything."

"She's not alone. She's got me now." Eric stood in the doorway in just a pair of jeans, his wet hair combed back from his face. Ellie's heart thumped at the sight, and she could tell from Charlotte's slack-jawed expression that her sister wasn't unaffected.

Ellie looked up at him, hope filling her. "You mean that?"

He nodded.

"You're not going to make me go into hiding or something like that?"

He took the mug of coffee Charlotte offered and sat down at the table. Ellie had to give him credit. He was great at pretending Charlotte wasn't ogling him openly. "We need to talk about that."

She tried not to take offense to that, knowing it was his twisted sense of chivalry—*protecting the little lady*—that got in the way of his good sense sometimes. Still, even after all that had happened, his overwhelming need to protect her was a little hard to take. There were a few things they needed to get straight, the sooner the better. "How about we discuss it *right now*?"

"Fine." He got up and followed her into the living room, but he didn't look thrilled. She knew Charlotte would hear every word, but at least she could pretend they had a little privacy.

"I need you to stop treating me like I'm some kind of helpless victim."

He shook his head. "I never once said you were helpless."

"You didn't have to say it. The way you feel is clear from your actions and the way you speak to me. I can't stand this anymore." She knew it was the stress talking, but she couldn't seem to clamp her mouth shut now that she'd started. "I need you to stop it or leave."

He gaped, affronted. "You want me to leave?"

"If you can't stop trying to take care of me, then yes, I want you to leave."

"Let me get this straight. You want me to go because I care enough to try to make sure nothing happens to you? You don't want me around because I threaten your precious independence? How is that any different from the way you take care of Charlotte and Becca, or your grandmother, or the way you took care of Marco before he met Amara? It seems to me that you spend so damned much time taking care of everyone else, that you forget that you need to take care of yourself."

She fell silent. As much as it killed her to admit it, he had a point there.

"Yeah, I thought so." He ran a hand through his damp hair. "If you want me to go, you're going to have to call the police and have me arrested. You're stuck with me until you leave, and you should be happy that I didn't run away every time you've tried to push me."

She almost smiled until she realized exactly what he'd said. "What do you mean, 'until I leave'?"

He brushed his finger across her cheek. "You need to go get changed. I'm going to take you out to lunch."

She dug her heels in, both literally and figuratively. "Not until you tell me what you meant by that comment."

"Carol's made arrangements for you and your sisters to go with her to see your mother for a while. Royce and I thought it would be best for you to spend some time away until we get things sorted out."

Ellie stepped back and stared at him, her mouth agape. "How could you do this to me? It's bad enough that you want to send me away, but I can't believe you got my family and friends involved."

"I'm just trying to protect you." He tried to pull her back into his arms, but she ducked away.

"I am so sick of you saying that to me! If you don't want me around, all you have to do is say so."

His eyes flashed as anger heated his gaze. "You know damned well that is not the case. I don't want you to get killed."

"I wouldn't even be in any danger if you hadn't approached me in the park!" She stood with her hands on her hips, not caring if Charlotte heard the whole conversation.

Eric's shoulders bunched and he took a step toward her, his agitation visible in every move. "Don't you dare blame this on me. You put yourself in danger when you slept with Royce Cardoso."

Her heart stopped and her mouth went dry at the comment. She heard nothing but the blood rushing in her ears. Just a few hours ago, she'd been so sure he cared. But now she knew he was just like all the rest. "That's it! I never want to see you again."

She turned and ran out of the house, her heart breaking a little more with every step.

* * * * *

"I screwed up," Eric said the second Liam answered the phone.

"What happened?"

"She's not going to go." He shifted the phone from one ear to the other. "I pushed too hard, and she ran away."

It had been three hours since their disagreement, and he'd been watching her house for most of that time. He'd had to leave briefly to take care of a few job-related errands, and when he got back, her car was gone. She hadn't been back since.

"Is that all? I'll take care of it." Liam's voice held a subtle hint of humor, but Eric failed to see anything funny about the situation.

"This is a big deal, Liam. Huge. Someone tried to kill her last night. She's in a lot of danger."

"What exactly did you say to her to make her run away?"

"I...I said a lot of things I shouldn't have. I was wrong, but now I can't find her to tell her I'm sorry." He'd do anything to get her to believe him. He just prayed it wasn't too late.

"I can fix this for you. Easy. Just trust me on this one. I'll get back to you in a couple of days." Without waiting for a reply, Liam disconnected the call, leaving Eric to listen to the blaring of the dial tone in his ear.

He shook his head and slipped his phone back into his pocket, hoping that Liam really did know what he was doing. He couldn't stand to lose Ellie over a couple of hurtful comments, and he at least wanted time to tell her he was sorry before he ran out of time.

* * * * *

Ellie sat on the old couch in Becca's living room, watching Liam closely as he spoke on the phone. From the hushed tones and furtive glances, she assumed the caller was Eric. Her mood darkened again just thinking about him. She'd let herself believe he cared, but in the end he was just like the rest of them.

Men sucked.

She'd come to Becca's house when she'd run out on Eric, needing someone to talk to. Charlotte had heard everything, so Ellie couldn't trust her to keep an open mind. She'd been surprised when a strange man—a big, tall one with a long black ponytail and tattoos covering a great deal of his arms—opened the door. She might have called the police if Becca hadn't come to the door behind him and assured Ellie that she'd spoken to Marco on the phone, and the man was safe. Liam, she'd learned, worked with Eric.

He was helping Becca pack while Tony was out.

At first she hadn't understood what was going on. But Liam had been all too happy to fill her in. It seemed her hunches about Tony hadn't been wrong. He was a dangerous man, one Eric apparently wanted her entire family away from as soon as possible. Though Liam hadn't come right out and said it, she knew it had something to do with the murders in town.

"That was Eric," Liam told her unnecessarily.

"That's nice," she replied, looking down at the hideous green shag carpet.

"He really thinks you should go to your mother's for a while." Liam spoke in a deep baritone she would have found sexy if she hadn't just had her heart ripped into tiny pieces. "And he's really sorry."

"Good for him."

"Maybe you should give him a chance."

Ellie was saved from further reply when Becca walked into the living room with her suitcase. "I'm all set. Now we just have to stop home and get Charlotte and Carol. Ellie can pack while we're there."

"I already told you. I'm not going." She got up from the couch and went over to give her sister a quick hug. "I've got a few things to do before I head home, but I'll get back as soon as I can to see you before you all leave."

"It's not safe to stay here," Becca protested, a worried frown marring her delicate features. "Liam said that there are dangerous demons around here, and that's what tried to kill you and Charlotte the other night. And Tony..." Her voice trailed off, and Ellie felt a stab of sympathy for the girl. She'd wanted to get her away from the man, but she hadn't wanted it to happen like this.

"I'll be careful, Becca, I promise." She walked to the apartment door, turning back to Liam before she walked out. "Thanks for taking care of my sisters and my grandmother. If you see Eric, kindly tell him to go fuck himself." She felt much better when she walked out the door.

Chapter 14

Ellie walked through the grocery store, absently tossing items into her cart. It had been three days since Becca and her grandmother had left for Georgia, and all had been quiet. *Suspiciously* quiet. She hadn't heard a word from Eric, but she didn't really expect to. He thought she'd left town.

A hand settled on her shoulder, and she whipped around, startled. Royce stood behind her, an angry look on his face. "You didn't answer your phone last night, or this morning," he said, his tone accusatory.

She shrugged. "I've been busy."

"Doing what?" he asked. "Or should I say, *who?*"

What was his problem? "It's a little late for jealousy. My private life is none of your business."

"It is when you put yourself in danger." He crossed his arms over his chest. "You're my friend, and I care about you. I'd hate to see something happen to you because of a lapse in good judgment."

She fumed, ignoring the elderly woman who walked by them slowly, her eyes trained on them with keen interest. "My judgment is fine, thank you very much. It's you I wonder about. You're supposed to be my friend. A little support from *someone* would be nice. I think you need to leave now. If you continue to bellow like a moron, someone is going to call the police."

She pushed her cart further down the aisle to the cash register, not caring if he followed or not. Lately the men in her life all drove her crazy. She was about ready to give up on the lot of them.

"Good. Maybe that's what it will take to knock some sense into you." Royce took some of her groceries from the shopping cart and loaded them on the belt. Just watching him do it made her hands clench into fists and her jaw tighten. She rubbed her temples, trying to ward off the impending tension headache.

"Knock it off. I can handle this myself." She took a box of cereal out of his hands and smacked it down on the belt, earning a curious look from the cashier. "Go home and pack for your trip. Aren't you leaving soon? Like, tomorrow maybe?"

"I postponed the trip for a little while when you decided to be pigheaded and not leave town. Somebody's got to watch out for you and your daredevil sister." He dropped a loaf of bread onto the belt, squishing one side.

She shook her head. "You know what? I'm just realizing now what a domineering jerk you are. You're just like Eric. Why don't you just stay out of my life?" She paid for her groceries and pushed the cart out of the store, her emotions well past the boiling point. Being a thick-skulled male and therefore unable to take a hint, Royce followed her out the door and grabbed her arm.

"If I didn't know you better, I'd think you had a death wish. Did you know that you've been sleeping with an assassin?"

Why is it that men would say anything to get their way? She narrowed her eyes and didn't even try to keep the sarcasm from her voice. "I'm sorry, you must have me confused with one of your simpering, agreeable women. Get this through your head, tough guy. I'm *not*!"

She stopped in back of her car and popped the trunk to load her bags. Royce moved her out of the way and did the job for her. She would have protested but by that point she was too furious to form the words. When he finished, he slammed the trunk so hard it bounced back open, and he had to shut it again. Ellie let out a frustrated groan as she shoved the grocery cart into the nearest carriage return.

"Go away. You're causing a scene."

"No, *you* are by making this difficult. Come back to Marco's with me so I can make sure you don't get hurt."

"I'm not going with you, Royce."

"Somebody's got to talk some sense into you. Come home with me."

"She said no."

They both turned as Eric walked up to them. "Go home, Cardoso, and leave the lady alone."

Royce started to walk toward Eric, his hands clenched into fists, but Eric spoke. "I wouldn't do anything stupid, Royce. You wouldn't want the lady to see you lose your temper."

Royce backed off, grumbling incoherently.

"Smart choice. I think you should walk away now, before Ellie decides to scream and call even more attention to you."

Royce walked away, but not without a parting shot. "He's using you, Ellie. You're just going to end up hurt in the end. Go ahead and ask him."

As soon as Royce walked away, Eric took her arm and walked her to her car. "Go ahead and ask," he told her as she unlocked the door.

"I don't need to."

"I find your trust a little baffling with the way you ran out on me."

"Trust isn't the reason I don't need to ask." She sighed and turned to him, hoping he'd understand what she had to say and just leave her alone. "I don't need to ask because I no longer care. Whatever I felt for you is gone."

He said nothing, but the look in his eyes spoke volumes.

"What, no domineering comments? No orders?"

Eric shook his head, his lips pursed. "I never meant to hurt you."

"You know, I actually believe that. Unfortunately, it doesn't change anything. I can't be with a man who wants to run my life. You lied to me. I don't know if I can forgive that."

"I didn't lie to you. Technically, I—"

"A lie by omission is still a lie."

"I'm sorry—"

She held up her hand to stop him. "Let me finish, Eric. I'm not a pawn in some childish game. I'm not to be used. I thought I made that quite clear before, but I guess I was wrong."

"I'm not using you." The hurt still filled his eyes, but anger was slowly taking root as well. "Why don't you understand that?"

She shook her head, ready to climb into the car, when Royce's words haunted her. She'd been too angry at the time to think clearly, but something he'd said struck her as odd. "Royce told me you're an assassin."

She'd thought it was a lie, but the look in Eric's eyes told her different. Rage ran across his features, contorting them into something that scared her. She backed up until she hit the side of the car. He took a step toward her, and she gulped. "Eric, don't."

"I'll kill him," he said, stopping just inches from her. "It wasn't his place to tell you that."

"Well, I'm glad somebody did." Her heart broke all over again. What would she find out about him next? Her hand rested on the cell phone clipped to her pants pocket. "You told me you were some kind of bounty hunter. That's a pretty far cry from hired killer. I think you need to leave now before I call the police."

"Fine, I'll go," Eric growled, pushing himself away from the car. "You made a mistake not leaving with your family. One of these days you're going to need me, and I'm not going to care. I'm not going to hang around so you can judge me for things you don't understand."

He stalked off across the parking lot, leaving Ellie to sink into the driver's seat of the car and rest her head on the steering wheel, her body wracked with sobs. The anger in his eyes had been unmistakable, but so had the pain. She'd really hurt him this time. Yes, he'd kept the truth from her. Yes, he'd tried to boss her around. But maybe, just maybe she was overreacting. If she really thought about it, he was a heck of a lot better equipped to deal with demon slaves and the like than she was.

She lifted her head and watched his retreating back as he walked across the parking lot. A sigh escaped her lips, both from frustration and longing for what they'd shared. Despite his behavior, and even though she didn't quite understand his reasoning, she didn't want him out of her life. Her anger dissipated, leaving a hole inside her.

She ran her fingers over her totem and wiped her eyes. Without really thinking about it, she reached out to him mentally. At first she felt nothing, but then his defenses came down and he let her in. She heard no words, only felt his comfort wrap around her like a warm blanket—like a hug. She smiled to herself at the gesture. When he slipped away, quietly closing the mental door, she felt bereft, and more alone than she ever had in her life.

Chapter 15

Eric walked up to the hotel room door and opened it with his key card. He was about to step inside when he felt it. There was someone out there, watching him. He let the door close and pocketed the card, turning slowly. He didn't see anyone, but he felt the presence in every cell of his body.

Ellie? No, it couldn't be, not after the argument they'd had that afternoon. It felt like her, though. Her energy had imprinted itself in his mind, and he couldn't shake her away. She'd done the unexpected when she'd reached out to his mind. He hadn't even known that kind of a connection was possible. His head hurt, and his muscles were weary. He had to find a way to make things right.

"Hi." Her voice came out of nowhere, and suddenly she was standing right next to him. She smiled almost shyly, a flash of nervousness across her delicate features.

"Ellie," he breathed, wondering if she'd dissolve into the air if he touched her.

"I'm sorry to come without calling first, but I had to talk to you."

"It couldn't wait until morning?" He hoped against everything he knew about her that she'd come to make amends. He didn't want to lose her—wouldn't allow that to happen—but he wanted her to make the first move. Had she by coming here tonight?

Her next words seemed to confirm his hopes. "I didn't want to wait."

"Do you want to come in?" He shoved the door open all the way and she tentatively stepped inside.

"So what was so important that it had to be said tonight?" he asked, his entire body tense with waiting for her response.

"I've been thinking about you all day."

He let out the breath he'd been holding with a whoosh of air, warning himself not to read too much into her words. Until she came out and told him she wanted to work things out, it would be best if he didn't assume anything. "Really?"

She walked toward the bed, slowly, her eyes taking in the details of the sparsely decorated room. His gaze locked on the sway of her slender hips under the long skirt she wore and his mouth ran dry. Something primal inside him turned over, making him want to take her in a way he'd promised himself never to do. He bit back the growl that threatened to erupt from his throat and wrestled the urge that beckoned him to claim her in every possible way—the way he was meant to take the woman he'd chosen as his mate.

Would she allow that?

He circled her slowly, coming to a stop behind her. She looked over her shoulder at him, her tongue darting out to wet her lips. The sight of the small, pink, bit of flesh was all it took to get him rock hard. He shook his head, fighting to not attack her like his body demanded. He couldn't make her understand the need coursing through his veins. The best thing for both of them would be to get her out, as far away from him as possible.

"Ellie, you have to go."

She shook her head slowly, almost imperceptibly, as she turned to face him. She ran a finger down his chest as she spoke, leaving a trail of electricity in its wake. "You don't have to hide yourself from me, you know."

"You make me crazy." He grabbed her hand and brought it to his mouth, nipping the finger she'd tormented him with.

"Is that a good thing or a bad thing?"

"A little of both." He drew in a deep breath, her scent enveloping him and adding to his agitation. "I'm more demon than man right now, Ellie. This would be a good time to run."

She glanced toward the door. "Why do I think you'd chase me and enjoy every second of it?"

She was probably right, but he had to at least try to keep her from getting hurt. "You don't understand. I'm trying to warn you that I could be dangerous right now."

The scent of her arousal filled the air, and he inhaled deeply. With every breath, he tried to fight the monster raging inside, but he couldn't hold it back much longer. He'd frighten her, if he showed her what he really wanted. Not only that, he might actually hurt her. He wouldn't mean to, but the urges were too strong for him to handle right now.

Her lips parted as he took a step closer. He expected to see fear in her eyes, but didn't. Instead, her gaze held the same raw arousal as his. It didn't make any sense. He wasn't like her. They were of two different races. Why did his body respond to her so strongly? And why did hers react in the same way?

He growled a low, harsh sound that reverberated through the room. He couldn't understand the desperate need to mate with her—a human woman who couldn't even carry his children. She could never be like him. Never. Mating should not have even been a consideration. He'd known her for days, not a lifetime, yet the connection between them told a different story. He *knew* her as surely as he knew his own name. She was made for him, as ridiculous as it sounded. She belonged to him, now and forever, even if she refused to accept that as fact. His groin tightened at the thought. Human or not, Ellie Holmes was *his*. He'd claimed her just as surely as she'd claimed him the second they'd met.

He'd heard all his life that when he met the woman destined to be his mate, he would know her without question. He'd scoffed at the idea, deeming it too crazy to believe. Now he knew different. But the fact that he cared didn't stop the animal need rampaging inside him. He threw his head back and fought for control in a last ditch effort to get a grip before he tore her clothes off and took her before she was ready. In the end, it didn't matter. It was already too late.

With all the self-control he could muster, he gently moved aside her hair and touched her neck. His senses went wild as flames of desire licked up his body. He sucked in a sharp breath and squeezed his eyes shut against the sensation. It was too much. He couldn't take it. Surely emotions this strong would kill him.

"What's wrong?"

He could barely breath, barely speak. He felt his control draining away, but was powerless to do anything about it. "I'm not exactly in very good command of myself here. You might want to leave."

"Eric?" Ellie's voice was suddenly uncertain, wavering. His gaze never broke from her as he circled her again.

"I'll warn you one last time, Ellie. If you don't leave right now, I will hurt you. I won't want to, but I won't be able to help it."

"You would never hurt me."

He shook his head, willing her to understand. "*I'm not human*. It's not the same, no matter how much I try to pretend. I want to be with you, but I need more than I can ask you to give."

"You can ask anything of me. Don't you know that by now?"

The thought left him a little bitter. He didn't need to add his…idiosyncrasies to her already long list of problems. Still, she was here and he couldn't help what happened. He circled her again, getting closer than ever. "I think between your family and friends, you have enough people to take care of. I'm not going to be another one of your projects." He pushed the strap of her tank top off her shoulder as he walked by. He stopped in front of her, leaning against the bed. She might take it as a casual pose, but he was ready to pounce.

"Stop it." Her command lacked authority, and he knew he had her.

"I don't think so."

She stood there, still and cool as a marble statue, but he felt the fire burning just beneath her skin. It mirrored the lava churning inside him, rearing to break free.

"I don't think you're ready to know who I really am, Ellie."

Even as he said the words, he knew how untrue they were. She was ready, more than that if he read the look in her eyes correctly. She was just as turned-on as he was, but could she handle him the way he wanted her? He really had no idea.

"I'm not walking away." When she spoke, her voice held renewed conviction. Her choice was evident in her heated gaze.

The energy in the room could barely be contained, and he needed more of it. He needed it all, whether she truly was ready or not.

Her body tensed as he pounced and wrapped his arms around her waist, flinging her to the bed. The air rushed out of her lungs audibly as they hit the mattress, Ellie on her stomach with him on top of her. Not in the mood to waste time on preliminaries, he stripped her out of her skirt, tearing the fabric from her body to bare her nude flesh.

It was quite a sight, his Ellie flat on the bed, her impossibly fair skin glowing in the dimly lit room. It almost put him over the edge. *Almost*, but he held tight to the thin thread that was left of the control he prided himself on. Pushing himself away, he stripped off his clothes and pulled her to her hands and knees, dipping his fingers into her already swollen sex. He wasted no time on seduction — it wasn't necessary. Ellie moaned and pushed against him. She was wet, *so* wet, and he couldn't wait. He pushed her forward on the bed, angling her toward the headboard and lifting her wrists in his hands. "Hold on," he told her, pushing her hands closer to the wooden slats that made up the headboard.

"What?" she asked, her tone confused. He bit down on her shoulder.

"Do it, Ellie. Hold on, and don't let go."

She did as told, reaching her hands out to grasp the wood. Her body bent at a ninety-degree angle, her arms outstretched in front of her—like an offering. He loved the idea.

"I can't hold on long like this. My arms will get too tired."

"You'll be fine." He caressed the smooth, unmarred skin of her back, running his hands across her to memorize every inch. Then, without any warning to her, he mounted her from behind. He pushed his cock into her tight sex, pulling her hips back against him at the same time. Ellie screamed with the force of his thrusts, pushing hard against him, but he knew he couldn't have hurt her—she was too wet for that.

"Quiet," he growled, not wanting the neighbors to call the police. He didn't need any interruptions. After a few more harsh thrusts, amazingly, Ellie came hard, her entire body convulsing. Still she held onto the headboard, quivering with the force of her orgasm. He felt her relax under him, going almost boneless. He leaned over her and clamped his teeth into the skin where her neck joined her shoulder. She cried out sharply as he tasted blood. It didn't take much more for him to follow her over the edge, filling her with his seed. He leaned hard on her when he came, and Ellie collapsed. He pressed her into the mattress with the entire weight of his body, running his tongue over her moist neck. Sweat clung to them—hers, his, it didn't matter. The moment had been incredible, and well worth the wait.

And then it hit him, what had happened. What he'd done to her, his human woman. A cold knot tightened in the base of his stomach and he rolled off, sitting on the edge of the bed. He should have had more control over himself than that.

"Eric?" Ellie asked softly, her tone filled with doubt. "What's the matter?"

She put her hand on his shoulder and he shrugged her away, his body felt bereft of the warmth almost instantly. "I'm sorry, Ellie. I shouldn't have done that."

"I don't understand what you think you've done." She sounded slightly insecure, and it made him feel even more guilty.

"I was wrong to take you that way. You deserve better than to be treated like some kind of animal."

She laughed behind him. "Is that was this is about? Do you think you've offended me? Trust me, Eric. It would take a lot more than sex to scare me off." She paused, and when she spoke again her voice was filled with wonder. "Actually, I kind of liked it."

"No. You can't. We shouldn't be together." No matter what his body told him. "I could really hurt you someday."

"You wouldn't. You just proved that. You'd never hurt me."

He turned around and glanced at the wound he'd inflicted on her neck. His teeth marks stood out red and angry against her pale skin. A drop of blood formed at the edge of the cut and he bit back the urge to lick it away. He felt his cock start to harden again, despite his efforts to leave her alone. He'd marked her, and his body didn't want to let him forget it.

She moved closer and cuddled him from behind, her front pressing against his back. Her arms came around him and she rested her cheek on his shoulder blade. "Please. You told me before to trust us. I have. Now I think *you* need to."

He extricated himself from her arms and walked across the room, needing to get away from her comforting warmth. It scared him. Set him on edge. What had he done to deserve her comfort? Nothing. He'd lied to her, seduced her mind, marred her perfect skin with the imprint of his teeth. He ran a hand over his face. He couldn't let this continue. She'd only end up resenting him in the end.

"What's the matter now?" she asked. He glanced down to see her standing right in front of him. He'd been so lost in his thoughts that he hadn't even heard her walk across the room.

"Nothing. You...you should go." She'd never understand his life. She'd never really accept him for what he was. He had to let her go before it was too late.

"No."

He looked deep into her eyes, the single word hitting him in the chest—knocking the wind out of him. She could stand up to him now, when she'd only seen a small bit of what he was capable of. She really had no idea what she'd be in for if she stuck around. He leaned forward and tentatively licked the wound. She shivered and made a small sound deep in her throat. The coppery taste of her blood was strange on his tongue, yet familiar at the same time. *His mate.* How would she feel when she found out the truth? He looked up at her and smiled weakly, still uncertain. "Are you sure this is what you want? Do you really want to be stuck with me for the rest of your life? Because that's what's going to happen if you don't turn around and walk out that door this minute."

"As strange as this sounds, that's all I've ever wanted." She glanced toward the bed before bringing her gaze back to his.

What he saw in there made his heart clench. She was too good for him. He didn't deserve her—but he was selfish enough to keep her, anyway.

"I don't know what's going on," she continued, confusion warring with a deeper emotion in her tone and gaze. "I...I feel as if I've been waiting for you all my life. I know that doesn't make any sense, but it's true. I told you I used to dream about panthers as a girl. I still do. And since I met you, the dreams have only gotten stronger. But they're different now. It's like you've always been there, in the back of my mind, but I didn't know it until you came here."

He opened his mouth, but closed it when he realized he didn't know what to say. Her confession shocked him, scared him, and made him believe that maybe everything would be okay. All his life he'd been trying to find that one force that held him down, anchored him to the world. Ellie did that, and more. Could it really be this simple? He shook his head. A deep sense of foreboding told him no. Nothing was this simple, and nothing this good could last. Had they been doomed from the beginning? He didn't like that thought at all.

He pushed away the sense of dread when Ellie took his hand and led him back to the bed. She smiled and lay down on the mattress, tugging his arm and bringing him with her. He rested on his back and she put her head on his chest, gently stroking his side with the tips of her fingers. "Whatever is haunting you, Eric, we can work it out. Everything is going to be fine."

Fine? He hoped like hell that she was right.

The longer they lay entwined on the mattress, the more he noticed the tiny jolts that ran through his nerves when her fingers grazed his skin. He placed his hand over hers, as if to still her movements. She kissed his chest, her tongue laving his nipple; his cock started to harden again. He groaned and she smoothed her hand over his abdomen, teasing him lightly with her fingernails and sending shivers through his gut. Letting his head drop back to the pillow, he closed his eyes and silently begged for control. He didn't want to take her again so soon, not when he'd been less than gentle with her only minutes ago.

She wrapped her hand around his cock, bringing him to full attention in seconds, and he snapped his eyes open. "What are you doing?"

"Just lay back and enjoy," she told him, a coy smile on her face.

"You should try to get some rest." He made one last plea for his sanity, because the way she stroked him was slowly driving him insane.

"Later," she whispered before she took the head of his cock into her mouth.

The unexpected sensation of her moist, warm mouth enveloping his erection hit him hard, making him arch his back off the mattress. He sucked in a sharp breath as she ran her tongue back and forth over the tip, cupping his balls in her free hand. She dropped her hands away so that only her mouth was touching him, and went up on her hands and knees.

Her silky hair draped over his thighs and stomach, tickling him and increasing his arousal. He threaded his hands through her hair and held her tight as she sank her mouth down on him. He groaned long and loud when his cock bumped the back of her throat. She pulled back a little and smiled, her lips stretching tight around him. When she took him deep into her mouth again, his hips lifted of their own volition to urge him further inside. She took as much as she could, licking and stroking with her soft tongue until he felt his balls begin to tighten and the beginnings of orgasm stir in his gut.

She seemed to sense how close he was and wrapped her fingers tightly around the base of his cock, pushing him over the edge. His come spurted into her mouth in gushing waves and she continued to suck, milking him dry. But she didn't release him like he expected. She worked his nearly flaccid cock with her lips and tongue.

"Hey," he said softly, brushing her hair from her face. "After that, I'm going to need a while to recover."

Her eyes took on a decidedly naughty expression and she let him slip from her mouth. "We'll see," she said before sucking him back inside the warm depths.

When he felt himself amazingly start to harden again, he sat up. He gently tugged on her hair to lift her off his swelling cock. She looked at him with glazed-over eyes, her cheeks flushed, her mouth open in a wanton way that made him completely hard all over again. The soft whimpering sound she made was nearly enough to drive him over the edge, but he held back. He pulled her up to him and kissed her hard as he rolled her onto her back, slinking down so that his mouth was level with her sex. He put his nose against the folds of her labia and breathed deeply. She smelled of sex, and the utter carnality of it made his blood hum. She smelled of *him*.

He thrust two fingers inside her cunt and she whimpered. The tiny sound turned into a moan as he sucked her clit into his mouth, scraping his tongue over the small bundle of nerves as he thrust his fingers deeply inside her. He swirled his tongue over her clit, circling the sensitive flesh, before he clamped down gently with his teeth, and he felt her body very nearly come off the sheets. Her cunt muscles contracted hard on his fingers.

Her hands fisted in his hair, and she screamed. He looked up at her, taking in the sight of her in the throes of an explosive orgasm. Her eyes were closed, her mouth open, her entire body flushed pink. She'd arched her back, giving him an incredible view of her breasts. Her legs were bent and drooping almost to the mattress. He'd never seen anything so beautiful in his life.

He crawled up her body slowly, kissing the soft thatch of black hair that covered her mound, the tiny swell of her abdomen, dipping his tongue into her navel and the valley between her breasts. He kissed his way up her throat, along her jaw, to her lush lips. As he kissed her, he settled his cock at the welcoming entrance of her cunt and thrust home, slow and easy this time. Still, she clung to him and moaned as he pushed inside completely. He echoed her sentiment silently in his head, pausing in his movements to memorize the way she felt around him, her slippery inner walls clenching around his cock.

He stroked into her with carefully measured thrusts, slow and even, until she gasped for breath beneath him. "*Eric.*" She said his name on a whisper of breath that tickled his neck. He looked down at her, and their gazes locked. It was impossible to break away.

"You mean so much to me." The words slipped out before he could stop them, but he didn't want to take them back. In just a short time, she'd become such an integral part of his life that he couldn't imagine going back to the way things were before. Whatever else he accomplished in his lifetime, he would make sure she knew—every day—how special she was to him. She deserved no less than everything he could ever give her. He just hoped he lived up to her expectations.

He pulled back a little and then thrust inside her, simultaneously attempting to push the doubts from his mind.

The further he sank into her, the further his mind melded with hers. He'd never dared to open himself up in that way during sex before, but now he found himself tentatively reaching out to her. The connection between them was strong, almost a tangible thing. He felt every emotion that crossed her mind—arousal, tenderness, passion...love. She wouldn't admit it yet, maybe didn't even know it, but he felt it there in her mind. It scared him a little to feel an answering emotion within him, equally as strong.

He watched her eyes cloud with passion and felt her tighten around him, her orgasm this time taking her slowly but steadily until she was limp in her arms. Just watching her was all it took. His whole body clenched as he came, not as explosive as the times before but just as powerful. Maybe even more so, given the emotional significance. With the last bit of strength he had he rolled to his back, pulling her on top of him. He looked up at her through the haze of sexual satisfaction, and she smiled.

"I told you that you wouldn't hurt me."

"No, but if you keep this up *you're* going to hurt *me*." He craned his neck to kiss her. "I'm not nearly as young as you. You have got to take it easy with me, woman."

"Oh, yeah. This is such a hardship for you." She leaned down and playfully nipped his lip.

If he wasn't so damned tired, he might have taken that as a sign that she wanted more, but as it was he could barely keep his eyes open. Any more loving would have to wait until morning. "Will you stay tonight?" he asked.

"If you'd like."

He kissed the top of her head even as his eyes closed and he drifted off to sleep.

Chapter 16

The telephone woke Ellie in the middle of the night. She rolled over in bed, reaching for the phone along the nightstand. It wasn't there. Bolting upright, she looked around the room. She wasn't at home. She'd fallen asleep at the hotel. In Eric's bed. As she woke up a little more, she realized the ringing came from her cell. She leaned over the bed, fumbling along the floor until she found the device. She answered quietly, not wanting to wake Eric after the tiring night they'd had.

"Ellie? It's Charlotte."

The terror in her sister's voice shook her. Nothing scared Charlotte. *Ever.* For her to sound this frightened was a big cause of concern. "Charlotte? Where are you? Are you okay?"

"No. It's *him.* He's got me."

"Who has you?"

"Tony."

Ellie's blood froze in her veins. Tony. Why hadn't she forced Charlotte to leave with Becca and Carol? Why hadn't she stayed home to watch over her sister, instead of selfishly coming to make amends with Eric? "Goddess, Charlotte. Are you okay?"

"I am for now," she spoke calmly, but Ellie heard the near-hysteria that edged her tone. "He wants you to meet him at the pier in ten minutes. If you don't, he says he'll kill me."

"I'll be right there."

She turned to wake Eric, to ask him to help, but he wasn't there. A chill ran through her as she wondered where he'd gone. Why hadn't he woken her? She shook her head. She didn't have time to think about it now. Charlotte needed her more than she needed Eric.

She dressed quickly, borrowing a pair of drawstring shorts and a T-shirt, and went out to her car. She tried to call Eric on her cell phone, but again got no answer. Swearing, she fished through her purse for the emergency number he'd given her. She dialed and pulled out of the parking lot while she waited for an answer.

"Kincaid."

She blinked at the deep, rough sound of the man's voice. Eric's boss. The edginess in his tone chilled her. She fought the urge to hang up, but at this point she'd do anything to help Charlotte. "I'm a friend of Eric Malcolm's. I have an emergency, and I can't get a hold of him."

"Is this Ellie?"

"Yes. My sister has been kidnapped."

"Where are you now?"

"I'm on my way to meet Tony at the pier to get my sister back."

There was a brief pause. "Didn't Eric warn you to stay put?"

Her voice was tight when she replied. "I can't even find him. My sister is going to die if I don't get there soon. I don't give a shit what Eric, or anyone else, has to say about it. My sister is a lot more important than hurting Eric's feelings."

"Okay. Relax," he said, his tone urging her to do anything but. "What I want you to do is drive to your house. I'll meet you there in a little while."

"Oh, no. I don't think so." How could he even suggest such a thing when her sister's life was at stake? "Where are you? How do you know where I live?"

"We all know," he answered cryptically. "I'm about five minutes from the pier right now. Eric and I will take care of Tony. Just go home and sit tight, and we'll be there as soon as we can."

Like *that* was going to happen. "I don't even know you. I'm not going to trust you with my sister's life. I'm going to meet him like he wanted."

"There's nothing I can say to make you turn around and go home, is there?"

"No." She pulled her car into a parking spot and got out, not even bothering to bring her purse. "I'm here now. I've got to go."

"Okay, fine. Have it your way. I'll get in touch with Eric, and we'll meet you. Try to hold the guy off until we get there, okay?"

How was he supposed to reach Eric when she couldn't? "Fine, whatever."

"Do you want me to stay on the line?"

She thought about saying yes, but ultimately declined. "I can handle it better without worrying about updating a stranger via my cell. Thanks anyway."

"Be careful. Eric will kill me if anything happens to you."

She scoffed at that and disconnected the call, slipping the small phone into the pocket of Eric's shorts. The wind, cool in the late night, wrapped around her legs and whipped her hair over her face. She shoved it behind her ears and walked around the small outbuildings to the boat dock. The smell of salt in the air seemed stronger tonight, sinister almost. She listened for some sign of her sister, but only the cries of the seagulls overhead filled the air.

"Ellie." The voice reached her out of the darkness. She strained to see through the moonlight. Tony was standing by the wrought iron fence that edged the sidewalk next to the water, his arm around Charlotte's neck.

"Okay, I'm here. Let go of my sister."

"Come closer." His voice was deep, alien. The knot of fear that had settled in her stomach when Charlotte had called tightened, making it nearly impossible to breathe. She stepped closer, slowly, feeling surreal. Surely this had to be some kind of terrible dream. When she stopped in front of him, he let Charlotte go and grabbed Ellie. Charlotte stood there, not sure of what to do. He laughed, the sound tinged with fear and bitterness. "Run, sweetheart. You've been spared, and that doesn't happen often. Get out of here before Aiala changes her mind."

Aiala? "Go, Charlotte. I'll be fine." Ellie assured her. "He won't hurt me."

Charlotte shook her head vigorously as she dug in her heels. "I'm not leaving you."

"She'll die if you don't," Tony said. "Go home now. Leave before it's too late."

Charlotte threw Ellie an uncertain look before she took off across the sidewalk and disappeared from view around the corner of an outbuilding. Ellie hoped she listened and left like she was told, but knowing Charlotte she'd gone only far enough to be out of sight.

Refusing to think about it until she was safe at home, she turned her attention back to Tony. "What do you want with me?"

"This isn't about what I want." Desperation filled his voice. "It's about what *she* wants. It always has been. Don't even try to run, because she'll stop you. She's here, even though she hasn't shown herself yet."

"What are you talking about?" she asked, the dread turning into a lump of ice inside her. "*Who* are you talking about?"

"Aiala. My Master. You're going to be a warning to your friends. I'm sorry. I can't disobey her."

He didn't give her time to react. He grabbed her hair and yanked her head up, sinking his fangs into her neck. It was the worst pain she'd felt in her life. He tore into her skin, ripping at her flesh. A scream caught in her throat as everything around her faded. She felt her heartbeat slow and her mind grow fuzzy. It was then that she knew, irrevocably, that she was going to die.

* * * * *

Eric's heart stopped at the sight that greeted him—Ellie lying on the sidewalk, her body still and lifeless. He ran to her and rolled her gently to her back, checking the pulse in her wrist. Weak. Thready. Fading even as he tried to decide what to do. Antonio hadn't drained her completely, but the gashes he'd made in her neck would insure she'd bleed out fully within minutes. He hadn't left her with enough to live, but with just enough to suffer before she died. Taking her to the hospital was out—the closest hospital was a good fifteen minutes away. She'd never last that long.

She'd called Sam, which meant she'd tried to reach him before coming out here all alone. He gave her credit for being brave, but she'd been walking into a trap. This was a setup, planned down to the last detail, and she'd fallen for it. He hated to admit it, but so had he. He'd left her alone because Antonio had contacted him, said he'd wanted to meet with him. He should have known it was a trap—would have if he hadn't been so tired and sated from his lovemaking with Ellie. But he'd been stupid and he'd left her.

His choice had cost his woman her life.

"Eric."

The cold feminine voice behind him made him turn. "Aiala."

"I warned you years ago not to mess with me. You didn't listen, and now your pathetic little human is going to die." Her laugh grated like fingernails on a chalkboard. "The world will be a better place with one less mortal to pollute it."

"I'm not going to let you get away with this." He stood and started to her, but Aiala held him off with a wave of her hand.

"Actually, I think I will. She's getting closer and closer to her last breath. If you chase me, she'll die alone." Even as she spoke the words, Eric felt Ellie's life draining from her body. The connection between them was severing, and his entire being ached. He'd only just found her. How was he supposed to live without her?

"It's too late," Aiala said, her tone harshly amused. "There's nothing you can do for her, Eric. Nothing. *It's too late.*"

"No, it isn't." Sam stepped out of the shadows of the buildings and walked toward Eric. "There's still something that can be done."

"You can't save her," Aiala's voice held real fear for the first time. "I won't let you."

"You don't have a choice." Sam raised his hand toward Aiala and made a pushing motion. She flew back into the fence, the air whooshing out of her lungs as she sagged to the ground.

"How dare you!" she yelled as she started for Sam. He didn't give her a chance to attack. When she got within a foot of him, he lifted his hand, palm out, and shot a ball of fire at her. It hit her in the face and a pained scream tore through the night. Her body disappeared into the air with a pop and a wisp of smoke. She'd be back, but at least Sam had bought them a few days while she recovered from the damage.

"What do you want me to do?" Sam asked Eric as he leaned over Ellie's body.

"What *can* you do?" Eric asked the question, even though he already knew the answer.

"I can make her one of us." Sam looked up at him, awaiting his answer. "Just say the word."

"No." Eric was adamant. "She'd hate me forever."

Sam shrugged. "Your decision. The lady's not up to making it herself."

"If you let her die, Eric, I'll never forgive you." Charlotte walked toward them, her hands on her hips. "I don't know what's going on around here, but I don't really care right now. If either of you is capable of saving my sister's life I suggest you do it, or heads are going to roll."

Eric felt Ellie's wrist for a pulse. *Nothing.* He closed his eyes and fought the grief that welled inside him. "It's too late now. It's over."

Sam looked from Eric to Charlotte, then back down at Ellie again. "I can still help, if you'll let me."

"I told you to do it," Charlotte insisted.

"It's not your decision. I need Eric's consent. Ellie is his mate." Sam sighed before he faced Eric. "It's not her time to die. I can save her, but you've got to understand it would be a sacrifice. She might very well hate you when she wakes, and she could try to hurt you if it doesn't go well."

"But if I don't agree, I'll lose her forever."

"Yes." Sam paused. "You might lose her still. I can't make any guarantees. Could you live with the fact that she might not want you after this?"

She'd want him. She'd have to. They'd formed a bond, and this could only make it stronger. At least that's what he kept telling himself. He really had no idea if any of it were true, but he had to take the chance, for Ellie's sake. She was so young, so beautiful, and he couldn't let her die because of his stupid mistake. "Knowing she's alive would be better than losing her for good."

"Thank you," Charlotte breathed, putting her hand on Eric's shoulder. He looked up at her and saw her fighting back tears.

"Fine." Sam knelt down, taking Ellie's lifeless body into the cradle of his arms. "I'll do this for you. *If* you go and try to find Antonio. He couldn't have gotten very far by now."

"But—"

"No, you can't stay and watch. You wouldn't want to see what I need to do." Sam turned his attention to Ellie. "Go, Malcolm, before I change my mind. And take your mate's sister with you."

"I'm not leaving Ellie," Charlotte said, crossing her arms over her chest.

"*Leave.*" Sam's eyes glowed red as he spoke the word. Charlotte squealed and turned, running in the opposite direction.

"Go after her before she hurts herself," Sam directed.

Eric stayed only long enough to watch Sam pull a dagger out of a sheath on his belt before he took off after Charlotte, trying not to think about what Sam planned to do with the dagger.

* * * * *

"You should have stayed with her," Sam told Eric as they settled Ellie into bed several hours later. "Or put someone on her. She's too strong-willed for her own good, going off like that."

Eric looked at him, ready to tear his throat out. "Don't you think I know that? I would have, if I hadn't had a *job* to do."

"If you'd called sooner, I would have sent someone to help. You know damned well you can always call if you need me. It isn't like you to be so impulsive."

"I didn't realize how bad it was until this happened."

"Aiala set her up." Sam paused to tuck a strand of Ellie's hair behind her ear. The small gesture made jealousy rise sharp and strong in Eric. "She set us all up."

Eric nodded.

"Is Ellie going to accept what I've made her?"

"She'd better. She doesn't have much choice." Eric sat on the edge of the bed and ran his fingers down Ellie's cheek. She was so cold. "She's strong. She'll be okay."

Sam nodded. He started to walk out of the room, but turned back when he reached the door. "You love her, don't you?"

Eric sighed heavily. "Yes, I do." That was something he hadn't even admitted to himself, not until he's seen what Antonio had done to her. Now he knew for sure that there was no way he was ever going to let her go.

"It will be fine, Eric." Sam spoke slowly and carefully. "Everything happens for a reason."

Eric thought about the charm Ellie wore. Something clicked inside him for the first time since he'd met her. "You knew, didn't you?"

Sam didn't speak, just frowned.

"I don't know how you knew, but you did. You knew Ellie was my mate. That's why you sent me to do a job that should have gone to Liam."

"Yes, I knew. I've known for years."

Eric closed his eyes and fought back the urge to ram Sam's face into the nearest hard object. In cat-speak, Sam was what was known as a Keeper—a cat who was given visions of the future of others, along with the means to manipulate fate to see that things happened the way they were supposed to. It chilled him to think that Sam had known all along what the outcome of this situation would be. "Why didn't you say anything?"

"I couldn't. It wasn't time."

"How can you be so calm about this? She died, Sam."

Sam nodded slowly, remorse filling his gaze. "If I'd known the way this would come about, I would have told you. But I didn't know it would be this bad." He sighed, turning his attention to Ellie's motionless body. "She was chosen for you years ago, when she was just a child. I know you won't believe this now, but together you're destined to do great things for humanity."

"Yeah, sure." Eric turned his attention back to Ellie, wishing she'd just open her eyes and give him a sign that she was okay. He knew it could be days before she woke, but that didn't make waiting any easier. "Come on, sweetheart." He kissed her forehead. She didn't even stir.

"She lost a lot of blood." Sam said. "*A lot.* She'll wake up when she's ready."

Eric looked up at him.

"She's been pretty much drained. Doesn't have much human blood left. It's going to get violent."

"What do you mean?"

"We'll have to tie her down once it begins, or she might kill herself with her thrashing."

Eric shook his head. He couldn't believe this was happening. He'd seen terrible things in his life, and they'd never affected him. With Ellie, everything seemed new. He didn't know if he could handle watching her change. Seeing her in the throws of so much pain would kill him. "What am I supposed to do? How can I help her?"

"You just have to wait it out. I've done what I can, and you just have to let the curse take care of the rest."

Eric nodded. He hoped like hell that Ellie would fight her way through this.

"Can I do anything to ease the pain for her?"

Sam shook his head slowly. "There's nothing. She may heal, and she may not. Most people would die after a wound like that."

"Can *you* do something?"

"No." Sam shook his head sadly. "I wish I could, Eric, I really do, but she's going to have to get through this on her own. Right now, you need to take a break and get something to eat. Your girl's going to be a cat by the time she wakes from this. She's going to need you, and you'll have to be strong."

With that, Sam walked out of the room, leaving Eric to stew in his own guilt yet again.

* * * * *

"Is there anything I can do to help?"

Eric snapped awake at the sound of the voice next to him. He blinked his eyes, trying to focus on the small form. He smiled when he realized who it was. "Hey, Merida."

"Sam told me you brought your woman here, and that she was sick. What's going on?" Eric's sister pulled a chair next to his and sat, crossing her legs on the seat. Her auburn hair was pulled back into a high ponytail, making her look about twenty years old.

"She's not sick. She died." He knew his voice sounded desolate, but he couldn't help it.

"But Sam brought her back. If he hadn't, she wouldn't be here."

He laughed bitterly. "Yeah, right. We'll see how she feels when she wakes up and realizes her former life is over. She's very much a creature of habit, Merida. She's not going to accept this."

Merida smiled and wrinkled her freckled nose. "I think you may be underestimating her. Give her time. She'll need it. But she'll come around. How can she not when she has a guy like you guiding her?"

He hoped that would be true. He allowed her a small smile. "You're just biased."

"Not everyone would do what you did to raise an annoying baby sister, Eric. Don't ever forget that. Now back to my original question. What do you need me to do?"

"Nothing. Stay here, stay safe."

"I want to go to Stone Harbor and get that jerk."

Eric shook his head. "I'm not going to put you in that kind of danger. Antonio's long gone. He'd already taken off before I could get to him. Aiala isn't someone I want you messing with. Even wounded, she's a nasty bitch."

She scoffed at that in typical Merida fashion. "It's not your decision to make. Sam's already okayed it. I'm leaving soon. I just wanted to come and see her before I left."

"I absolutely forbid—"

Merida held up her hand to stop him. "Think before you forbid, Eric. You have enough going on. You don't need to add a couple of broken bones to your list."

He nearly laughed aloud. She was serious. And she could do it. His sister didn't look like she could defeat a housefly, but he'd seen her take down men three times her size with relative ease. He knew she could—and *would*—defend herself, but he still didn't want to see her get hurt. He'd tried to forbid her to work for Sam when she'd gotten old enough, but she'd reacted the way she always did. She'd laughed at him. He had to admire her strength of character, but he still didn't want to see her get in over her head.

He also didn't want her subjected to Antonio and Aiala, but what could he do? She was already set to go, and as much as he hated to admit it, he really had no control over her. None at all.

"She's pretty," Merida said absently, twirling a curl that had escaped her ponytail around her finger. For a *Panthicenos*, her light coloring was unusual. It was close to albino, as far as cats went. The coloring combined with the underlying sense of power was an intriguing combination. When she'd been a teenager...he hated to even think of that. Men noticed her wherever she went. Even Sam had noticed, but he knew Eric would beat him to within in inch of his life if he laid one finger on Merida.

"If you insist on going, I guess I can't stop you." He smiled sadly, hoping the tragedies had stopped, at least for a little while. "Be careful, though. Don't do anything stupid."

She laughed at that. "Stupid is such a relative word. I'll be careful. You take care of your woman. Don't worry about me. I'll be in touch." She kissed him softly on the cheek before she turned and walked out of the room.

Chapter 17

Ellie opened her eyes slowly, gradually becoming aware that something pressed against her lips. She moaned softly and forced her eyes open. It was a straw. She took a sip, and the salty taste made her nauseated.

"Drink. It will make you feel better."

"Eric?" Slowly he came into focus.

A smile spread across his handsome face. "Hey. I was beginning to think you'd never wake up."

"How long have I been out?"

"A couple of days. You've been in and out of it, awake enough at times for me to make sure you got fed."

She managed a small laugh, her voice rusty from disuse. "I thought I was dead."

He was silent for a long time. Too long. When he spoke, she had to strain to hear him. "Actually, you were."

She swallowed hard. She must have heard him wrong. She couldn't have died—she wouldn't be here now if she had. It simply wasn't possible. "Am I in the hospital?"

"No. There was no time." He tried to force the straw between her lips again. "Please drink some more, Ellie. You need all the nourishment you can get. You're healing well, but it's still going to be a couple of days before you feel like your old self."

Well, that relieved her. She couldn't believe she'd thought he said she'd died. Whatever happened to her must have affected her hearing. She sucked on the straw, but the taste of the liquid was strange. She coughed as it hit her tongue. "What is that?"

Eric stood up and set the mug on a nearby table. He sighed heavily. "It's soup. Just chicken broth."

"Why does it taste funny?"

He glanced at her quickly before he looked away.

"What is it that you're not telling me?"

It took a while for suspicion to sink into her injury-fogged mind, but when it did, it hit with the force of an explosion. "What did you do, Eric?"

"I did what had to be done, in order to save your life. I had to make the decision quickly, and I couldn't bear the thought of losing you when I could have prevented what happened."

"Did he really hurt me that badly?"

Eric nodded, his mouth set in a grim line. "Unfortunately, yes. He tore your neck apart."

Her hand flew to her neck to feel for an injury. What she felt was the smooth line of a scar. "I thought you said I was only out for a couple of days?"

"That's all it takes for you to heal now."

She drew in a deep breath, catching the scent of the soup in the mug. How could she smell that from this far away? "How? What did you do, have Royce or Marco turn me into a vampire?" She braced herself for the answer, not sure how she felt about it all. If she'd wanted to turn, she would have asked Marco years ago. But what other explanation could there be?

"I wish it were as simple as that." He paused. "No, Ellie. You're not a vampire."

"Then what am I?"

"You died that night, Ellie." He shook his head. "I would have given anything to save your human life, but fate obviously had other plans."

"My human life?" Her mouth went dry and her pulse sped up, the blood pounding in her ears. "What am I?"

"You'll be weak for a while. Your body didn't react well to the change. I had to restrain you to keep you from hurting yourself."

She looked at her wrists, lightly bruised with ligature marks. It sickened her.

"I didn't want to do it," he said softly. "I wouldn't have done it if it wasn't a necessity."

Every muscle in her body ached. "I can only imagine."

He shook his head. "Not in your wildest dreams. It nearly killed me to watch you go through it and know I couldn't do a thing to ease your pain."

"I was told it wasn't painful at all." Her mind drifted to what Amara had told her.

"The change from human to vampire is not. The change you've undergone is very different." He smiled sadly. "Sam saved your life."

"Sam?" This was entirely too dreamlike for her to accept. "What exactly did he have to do to save me?"

"He had to bring you back to life." Eric sighed heavily, and she wished he'd just get on with it. "He had to...in order to save you, Sam had to curse you."

"Curse? Oh, okay." She was still waiting to wake up from this incredibly strange dream. "So I'm a zombie or something? Living dead?"

"Humans cannot become *Panthicenos* unless they are cursed," he blurted, but his admission didn't make her feel any better. "You're a cat now, Ellie. I'm sorry."

"No." He had to be lying. She didn't want this. She wanted her old life back—her house, her family, her painting. This couldn't be happening.

"We'll talk about it a little more when you've had a chance to recover," Eric said, his voice breaking through her hysteria. "I want you to know that I never would have consented to this, if it hadn't been the only way."

She shivered at the thought. "Do you want me to thank you or something?"

The darkness in his expression frightened her. "No, I don't expect your thanks."

"Tony meant to kill me."

Eric stared at her for a few seconds before he stood and paced the length of the room. "No, I don't think he did."

"He took most of my blood!"

"Antonio isn't in control of himself. Aiala meant to kill you." He paused again, looking at her sadly. "He called me, Ellie. He told me exactly where I could find you."

"Why would he do that?"

"He did as he was told. Aiala wanted revenge, and this was her way to get it." He shook his head. "I'm so sorry I dragged you into all of this."

"It wasn't just you. He told me she wanted to hurt you, but also Marco and Royce."

"And you'd be the perfect victim." He came back over to the bed and sat down, brushing his fingers through her hair. "How are you feeling?"

"Tired." Her life had changed so thoroughly and completely she didn't think she'd ever recover.

"We'll give you a couple more days to rest, but then we've got a lot of things to discuss. You'll have to learn to control yourself so you don't slip into other forms unknowingly."

"Other forms? Excuse me. I think I'm going to pass out." She took a deep breath. Why did she feel like she'd been sucked into one of Amara's horror movies? "I can't handle this. I don't want to change into *anything*."

"Don't worry about it. I'll be there for you, for whatever you need. Or Sam could show you, if you want him to. I'm sure he wouldn't mind. All you'd have to do is ask."

She didn't miss the disdain in his voice when he said Sam's name. "What's the problem you have with the man? Didn't he save my life?"

Eric nodded, jealousy flashing in his eyes.

"Oh, I get it now. You think because he saved my life, I'm going to run off with him."

"I didn't say that."

"You didn't have to. Sometimes you're entirely too easy to read." She shifted in the massive bed. "I've never even met the guy. I talked to him on the phone once. There's no chance of me leaving you for him."

Eric looked a little relieved, but she still saw worry shadowing his gaze. "You've got a lot to learn, sweetheart. You're going to have to stay here with him for a while."

"What about you?"

"I'll stay, too, if that would make you happy."

"Let me put it this way. If you don't stay, I won't stay, either. I go where you go, Eric Malcolm, so you'd better get used to it." That, at least, earned her a small smile. He really was worried about Sam.

He laughed uneasily. "We'll talk so much more about this a little later. Now you need to eat a little and take a nap."

"I've been napping for days," she protested even as fatigue hit her hard. "I'd rather get up and get moving."

"No. You stay in bed for at least another day." His smile this time was genuine.

"How much longer do you think it will be before I'm well?"

"Not long at all. You'll heal much quicker now, in any situation."

She did feel different, but she couldn't quite explain it. It had something to do with her energy, and the way it moved through her body more noticeably now. "Why did you say you had to give Sam consent to save me?"

He took a deep breath. "We haven't known each other that long. I don't want to rush you."

"Please tell me."

He smiled. "I can't imagine being without you. When cats find their true mate, it's for life. It's a stronger bond than marriage, than even love."

"And that's what you feel for me?"

He didn't answer, but his eyes said it all. "We'll talk more about it in a couple of days. Now I want you to get some rest."

He stood up and brushed a kiss over her forehead. The thought that he planned to leave her alone made her suddenly panicky. She clung to his arm, not wanting to be by herself with what he'd just told her.

"Where are you going?"

"I have some things to take care of, and you really do need to sleep."

"No. Please stay." Even as she spoke, she felt herself begin to fade. Her body had been through a lot, and it was starting to go into standby mode without her consent. "Come back soon, please," she said as her eyes drifted closed.

"I will." He took the mug and left the room, shutting the door behind him.

* * * * *

"Should I take your presence as a sign that she's not doing well?" Sam asked when Eric walked into the kitchen with the nearly full mug of soup.

"Actually, no." He set the mug in the sink, wishing she'd taken just a little more before drifting off. "She's doing better. She woke up and talked to me for a little while, but she's back to sleep now."

"You really think she's going to be okay?"

"I think she's going to kick my ass, and probably yours, as soon as she's up to it."

Sam laughed. "She'll definitely be fine. She's through the worst of it."

"I really hope you're right."

"Give her a while. She just needs some time to make the adjustment." Sam shook his head and took a swig of beer from the bottle in his hands. "How are *you* handling this?"

"It's getting easier."

"Good. I don't think I've ever seen you that distraught over anything. Frankly, it bothers me to see you so out of sorts."

Eric slumped in a chair and leaned on the table, taking a deep breath. "She had me really worried there."

"She's the only one, in all the years I've known you, whom you've ever bothered with."

"Yes, she is." And it scared the hell out of him, too. But it was much too late for regrets. "I just hope she feels the same way about me."

He loved Ellie, but he didn't own her. He'd do all he could to keep her, but he was too proud to beg. He had to draw the line somewhere. The decision was out of his hands. If she wanted him, she'd have to be the one to make the first move. Right now, he wasn't sure of anything, and he wasn't going to give her the chance to reject him.

"Maybe you should ask me."

They both looked up at the kitchen doorway where Ellie was standing. "You're supposed to be sleeping," he said, his body tight with nerves. How much had she heard?

"I've never been very interested in naps." She smiled a little when she replied, even though fatigue etched her face.

Her gaze fell on Sam, and Eric noticed her eyes visibly widen. "Ellie, this is Sam."

"Hi," she said hesitantly.

"Don't let him scare you." Eric said to her. Ellie's expression was a mix of fear and fascination. With his rugged build, harshly defined features, and the jagged scars that ran from his nose to his jaw on the left side of his face, he tended to have that effect on people. Especially women.

Ellie would be no different. Sam had cursed her—*recreated* her—and it was inevitable that she would feel a very strong bond toward him. Eric had to face the possibility that he might lose her to Sam, even after everything he'd done to ensure she stayed with him. That thought chilled his heart as well as his bones. He could very well lose his woman, and the man who had become his best friend. If Ellie chose her creator, Eric wouldn't be able to hang around anymore. He'd have to leave his job, his home, and move far enough away that he'd never have to face either of them again.

That thought alone was enough to spark his territorial instincts. His body tensed, and his hands clenched into fists at his sides. He couldn't give her up without a fight.

But he couldn't fight Sam—not if he wanted to walk away with all his body parts intact. In a fight over her, Eric would lose—hands down. He didn't doubt his power, but he didn't doubt Sam's either. Power came with age, and Sam was nearly twice as old as Eric. The man had also spent a lifetime studying the spells and incantations Eric had shunned. If he went up against Sam, he was a dead man.

Ellie made a small noise—a cross between a whimper and a sigh. Eric glanced at her, and saw she'd gone even paler, if that was possible. She looked like she was ready to collapse. He stood up and rushed to her side.

"Sit down, Ellie, before you fall over."

She shook her head. "I want to take a shower, and I really want to brush my teeth. I'd feel a lot better of I could get clean."

"Not even an option," Sam told her. "If you can't stand up for five minutes without falling over, I'm not going to trust you to stand up in a ceramic tiled shower. You don't need to add a head injury to your list of complications."

Ellie narrowed her eyes at Sam. "Last time I checked, I didn't answer to you. I'm twenty-eight years old, and I don't need to ask permission. Eric, will you please help me find a couple of towels so I can get cleaned up?"

"Yeah, no problem. I'll see if I can get a toothbrush for you, too." He shot an amused look at Sam, who shook his head.

"No, she's not going to be difficult at all." Sam finished off his beer and set the bottle on the table. "There's an extra toothbrush or two in the linen closet in the hall. Eric can show you where everything is." He turned his attention to Eric. "Just be careful."

"Of course." Eric couldn't help the tiny flash of resentment that built in him with Sam's words. He'd stopped needing a father figure hundreds of years ago. "Go back upstairs, Ellie. I'll be right there."

"Is she going to be a problem for you?" Sam asked when she was out of earshot.

"Probably," Eric answered with a smile. "I hope so."

"I can imagine. She's a tough one, huh? I never would have imagined…" The look on Sam's face had Eric's instincts up again, despite his fight to keep them at bay.

He clenched his teeth. "She's mine."

Sam laughed. "I can see that. It's plain on both of your faces. Just don't push her too hard, too soon, or you'll lose her."

"I'm trying." Eric shook his head. "This is killing me. She's too complacent, too at ease with the whole thing. I keep expecting her to tell me to go jump off a cliff or something."

"That won't happen. You've already bonded with her. That won't change."

"God, I hope you're right."

"Of course I am. I'm always right." Sam laughed again, and some of Eric's tension eased. "And just for the record, I promise to try to keep my hands off her."

"*Try?* You *will*. I'll kill you if you don't."

Sam snorted. "That'd be the day."

"Don't push me, Sam."

Sam was silent for a long time, his intense gaze boring into Eric's. "I have a feeling that, where you're mortal-turned-cat mate is concerned, you might actually be able to do it."

"Don't ever doubt that I could."

* * * * *

Ellie stood under the shower spray, letting the hot water run down her body. She imagined the steam and water cleansing her, body and soul, taking away all the bad things that had happened in the past couple of days. Her life had changed, but she could get through it. Her mother and grandmother had raised her to be strong.

She leaned one hand on the black tiled wall for support, feeling weaker than she'd first thought. Her legs still felt like they were made out of gelatin, and her stomach still felt queasy. She needed to eat something, but she didn't know if her body would accept it. When she'd sipped the soup, nausea had hit her in strong waves.

"You should have waited for me. I told you I'd be right there."

She jumped as Eric pushed the shower curtain aside and stepped in behind her. Naked. Despite her weakened state, she couldn't help but notice that. She noticed him now on a whole new level—primal and instinctual. The energy thrummed through her body and she reached for him.

He disappointed her by shaking his head and turning her around to face away from him. "Not until you're better. I just want to make sure you can wash up without losing your footing and cracking your head on the tub."

Indignation rose in her and she frowned. "I'm perfectly capable—"

"Shh," he whispered in her ear. "Just let me take care of you for once, okay?"

She leaned back against him, absorbing his warmth. His *essence*. She hadn't been able to do it before, but now she felt like she was absorbing part of him into her. He felt so good against her, but it was hard to ignore the way his erection pressed into her ass. He took a bar of soap and ran it over her skin, cleansing every inch of her body with slow circles of his hand. Her skin quaked under his touch, driving her to the edge of a need she didn't quite understand. By the time he finished soaping her and started to run his hands over her to rinse her, she was ready to tear him apart. A low, incoherent moan escaped her lips and she tried to turn to him. He wouldn't let her.

"Just relax, Ellie. The shakiness will pass," he said soothingly. "We can't make love yet, as much as I'd like to. I won't put your body through that. For now, just breathe slowly and let it go. You can control it, you just have to focus."

She felt him in her mind again, his words calming her inside and out. She felt herself get weaker as he turned off the shower water and helped her out, drying her slowly with a plush towel. He dried himself quickly and took her back into the bedroom, climbing into bed with her and wrapping her naked body with his.

"How are you feeling now?" he asked, his tone tinged with worry.

"A little better, but still tired." She was just beginning to realize how much she ached. Everywhere. She felt like she'd just jogged down the entire East Coast. Her mind had started to clear, but some things were still foggy. "Where are we, anyway?"

"My bedroom," he answered softly.

Up until that moment, she hadn't even asked where he lived—or *how* he lived. She glanced around the room, taking in the masculine décor done in black and beige. The bed was large, the linens soft, probably very high quality cotton. His manner, his clothes, even his furnishings spoke of money.

"Where exactly do you live?"

"Right now, in southern Maine. We're about two hours north of Stone Harbor."

"That's it?" She didn't know what she'd expected, but it certainly wasn't that. "Do you and Sam live together?"

"Not really. None of us are here that often. We live here, yes, but nobody ever really stays here for more than a few weeks at a time."

"Nobody? There are other people here besides the two of you?"

"Merida, my sister, is here more than anyone else. She kind of keeps the place running."

His sister. "Will I get to meet her?"

"Absolutely. She's out right now, but I think she'll be back in a couple of days."

She licked her lips and drew in a deep breath, not sure how to ask the next question. "So what happens now? With us, I mean."

He sighed into her hair and pulled her closer. "We'll work it out in time. For now, let's just get some sleep."

* * * * *

Royce stood in the shadows, watching the empty streets. No one dared venture out after dark anymore. It had been a week since Ellie's disappearance. He was worried sick about her. They all were. All that had been left on the pier that night were a couple small puddles of blood. Was Eric taking good care of her? Was she even with Eric at all? Charlotte knew more than she let on, but she wasn't talking. She'd left right after Ellie disappeared, going to Georgia to join the rest of her family.

Eric had disappeared, as well as Antonio. Something about this didn't settle well. It sat like a nail in his gut, twisting and turning and tearing him apart. He needed to know Ellie was safe. Until then he wouldn't be able to rest.

Hearing someone creeping up behind him, he stood as still as he could. *Cat.* Just what he needed right now. In one fluid motion, he turned and grabbed the visitor's arm, dragging him into the glow of the street light.

His eyes narrowed when he saw it wasn't a man standing before him. It was a very pissed-off looking woman with fiery-red hair and green eyes that sparked daggers at him. She looked like some kind of high school cheerleader. Definitely not a threat. He snorted and dropped her hand. "Merida?"

"Nice to see you, too, Cardoso." She winked at him and gave him a big smile. "I thought you could use some help around here, seeing as you and your vamp friends can't seem to stop Aiala."

He didn't have time for childish games, not when he had a killer to catch and a woman to rescue. "Don't you know how dangerous it is to be wandering the streets tonight, honey?" he asked in his best condescending tone.

She raised an eyebrow and sneered at him. He would have laughed, if the situation had been different. "Do *you*? You're out here all alone, with just those wimpy little fangs to protect you. If you don't want my help, I'll just go find someone who does."

She smiled wickedly and started to walk past him. He grabbed her arm, trying to convince her she was in danger. Big mistake. She twisted his wrist in a death grip and shoved his hand away. "If you touch me again, I'll make you wish you were never born. And then I'll make sure there's no way in hell you'll ever be able to father children." With that, she turned again to stalk away, looking over her shoulder after a few seconds. "You coming or what?"

"Excuse me?"

"You're not even going to try to follow me?" She cocked her head to the side and laughed at him. "What if I told you I know exactly how to stop Aiala?"

"I'd say you were lying."

"So you're too macho to accept my help?"

Of all the nerve. Who did she think she was coming here and acting entitled? "What the hell kind of a question is that?"

"An honest one. I deserve an honest answer." She shrugged. "If you don't want to give me one, fine, don't. I couldn't care less. You should feed if you're planning on being out here much longer. I can see in your eyes how hungry you are. It's not good to go very long. You might go nuts, like Antonio did, and start killing people."

"How much do you know about that?" he asked, taking a dominant stance. She didn't shrink away like he'd expected — like *most* women would have.

She put a hand on her hip and glared right back. "I know you're accusing the wrong guy. He's not in control of himself — at all. Aiala is the only real danger here."

"*Bullshit,*" he said before he could stop himself.

She nodded. "Yep. That's what I thought. Typical male, always flying off the handle for no reason at all. You know, it's a wonder there's life on this planet at all, with the way you men behave. You guys are lucky you can get a woman to even look at you, let alone sleep with you."

"What gives you the right to talk to me like that?"

"Oh, relax." She sighed and shook her head, obviously fed up with him. "Are you going to let me go about my business, or are you going to follow me? If you could decide sometime tonight, that would be great. I've got a lot to do, and I don't want to waste too much time goofing around with you."

He resisted the urge to slam his fist into something. "Are you working for Sam now?"

"Yep. Okay, conversation time is over. I have to worry about is finding the psycho demon bitch before she kills someone else, not appeasing some macho vamp's fragile ego."

"Go back home, Merida. We've got it covered here."

"Yeah, you keep telling yourself that, buddy, until another body is found. I, on the other hand, am not willing to take that chance. I'm going to find Aiala, and if you get in my way I'll have to hurt you."

"Hurt me?" He almost laughed at the idea of a little thing like Merida doing him any kid of harm.

She shrugged again. "It wouldn't be any big sacrifice, you being a vamp and all."

She walked away, and he followed. It was no secret that cats and vampires didn't get along, but she seemed to be taking it to a whole new level. "Do you have a personal vendetta against vampires?"

"They're not my favorite creature." She walked faster. "Besides, maybe it's you personally that's the problem, and not your race. Do you mind walking away so I can get my job done?"

She had a personal beef with him? That didn't make any sense. He barely knew her, hadn't seen her in literally hundreds of years.

"Where's Ellie?" he asked. If she'd spoken with her brother, she had to know where he was keeping her. The only information Marco had been able to get out of Charlotte before she left was that Ellie was safe, in no danger, and she would contact them as soon as she could.

"Your friend is safe. She'll be safe as long as you don't try to find her. Let Eric take care of her. He knows what he's doing. If either Aiala or Antonio is led to her, Eric and Sam are going to be pissed. If you've seen Eric mad, you *know* that's not a good thing. And, trust me on this one, Sam is ten times worse."

"Sam has enough emotions to actually get mad?" Back when Royce had worked for him, Sam was the coldest son of a bitch he'd ever met. The man had no emotions whatsoever, at least none he'd ever shown.

"So you don't know everything after all." She laughed and kept on walking. If he wanted any answers, he had no choice but to follow. "If you screw up and get Ellie killed, then you'll get to experience his murderous temper firsthand. If you play this right and let me take out your killer, you won't have to worry about it."

"What happened to you? You used to be so quiet."

"You're just full of questions, aren't you?" she asked. She stopped in front of a big black sedan, unlocking the doors with a remote attached to her key ring. "I told you why I'm here. I offered you a chance to work together. You didn't take it. Now go away."

She made a shooing gesture with her hands. He almost laughed at it. She was so small, so petite. Did she really think she could shoo him away like a common housefly? "Listen, kiddo, I think we need to get something straight. When I find your brother, and I *will* find him, I'm going to kill him for taking Ellie away and not even having the courtesy to let me know where he was going. And believe me, sweetheart, I'm going to enjoy every second of it. If you get in the way, I have no problem taking you out along with him."

It was a lie, and she knew it. She snorted. "Like I'm supposed to believe that one? Most of you vampires don't have it in you to follow through with a kill, at least not while enjoying it. That's the problem with having a conscience. It gets in the way. Now again, if you'll excuse me, Cardoso, I have a job to do. If I don't do it, I don't get paid, and that could be a problem."

He raised his eyebrows in disbelief. Was she for real? God, she was like Amara on crack. Definitely not the kind of woman he needed in his life, in his *way*, with all that was going on. But if she really knew what needed to be done to get rid of Aiala for good, listening to her might not be a bad idea.

"What are you planning to do?"

"Whatever needs to be done. In this case, getting rid of your vamp with his demonic obsession before a bunch more women end up dead. I'd listen to me for a little while, if I were you. Aiala has a personal grudge against you and Eric. I'd be a little worried about Marco's wife."

"Is that some kind of a threat?"

"Of course not. It's just a warning." She opened the driver's door of the sedan. "It seems like we're both after the same thing. Why don't you just stop your stupid macho protests and get in the damned car? We could get the job done quicker together, and then I can get the hell out of the crazy town before I end up as nuts as you."

"Yeah, I know exactly what you mean." Getting rid of Aiala was his number one priority, but he didn't know if he could work with Merida without wanting to kill her. Women weren't supposed to be so rough around the edges. They were made to be soft, pliant, and sweet—at least for the most part. What had gone wrong with this one?

"We've only got a few hours to plan before daylight. If you want to help me, it would be nice if you'd let me know."

"Yeah, okay. Whatever." He got into the car with her, hoping by the end of this one of them didn't end up dead.

"You need me to stop somewhere so you can find some food?" she asked after a few minutes.

"No, I'm fine." He leaned back in the plush leather seat. "If I get hungry enough, I'll just feed on you." He gave her his best leer, and was surprised when she smiled. "I've got to warn you, babe, I like it." Maybe working with Merida wouldn't be such a bad thing after all.

Chapter 18

Ellie sat on the edge of the bed, brushing her still-damp hair. It hung in long, limp strands nearly down to her waist. Usually, it was healthy, but now it seemed dull and tangled. She hoped that was temporary—she'd always thought of her hair as her best feature.

Over the past week she'd spent an obscene amount of time in the shower, scrubbing the memories of what had happened off her body until her skin was bright pink. She still felt skewed, like her life had been shattered and not put back together properly. It was an odd feeling, one she could do without. She didn't like the sense of unbalance it left her with. Though the pounding she'd felt in her head for the first couple of days had dulled to a low throb, her nerves still tingled and everything felt...weird. She had yet to accept the fact that she now looked at life through a demon's perspective.

If it hadn't been for Eric and Sam, she wouldn't be here right now to perceive anything.

That thought chilled her to the bone. She owed them her life, literally, even if it had changed permanently in the process.

"Are you doing okay?"

She'd been so wrapped up in thought that she hadn't even noticed Eric had come into the room until he spoke. "Fine, thanks." She tried to smile, but it fell a little short.

"You don't look fine." He scooted up on the bed behind her and took the hairbrush from her hand. He started gently brushing her hair.

It was an amazing feeling, another new experience for her. He'd been so kind and caring while she slept much of the week away. She couldn't have asked for a better caretaker. The problem was, she hadn't asked for anything. He was smothering her with kindness, and she just needed a moment to breathe.

"I have something to say," he told her, stilling his movements with the brush. "I know you don't want to hear this, but please just give me a few minutes to say what's on my mind. I know you probably resent what I did, and I understand. I just hope you can find a way to forgive me someday, because I'd really like things to work out between us."

She'd had the whole week to think about what had happened, and at some point during her recovery she'd come to an important conclusion—she wasn't upset with him anymore. Hanging on to her anger wouldn't do her any good. It would just eat away at her inside. "I don't resent you. Not really. If you hadn't done what you did, I wouldn't be here at all right now."

"If I'd left you alone in the park that first evening, none of this would even be an issue."

"And then I'd still be sitting at home on Friday nights, bored out of my mind." Of course, this was a little extreme as far as cures for boredom went.

He laughed and kissed her hair. "Do you always look at the bright side of things?"

When the dark side is enough to give a person nightmares... "Sometimes life changes. We have to just accept that."

"This will be a tough life for you to adapt to."

She placed her hand over his. "I'll be fine. I have to tell you, though, I'm not crazy about your job."

"It's an old habit, I guess," he said, pulling away from her slightly. "Times were different when I was born. Cats had to struggle to survive, constantly watch our backs for people who'd grown suspicious of what we were. You'd be amazed at how quickly the masses leave you alone when you make an example of a couple of would-be killers."

She froze. "Torture?"

"What do you think they did to my mother? That's how she died, you know."

"An eye for an eye."

"The law was different then. That's just the way it was. I'm older, and I've moved past the vindictive stage. Now it's just a job."

She shook her head. What he was telling her should have bothered her, yet it didn't—not when he'd given a compelling reason. She couldn't imagine anyone doing something like that to her mother.

Thinking someone was doing it to her sister is what had gotten her into this mess.

"Your heart is beating fast." She made the comment offhandedly, but he stopped brushing.

"Yeah, I guess it is. You'll notice that more often now. Are you hungry? You haven't really eaten much this week."

"No, I don't think so." She didn't know what she was. Her emotions and physical needs were a jumble of confusion and it was going to take a while to sort them out. It wasn't a bad feeling, it was just different. Once she got used to it all, she'd be fine.

"Anything I can do to help you?" Eric asked, leaning over to kiss her jaw.

"Just be there for me." Could the change she'd been through really be so different from what she'd been before? Her body said, yes, it could. She'd never felt anything like this in her life. An adjustment period was definitely necessary.

"Always." She felt his smile against her cheek. "The way things happened isn't what I would have chosen for us. But, if I hadn't met you...well, I hate to say this, but I don't regret making the decision to let Sam save you. The only thing I regret was not getting there sooner. If I'd been a minute or two earlier, you wouldn't have lost so much blood, and maybe you would have been able to live as a human. But whatever you are now, it doesn't change the way I feel about you. In fact, it even makes me feel stronger knowing we can be together fully and completely now. I've missed you this week, Ellie. Did you miss me, too?"

He set the brush down and moved her hair aside to kiss her neck. His lips brushed over her skin and her senses went wild.

She felt everything magnified, and all it took was the brush of his skin against hers to arouse her beyond reason. He hadn't so much as touched her intimately all week, and the arousal she'd felt that first day in the shower hadn't completely faded. Now it was front and center. She nodded, not able to speak with the way he was touching her. If she thought it had been good before, she didn't even know how to explain what was happening now.

"I know this has you a little nervous. You'll get used to it. I promise." He dragged his lips across her neck, and she felt the slight scrape of his teeth. Sharper than before, almost like a fang.

She stiffened in his arms. "What was that?"

"What?" Eric asked, his lips hovering over her neck.

"Your teeth. I felt them like that before." Or was that in her dream? She couldn't remember. "Why do they seem so sharp?"

"I'm sorry if that scares you. When I'm with you, I don't always have as much control over myself as I'd like. Sometimes things slip into more demon form than human."

"Oh." She couldn't think of anything else to say.

"I know it sounds scary, but it's not. It's just part of who I am." He ran his tongue over the shell of her ear. "Part of who *you* are, too." He kissed her neck and moved aside the straps of her tank top to kiss the backs of her shoulders. She leaned into his touch, her body craving it after going so long without.

He continued to kiss his way down her back as he grasped the hem of the tank top and lifted it over her head. His hands came around her front to cup her breasts. He held her almost reverently, and it made her breath hitch in her throat.

She rushed to ask the questions she needed answers to before he stopped her brain function all together. "What about my family? I can't just leave my grandmother."

"She's being taken care of. Charlotte, Becca, and Carol are all fine."

She melted against him as his hot breath fanned across her back. "How can you be sure?"

"Trust me to take care of you, Ellie, at least until you've gotten your strength back. As soon as you're ready, we'll go back to Stone Harbor. But let's take it slowly, okay?"

"I can't leave them, Eric. I don't want to leave my home."

"What makes you think I would ask you to?" He trailed his tongue up the length of her spine, and she shuddered, remembering how he could bring her to climax so easily. Then, it had been amazing. Now it was like every nerve in her body had multiplied, and just the slightest touch drove her insane with arousal.

He laid her down on her back on the bed and kissed her stomach. "You're doing it again, assuming too much about me. Don't." He brought his mouth to her breast and suckled her nipple. Tiny waves of pleasure washed over her as his wet mouth devoured her. She didn't know if he meant he wouldn't move her away from her family, or if he wasn't planning on there being a lasting relationship between them.

"Eric," she pleaded, her voice raspy. "I don't need any more change in my life."

He looked up and her nipple slid from his mouth with a pop. "Nothing will change. We'll live wherever you want."

She watched his gaze, checking for insincerity but finding none. She smiled as he went back to sucking gently on her flesh. That was all she'd wanted, a promise—a commitment. Things would get difficult when they went back, and she wanted to know he'd stand by her no matter what. Whatever else happened, she'd deal with it when the time came. For now, it was time to concentrate on the present.

"Eric, touch me. Please."

He ignored her, moving his lips over the skin of her belly. She'd have just about all she could take. "It's been *days*, Eric, and I'm going out of my mind. I need you now. I don't want to wait."

He looked surprised for all of two seconds before he pulled off his shirt and kissed her hard on the lips. "I've missed you so much." He paused to gently nip her chin before he rolled on top of her. "I've missed *this*."

He ground his pelvis against her and she felt the hardness of his cock through his pants. Something in her snapped and she had trouble reining it back in. The world around her became a white haze, Eric being the only thing she could see clearly. She clutched at him while he kissed her, dragging her nails over his chest and arms. He cried out and pulled away, sitting up in the bed.

Ellie rolled over onto her side to face him. The ribbon of blood that ran from a deep welt in his arm dismayed her. "Did I do that to you?"

He laughed, but she saw the flash of pain in his eyes. "You're going to have to work on keeping your claws sheathed in bed, or I'm going to end up torn to ribbons."

She brought her hands up to her face and looked them over. They looked the same as they always had. "How could I have done that?"

"You're still so new at this. It'll be some time before you really learn to control it. We'll have to make sure to practice lots, until it doesn't happen anymore."

"I'm so sorry." She felt terrible. At the same time, she felt...hungry, watching the blood drip down his arm onto the sheets. That wasn't right. Was it? She wasn't supposed to crave blood, yet for some reason she wanted to taste his. She leaned forward and ran her tongue over the wound.

Eric sucked in a sharp breath. "Easy."

She lapped the thin trail of blood from his skin, and it only whetted her appetite for more. She felt like someone else was taking over her body, yet in some strange way she was the same. She couldn't explain it, but this new side of her reacted to Eric in a very big way.

He didn't protest, but when she glanced up at him she caught his wince.

"Do you want me to stop?" she asked, not wanting to cause him any more pain.

"No" he rasped. "Whatever you do, don't stop."

Eric wrapped his hands in her hair and pulled her down against him. She was out of control, and it did wonderful, amazing things to his body. Her mouth was harsh, inexperienced, and a jolt of pain shot through him as she licked his wound. He tensed at first, but soon relaxed and dropped his head back on the pillow. It didn't take her long to find her rhythm, the seductive power of the cat taking over as she caressed him with her mouth. He hadn't had a chance to explain this part of her new life to her, but she seemed to be doing just fine running on instinct alone.

She ran her hands along his chest, followed by her tongue, damn near driving him insane. His arm throbbed, but he no longer noticed. It wouldn't be long before it healed, anyway. His cock ached, straining against the fly of his jeans. Then Ellie's fingers were at his pants, unbuttoning and unzipping. Her fingers, again tipped with razor-sharp claws, tore his clothes into ribbons to get them off his body. He winced when she got to his pants, hoping she didn't hit something vital. Thank the goddess, she missed.

"Touch yourself for me, Eric." Her whisper was soft, too seductive to refuse. He wrapped his hand around his cock and stroked up and down a few times.

"More," she spoke softly, stripping out of her shorts and panties. He hesitated, but continued to stroke himself. Being so open, so vulnerable made him nervous, but at the same time turned him on beyond belief. The way she watched him, the hungry gaze in her eyes, almost made him come right then. He eased his strokes, fighting for control. Ellie moaned softly, her gaze focused on nothing but the motion of his hand as he stroked his cock.

"*Yes*," she whispered as his thumb skimmed over the tip. He settled into a good, fast rhythm, his hips bucking off the mattress. He groaned, gripping himself tighter. Ellie ran her tongue over her lips, apparently enthralled. She watched him with utter fascination, and he in turn watched her.

"Ellie, I'm about to come." His voice was a harsh growl. He wanted to come in her, not all over the mattress.

"Please do."

"I want...to..." He ended the sentence with a deep moan. "Shit. I can't wait."

Seconds later he came hard, his come spurting from his cock in hot rushes. Ellie leaned over and put her lips over him, catching the last of the spurts in her warm, wet mouth. She swallowed and crawled up his body, kissing him hard on the lips.

"Happy now?" he asked when she broke the kiss to lap at his chest again.

"Very. Feel like another round?" Her fingers curled around his flaccid cock. He felt it start to harden almost immediately as she stroked him.

His answering laugh was tinged with bitterness. "Yeah, but only if you're involved."

She paused in her ministrations. "You have no idea how involved I was." She brought his hand to her sex. "Feel for yourself." He closed his eyes and slid his fingers into her sopping cunt. She whimpered and bucked against his hand.

"Watching me actually turned you on that much?"

She nodded. "*So* much. I need you to help me with that."

"I'm going to watch you someday," Eric promised. "But not tonight. Tonight, I want to bury my cock in your sweet cunt. I'm going to come inside you this time, sweetheart, and every other time for as long as we have."

"I hope you do." She bit into his chest, hard, and he sucked in a sharp breath. She pulled away. "Did I hurt you?"

"A little. It's good, Ellie," he added when she started to pull away. "Trust me. I can take whatever you want to give."

"I don't think I can control myself much longer," she said softly.

"So don't."

Ellie released her hold on him and pushed him onto his back. She straddled him and lowered her sex onto his cock. He groaned and raised his hips, pushing the head into her cunt.

"You feel so good," she whispered, her eyes closing.

So did she. He'd never felt like this in his life. She rode him hard and fast, bringing out a frenzied need in him he didn't even known he'd had. Her nails scraped his chest, leaving little welts as she went. He wanted to possess her in every way possible, but it was Ellie who possessed him. He hadn't been able to sleep, he'd barely had anything to eat, and all his thoughts had revolved around getting her back into his bed. Now that he had, he realized his dreams and fantasies couldn't even begin to compare to what they shared.

She raised herself up until his cock nearly slipped from her before she brought herself down hard, their flesh smacking together. She whimpered, and Eric knew she was close. He reached between them, stroking her clit with the pad of his finger. One touch and she came, bucking wildly on top of him.

It was then that the real problems started. Ellie's fingers tore at his skin as she thrashed over him. He grabbed her wrists and flipped her over onto her back, settling her hard against the mattress. She hissed and bit at his lip when he kissed her. He thrust hard and fast, needing desperately to find release—but needing to keep his skin intact at the same time. She wrapped her legs around his waist, digging her heels into his ass and pulling his cock deeper inside her cunt.

He pinned her arms above her head and latched his mouth onto her breast, biting gently into her nipple. She gasped as his teeth clamped down a little harder. Her eyes darkened, and she arched her back, a moan escaping her lips. Encouraged, he moved to her other breast and bit her nipple, suckling her hard. She pulled her wrists out of his grip and raked her nails down his back as she came again. The pain of her nails tearing into his flesh sent him into the most explosive orgasm he'd ever experienced. He came hard, spending himself inside her before he collapsed on top of her, thoroughly and completely sated.

They were both silent for a long moment, and Ellie's voice was hoarse when she finally spoke. "I think I may have underestimated you, Eric Malcolm."

"How so?" He raised his head a little so he could look at her, but was too worn out to hold it upright for long.

"I think you're dark side runs very deep."

That caught his attention. He rolled off her. "I didn't hurt you, did I?"

She laughed and gently scraped her nails across his stomach. "Hurt? No. How are you feeling?"

"I think I'll survive." He laughed, gently rubbing the healing gash in his arm. "This is definitely going to take some getting used to."

She was different now—untamed and wild. Part of that was being a new cat, but most of it was the nature of the cats themselves. He didn't think he'd have a difficult time getting used to this new side of Ellie—he relished in it, actually. He liked it a little rough, and if the state of his body was any indication, so did she. It would take her some time to get used to her new powers, and until then he hoped she didn't tear him completely apart.

He'd just started to doze when she lifted her head and looked at him, her expression tentative. "I want to go back home."

"What's wrong with staying here for a little while? You still need more time—"

"No. I don't. I'm perfectly fine now. It's been a week, Eric, and I'm sure Marco and Amara are worried. I miss my painting, my house, my *life*. I just want to go back and make sure everything is okay." Her pleading gaze nearly did him in. "Don't you have a job to finish?"

He sighed, weighing his options. If he took her back, he'd be bringing her right back into the danger. But Merida was there, in danger herself. If he went back, he could watch over both Merida and Ellie. "If it will make you happy, we'll go back tomorrow. But if it gets bad, don't think I won't ship you back here."

She raised an eyebrow at him. "Don't even try it."

With any luck, he'd be able to make sure both of the women in his life were safe, and Aiala was destroyed before she could thoroughly possess Antonio. He kissed the top of Ellie's head and tried to tamp down the feeling that something could still go horribly wrong.

Chapter 19

Eric pulled his car into the driveway and shut off the ignition, but didn't get out. "Are you sure you want to do this now? You can wait to talk to them in a couple of days if you don't feel ready."

"I'm ready. More than ready." Ellie struggled to give him a smile. "I think."

Before she could chicken out, she got out of the car and walked up to the front door. She heard Eric walk up the steps behind her, felt his hand on the small of her back in a gesture of support, but she barely noticed any of it. Her nerves were fried, her stomach clenched in knots, and her palms sweaty. She'd wanted so badly to come back to Stone Harbor, but now that she was here, she wanted to turn around and run.

Amara opened the door after what felt like an eternity. She blinked hard when she saw them standing on the porch. "Ellie. How are you?" She looked even more shocked than Ellie felt.

Ellie forced another smile, more for Amara's benefit than her own. "Great. How has everything been here?"

Amara licked her lips and glanced behind her. She looked Eric over, an uncertain expression in her eyes. Finally, she sighed and opened the door wider. "You might as well come in. Marco and Royce have been out of their minds with worry."

Amara ushered them into the foyer and closed the door. She pulled Ellie into her arms for a hug—very unusual for Amara—not letting her go for a long time. "I was worried about you, too."

"As you can see, I'm just fine."

"Yeah, right." Amara's tone dripped of disdain and she focused a glare on Eric. "Maybe you should have waited in the car."

"He saved my life, Amara," Ellie butted in, not wanting an argument. "I want him here."

Amara ignored Ellie's comments. She crossed her arms over her chest. "Is there something wrong with your brain? Wasn't it bad enough that you had to draw my friend and my brother-in-law into danger? Why did you have to drag my husband into it, too? All they talk about is that demon, and how they're going to kill her. I'm sick of hearing it. Thanks a lot, Malcolm. And then you had to go and…well, do whatever you did to Ellie to make her what you are. I don't like it one bit."

"How did you know?" Ellie asked, standing in between Eric and Amara.

"Please. It's so obvious." She shook her head. "Don't worry, though. I won't hold it against *you*. Just him."

Eric, wisely, remained silent. Amara was relentless — no one ever won an argument against her so it was better to not even try.

Amara opened her mouth to speak again, but before she could say anything Royce came around the corner from the living room with Marco right behind him. They stopped and stared for a full minute before Royce finally spoke. "What the hell happened to you?"

"It's a really, really long story, one I'm not going to bore you with right now." She hoped he'd leave it at that, but life just wasn't that easy.

"You disappear off the face of the planet for more than a week, you don't let anyone know where you're going to be, you don't call to say you're okay…do you really expect me to just drop it?"

"Actually, yes, I do." She never knew what to expect from him, but she hadn't expected anger.

Marco's reaction was easier to predict. She'd known him long enough to be able to judge how he'd react. With him it was always the same—act first, think later. He lunged for Eric, but Eric stopped him easily with a hand in the air. Marco stumbled back, but held his ground.

"You couldn't be satisfied with just having her with you, could you?" Royce asked Eric, barely contained rage in his voice. "You had to go and make her into one of your kind."

The way he said "your kind" didn't sit right with Ellie. "Shut up, Royce. It's what I am now, so either accept me or don't. But it was either that or die, and I really would prefer to live. Stop blaming Eric. It's not his fault."

"Did he ask your permission?" Marco asked, his tone surprisingly rational.

"Gee, it's kind of hard to ask a dead person's permission. At least he did something instead of just leaving me there. Would that have made you happy? Would you rather see me dead?" She did her best to keep her voice calm, but given the situation, it wasn't easy. Tears of hurt, anger, and stress welled in her eyes, and she balled her fists.

"No. Of course not." Marco pulled her into his arms and hugged her, earning a growl from Eric. "Don't even talk like that. You know that's not what I want, I just want to make sure he's not going to force you into things you're not ready for."

Eric stayed where he was, but Ellie could see he wanted to tear Marco's head off. She shook her head slowly and Eric relaxed a little. She pulled away from Marco and explained what Eric had told her about her situation. "I'm hoping you would have made the same choice."

Marco stared at her for a moment before he finally relented. "Yeah, I probably would have." He glared at Eric. "But I'm not a killer, either."

"Oh, stop being such a jerk. Eric didn't kill anyone."

"At least not yet this month," he spoke from behind her. "There's still time left."

She whirled on him. "You're not helping, you know."

He just smiled and winked at her.

She rolled her eyes. "At least someone around here has a sense of humor."

Eric shrugged.

"Are you really, absolutely sure you're fine?" Marco asked.

"Of course I'm fine. Geez, Marco, get a grip."

He smiled at her before he glanced at Eric, his expression a blatant challenge. "If you ever hurt her, I swear I'll kill you."

Eric leaned against the wall and crossed his arms over his chest. "Funny, I was just going to say the same thing to you."

Sick of the male power play, Ellie left the room and walked into the kitchen. She got a glass from the cabinet and filled it with water, draining the entire glass before she set it in the sink with a sound thump.

"Get used to it. If Eric is anything like Marco, it's not going to get any better," Amara said from the doorway.

"He's really not. At least I didn't think so until today." She rolled her eyes, sick of the whole thing. "Why is it men have to be so territorial?"

Amara shrugged. "Beats me. You'd think they'd have grown up by now, but I guess even a couple centuries isn't enough time for some people to mature."

Ellie laughed.

"You know, I think we can find this sorceress before they do," Amara continued.

"How?" Ellie asked.

"Merida will help. She can't stand Royce, and I think she'd do just about anything to piss him off. What do you think?"

What would Eric think of she and his sister getting involved? He wouldn't like it, that was for sure. "What can she do?"

Amara shrugged. "She's been one step ahead of Marco and Royce the whole time you were gone. She knows where Tony is hiding, but she didn't want to go after him alone. I guess Aiala is really powerful, and she's literally been half living inside Tony's mind. Maybe with three of us, we can take care of her."

Ellie laughed. "I guess it can't hurt. Why not?"

Amara nodded. "I'll give her a call."

"Call whom?" They looked up to see Marco standing in the doorway. "If you're planning on calling Merida for help, don't. Royce has been a bear lately as it is. Seeing her again will put him over the top. She spends enough time around here without asking her for more."

"An added bonus." Amara smiled too sweetly at Marco and brushed past him on her way out of the kitchen.

Ellie went back into the foyer to find Eric. She didn't see him anywhere, but Royce sat on the stairs, still looking angry. "Your *boyfriend* is outside."

She didn't care for the way Royce said "boyfriend", but she ignored it for now. Whatever his problem was, he'd get over it. She hoped. Life had changed enough without losing someone she'd come to think of as a close friend.

She walked out the front door, letting it shut quietly behind her. Eric was standing on the porch, looking out over the water in the distance. He turned and smiled when she approached.

"How are you holding up?"

"Fine." She smiled back. "Everything is still a little surreal, but I'm okay."

"Sorry about that in there. I guess it couldn't be helped."

She shrugged, not wanting to admit that Royce and Marco's reaction had left a hole inside her. She needed them now more than ever, but she didn't know if they'd ever learn to accept what she'd become. "So what do we do now?"

"We're going to check into a hotel, a different one than the one where I stayed, and we're going to wait until I hear from Sam."

"Why wait?"

"Sam has some connections I don't. He's going to look into some things and get back to me."

"We can't go back to my house?"

He took a deep breath. "It's not safe there. That would be like dangling a steak in front of a pit bull. I don't want anything else to happen to you."

As much as she hated to do it, she relented. He had a point. There would be plenty of time later to go back home and settle in again.

* * * * *

A little while later, Eric had checked them into a hotel under assumed names. Ellie walked into the room and flopped down on the bed, more tired than she was willing to admit. She closed her eyes and felt the mattress dip when Eric joined her.

He ran his fingers through her hair and kissed her temple. "Hungry?"

She nodded.

"Do you want to go get something to eat, or would you rather take a walk on the beach first?"

"I'm not really up for walking right now."

"Okay, dinner it is." He left her and walked to the corner of the room and took out his cell phone.

She didn't know who he was calling, and she really didn't care. She didn't know what she wanted, or even who she was anymore. She'd thought coming back would be the best thing for her, but the people she considered friends didn't exactly welcome her warmly.

"All set?" Eric asked as he slid the phone back into his pocket. Ellie got up from the bed and followed him out the door, going over and over in her mind what had happened earlier.

She was surprised when he led her to the small coffee shop on the first floor of the hotel. "I hope you don't mind eating in a dive like this, but I have to meet someone."

Not in the mood to meet anyone new, Ellie dug in her heels. "Why don't I go back to the room and you can bring me back something later. I'm not really in the mood to sit in on some kind of business meeting."

Eric frowned at her. "It's just my sister. Come on. She'll love you."

He led her to a table in the corner, where a petite woman with reddish brown hair and fair, freckled skin sat. She smiled when she saw them and jumped up to give Eric a hug. Her smile widened when she looked at Ellie. "It's nice to meet the woman who's finally gotten my brother to settle down."

Eric sighed. "Don't start. Ellie, this is Merida."

Eric's phone rang just after the waitress came to take their orders. Ellie rolled her eyes, already sick of the thing. One of these days she was going to pitch it into the ocean. "I have to take this," he said, getting up from the table. "It's Sam. Be right back."

As soon as he was out of earshot, Merida leaned across the table. "Antonio hasn't left Stone Harbor, you know."

"He hasn't?"

Merida shook her head. "He's staying in some cabin out in the woods. Aiala won't let him leave since he didn't do his job." She bit her lip. "I think she might have hurt him again."

"Again?" That was a story Ellie had yet to hear.

Merida glanced around, looking in the direction where Eric had gone. "Okay, I guess Eric hasn't told you everything yet. It was three, maybe four hundred years ago or so, ago when they all worked for Sam—Eric, Royce, and Antonio. Antonio got mixed up with Aiala. Eric tried to warn him away from her, but he didn't listen. Aiala's a black sorceress, and she gets her kicks out of enslaving and killing men. I swear, she would have done well as a succubus. Anyway, she made the mistake of killing Sam's son. Well, you know how Sam is. He wasn't going to let her get away with that."

Ellie watched Merida in wonder, thinking she couldn't possibly be related to Eric. They had absolutely nothing in common, and didn't share a family resemblance at all. "That's horrible." Ellie's heart went out to Sam. She hadn't known any of this, and she felt terrible.

The waitress brought their food, and Merida took a bite of her hamburger. Ellie shook her head, the story making her lose her appetite.

"Yeah, it gets worse," Merida continued, absently munching on French fries. "Sam sent everyone he had after Aiala, but he didn't know Antonio was having an affair with her. By then she'd already burrowed into his mind so that when they went after Aiala he attacked them—his friends. Royce cornered Antonio, but in the end, he couldn't kill him. He hurt him pretty bad, though, and Aiala too. We all thought she'd died when we didn't hear from her for so long, but obviously she's a lot stronger than we've given her credit for. All these years she's kept Antonio, but from what I gather she's never been able to fully possess him since. Do you know what demonic obsession is?"

"No." And she wasn't sure if she wanted to.

"It's basically when a demon constantly bombards a person with harassment, kind of like a mental stalking, when a demon becomes obsessed with a human. It's not the same as a full-blown possession in that the demon can't control the person's actions, just try to influence them. Usually it manifests itself in bad habits, stuff that can be considered sinful—lying, stealing, alcoholism, sex. Aiala's in Antonio's head, but not completely. She can't really control him with her mind, so she has to resort to bombarding him with suggestions until he breaks, using physical punishment if he refuses. He's teetering between obsession and possession, and that's a very bad thing. The weaker he gets, the more she can push inside his mind. When she's finally completely inside, like she was years ago, she'll get all her powers back and he'll snap. We have to keep that from happening. She's pretty much indestructible now. If she gets her abilities back to their fullest...well, you don't even want to know what could happen then. "

"So what's the plan?"

"We have to hurt her enough so that she has to disappear for a couple more centuries."

Ellie blinked at her. "A couple of centuries? That doesn't seem long enough."

"It will buy us some time. We can hope that, by then, someone like Sam will have developed his powers enough to get rid of her for good."

The thought made her blood run cold. "You mean, no one can...?"

"Kill her? Unfortunately, no. At least no one has been able to yet."

"Then how do you expect to keep her from burrowing into Tony's mind?"

Merida stopped eating, her gaze growing serious. "We kill him."

Ellie gulped. Despite what she knew about him, taking a life was something she was not capable of.

"How long do you think we have before she takes Tony over completely?" Ellie asked as she pushed her plate away. It baffled her that she was sitting in a little coffee shop, discussing the differences between obsession and possession with a demon.

Merida shrugged and polished off the last of her fries before picking up her burger. "Don't know. The more he feeds and kills, the stronger she gets. A day, maybe two. Something's got to be done quickly if we want to avoid a big, bloody mess."

Avoiding a big bloody mess was definitely on the top of Ellie's list. "Do you have something planned?"

"Yep." Merida detailed her plan to Ellie just before Eric came back to the table.

"What did I miss?" he asked as he slid into the booth next to Ellie.

Merida rolled her eyes. "Lots."

"Do you want to fill me in?" he asked when she went back to eating her dinner.

"Not really." She gave him a big grin and concentrated on her food. Ellie smiled at that. She was really going to like the other woman.

* * * * *

"I'm glad you and Merida got along so well," Eric said as they walked across the darkened beach a few hours later. "What did you two talk about while I was gone?"

No way was she telling him any of that. "Did everything go okay with Sam?"

"Yeah, fine." She heard the brush-off in his voice, but chose to ignore it since she was doing the same thing to him. "So…"

"So," she repeated, at a loss for words.

He stopped suddenly and turned her in his arms to kiss her. His tongue traced her lips before delving inside. He ran his hands along her hips, sending tingles through her. She heard his soft growl as he pressed his pelvis against her. He'd already started to get hard, and the idea thrilled her. By the time he broke the kiss she'd just about forgotten the plans she'd made with Merida.

He pushed her back against a tall sand dune, lifting one of her legs up over his hip. "You look so beautiful in the moonlight."

"I was just going to say the same thing about you." Arousal coursed through her, and she was barely able to keep control of herself. She had no idea why the thought of making love in such a public place did so much for her, but it did. Her panties were damp just thinking about Eric taking her in the middle of the beach. She smiled up at him and moved her hand to the front placket of his pants. He was completely hard now, and so hot she felt heat radiate through the fabric. She moaned as out-of-control arousal ripped through her.

Eric sucked in a sharp breath. "I want you, Ellie."

She nodded.

"We're out in a very public place."

She shrugged.

"We could get arrested."

"I don't care."

Whatever it was that had come over her, she liked it. She didn't know if it was from the new power thrumming through her, or just being with Eric, but she'd never felt so incredible in her life. He was so warm and solid, so sexy, that it was all she could do to keep herself from ripping off his clothes right then and there. She unbuttoned his shirt and spread it wide, running her hands over his chest. The crinkly hairs tickled her palms.

Eric kissed her, his lips crushing hers. She wrapped her arms around his neck as he ripped her panties off her and unzipped his pants. He slid inside her without any seduction whatsoever, and she didn't need any. She was so ready for him it wasn't funny. She moaned and clutched his shoulders, her leg ready to drop out from under her. The dune against her back was rough and soft at the same time, while Eric was all hard. He slammed his cock into her, his urgency evident in his forceful thrusts. Before long he lifted her other leg around his waist, leaning down to nip her shoulder at the same time. She clung to him as she felt the first tremors of orgasm low in her belly, afraid she might fall if she let go. Just as she felt the full force of her climax, Eric growled with his own release and collapsed to the sand below.

Ellie's back hit the bottom of the dune hard, nearly knocking the wind out of her, but she was too sated from their quick bout of lovemaking to care. She sucked in a sharp breath as Eric withdrew. "Where are you going?"

He shook his head as he tucked his flaccid cock back into his pants. "We need to get back to the room before the couple that just walked by calls the police and we get arrested."

Ellie froze as a sliver of fear knifed through her. "What couple?"

"That one," he pointed to the retreating forms of two people before he bent down and helped her to her feet.

"Do you think they noticed?" She picked up her torn panties off the ground, trying to control her shaking. To say she was mortified would be a huge understatement.

"They probably stopped and watched. Come on." Taking her hand, he walked her back to the hotel room and let them inside.

"Do you really think they'll call the police?"

He shrugged. "Beats me."

She wrapped her arms around herself, shaking at the thought of strangers watching her and Eric make love. It scared her, but at the same time thrilled her. She laughed at herself when she realized she couldn't wait to do it again.

She stripped off her clothes and climbed into bed with Eric, curling around his warm body. As excited as she was, she knew she needed to settle in to get some sleep. Tomorrow was going to be a very long and difficult day.

If things went the way they'd been planned, Aiala would be destroyed and Tony freed from her forever. If something got screwed up and the plan went wrong...well, she'd think about that if the time came.

Chapter 20

"He's in there," Amara said with certainty.

Ellie, Amara, and Merida crouched in the woods outside a small cabin, one where Merida had learned Tony was staying. Ellie didn't know how Merida had done it, but she'd found him with apparent ease. It made her wonder if, somehow, she had inside information. When Ellie had asked her about it, though, she just shrugged and smiled.

"What do we do now?" She squinted against the broken sunlight that came through the canopy of trees, wishing they could get this over with so she could just go home. She had a very bad feeling about this.

"We need to get inside," Merida said softly. "And then we take him out before he even wakes up."

"What makes you think he's going to sleep that long?"

Merida shrugged. "Wishful thinking?"

Amara laughed nervously, but Ellie remained silent. This whole situation bothered her.

"Do we have to kill him?" Amara asked.

"No, but we have to hurt him enough to make him useless to Aiala." Merida frowned in concentration. "That will draw her out. Then, we incapacitate her enough that she has to go back to the demonic plane to heal. Fairly simple, but effective."

Oh, yeah. It was that simple. "How are you planning to do that?"

"Easy." Merida waved her hand in the air and scoffed, making it sound like destroying killer demons was a common occurrence for her. Maybe it was. "Sam got her good that night you…well, she's going to be weak, and it won't be hard if she can't draw her strength from Antonio."

They crept up to the front door. "He's sleeping soundly," Amara confirmed. That was all they needed to know. For now, they were safe. How long that would last was anyone's guess. She knew they had to act quickly, but suddenly she second thoughts filled her. "The door's locked. How are we going to get in?"

Merida didn't answer. She grabbed the doorknob and gave it a sharp tug. The knob came off in her hand.

"Oh. Okay." Ellie backed up a step, not at all sure if she should be standing so close to Merida. She barely knew her, and her powers were downright scary. Eric had promised her that someday she would be as powerful, but she had yet to even try to use her abilities. If she did, that would be admitting she'd become something other than the human she once was.

Merida gave the door a shove and it swung open, surprisingly soundless. They walked inside. The creepy factor in the cabin was a little too high for Ellie's tastes. The inside was dark, so dark that if she were still human she wouldn't have been able to see at all. As it was, she could barely make out the furniture with her newly improved eyesight. The smell of mold and must hung in the air, creating a thick aura of decay over everything. Two steps down the hall Ellie walked through a cluster of cobwebs hanging from the ceiling. She sputtered and brushed at them to get them away from her eyes. How anyone could live in a place like this baffled her.

Amara turned the knob on the only closed door in the hall, what they assumed would lead to the bedroom, and it swung open with a low groan. Ellie followed Merida further into the room. They stopped by the double bed, and alarm washed over Ellie as she realized it was empty. The covers were tossed aside, the indent of a body still on the mattress. He had been lying there until recently—so where was he now?

Merida blew out a frustrated breath, and Ellie echoed the sentiment wholeheartedly. Something about this seemed off. She couldn't brush off the feeling that they'd been set up.

Merida seemed to be thinking the same thing as she walked back out into the hall. "Okay, I think we might be in just a little over our heads here."

Ellie followed, with Amara close behind. The aura of the house seemed to change from decaying and abandoned to sinister. "What are we going to do now?" she asked, hoping Merida had some sort of a backup plan.

"My gut instinct is to get the hell out of here. I think it might already be too late," Merida answered. She walked in the direction of the front door, which still swung knob less on its hinges. As they approached it the door slammed shut with a rush of wind strong enough to make Ellie stumble.

An impossibly deep voice came from behind them. "Looking for something?" They all spun around. Antonio—Tony—was standing not three feet away. His shoulders were hunched, his hair and clothing disheveled, his expression desolate.

"You shouldn't have come here," he said. "That was a big mistake."

A small blonde walked out from behind him. Merida took a step back, and Ellie and Amara followed.

Merida glanced from Ellie to Amara and back to Tony. "Oh, shit."

"What's the matter, ladies? Too shocked to speak?" Her laugh was menacing. "Ann Elizabeth, dear. It's wonderful to see you out and about. After that terrible accident, I'm surprised you lived. And Mrs. Cardoso, be sure to give your brother-in-law my regards. *If* you make it home this morning."

She turned her attention to Merida. "Ah, little one. I see you were finally able to find me."

"Fuck off, Aiala." Merida sneered as she spoke, her voice very close to a growl.

Aiala? Ellie looked the woman over. She didn't look injured at all. In fact, she looked downright scary. Ellie hoped Merida knew what she was doing, otherwise they were all in very big trouble.

"What was your name again? Oh, well. It doesn't matter. You won't live long enough for me to bother with."

Merida cocked her head to the side and snorted. "What makes you think you can kill me?"

"Compared to me, you're just a child." Aiala stalked toward Merida and circled her slowly, stopping in front of her. "You overestimate yourself. You're very much like your brother." She raised her hand to Merida's face, but just before her fingers made contact, Merida's hand snaked out and snagged Aiala's wrist. Aiala sucked in a sharp breath and yanked her hand away as if Merida's touch had burned.

"Don't toy with me, child. I'll make your death more painful than you can imagine."

Aiala turned toward Ellie, her eyes glowing red in the darkness. "You weren't supposed to live."

"Obviously I'm a lot harder to kill than I look." Ellie fought to keep from showing her fear, although she suspected the demon already knew how scared she was. Ellie locked her knees so she didn't fall to the floor.

"By yourself, you would have been such an easy kill." Aiala shook her head. "Sam is not here to save you now. At first I'd thought to kill Eric, but now I think I'll kill you instead. Living his life without you would be torture for him. So much worse than a simple death. I'd much rather make his pain everlasting."

Merida went silent. Her hands were clenched into fists at her sides, and her eyes were closed. Ellie thought she was fighting anger, but knowing Merida she had something else planned. She knew it was the latter when Merida opened her hands, blue electricity glowing over her palms.

Ellie turned back to Tony, and she felt a sharp rise in her anger. A tingling started in her palms, moving slowly up her arms.

"Your silly organic magic won't be able to hurt me," Aiala said to Merida. "I know what you are, and I know what you're capable of. I'm too quick for you."

Aiala lunged for Ellie, but Tony grabbed a handful of her hair and pulled her back. "Stop."

She spun on Tony, fury in her eyes. "How dare you go against me, slave?"

"I've had enough. I'd rather be dead," he growled, giving her hair a sharp tug. She slashed her hand across his face, her long fingernails slicing the skin. Blood dripped from the welts and Ellie caught the scent of burnt flesh in the air. He pushed her away, clutching his face.

Aiala dismissed him with a wave of her hand, obviously thinking he wouldn't be a threat to her, and turned her attention back to Ellie.

Ellie glanced to Merida, silently begging for help. Merida gave a slight nod before focusing an intense stare on the beautiful demon. She raised her hands, the blue light jumping between her palms and crackling through the otherwise silent air.

Despite her protests, Aiala moved in back of Tony where she would be at least partially protected from Merida. The bleak look on his face made Ellie's heart clench. As much as she wanted to hate him, her mother and grandmother had raised her better than that. His interference had saved her from certain death at Aiala's hands. He'd been under her spell for far too long, and maybe now it was time to do something about that.

She closed her eyes and concentrated on the totem around her neck — the animal that had given her strength all her life and now was an integral part of it. She let herself imagine what the panther would see, what she would feel. She imagined her muscles and bones changing shape, stretching and elongating. It wasn't until she opened her eyes that she saw the changes weren't imagined. She'd *become* the panther. Just as Merida released the electricity gathering in her hands, Ellie leapt at Tony and pushed him out of the way.

The jolt hit Aiala in the chest, sending her slamming into the decrepit fireplace across the room. She slid to the floor amid a shower of brick bits and mortar dust, writhing for a few seconds before exploding into light and dust. *Lots* of dust. It filled the room and caught in Ellie's throat. She coughed as she sat up off the floor, realizing she was now back in her human form, lying on top of Tony. *Naked.* She squealed and slid off him. "What happened to my clothes?"

"They get destroyed if you change into panther form with them on," Merida told her matter-of-factly, as if it was a common occurrence in her life. "Antonio, the woman just saved your miserable life. Go and get her something to wear, will you?"

Ellie wanted to protest—she'd been wearing other people's clothes more than her own lately—but common sense told her it wouldn't be good to go wandering around in the buff, so she held her tongue.

Tony disappeared into the bedroom, emerging minutes later with a long T-shirt and a pair of cut off sweatpants. He handed them to her, his eyes locking with hers. "Thanks. I didn't deserve that."

She didn't know whether she agreed or not.

"You'd better get out of here," Merida told him. "Or else I might kill you myself."

He looked at Ellie again before he turned and ran out the door.

"What happens now?" Ellie asked as she watched him disappear into the trees.

"Now we go home. There's nothing else for us to do here." Merida waved her hand in front of her face and coughed as a remnant of smoke fluttered near. "Aiala will be out of commission for a long time, and hopefully by the time she resurfaces Sam will have figured out a way to kill her."

Amara cleared her throat. "What about Tony? Will she try to possess him again?"

Merida shook her head. "No. I don't think so. She'd probably try to kill him instead. He failed her, and I don't think she's going to take that lightly." She sighed and shook her head. "I guess that's something he's going to have to deal with when the time comes."

"If he doesn't stay away from my sister, he's going to find out about problems a lot sooner." Ellie put the way-too-big clothes on and they walked out of the house. The air outside was fresh and clean and, despite the oppressive humidity, Ellie drew a deep breath. At least for now, it was over.

But some of her problems were just beginning. They'd only made it a few steps down the path when Eric approached. He glared at them, barely contained rage in his eyes.

"What the *hell* do you think you've been doing?" he yelled.

"Just doing my job." Merida said, smiling smugly.

Eric apparently didn't find it at all funny. "Do you have any idea how much danger you put yourselves in? You could have been killed." He shook his head at his sister before turning his attention to Ellie. "What were you thinking? I told you to call if you ever got into trouble."

"I wasn't in trouble," she lied, frowning at him.

"You snuck out, came down here to do something you had no business doing. You had to have known that it would make me angry, or you wouldn't have done it." He growled before he pulled her into his arms. "I was so worried about you. Don't you *ever* do that again."

His embrace was so tight she had to struggle to draw a complete breath. At the same time, it felt good. She'd never been so glad to be alive. "Believe me. I won't."

"I should have known you'd pull something stupid like this, Merida. I'm just surprised you got these two to go along with you." Eric shook his head in utter disappointment.

"It was their idea," Merida scoffed, turning her attention to Ellie and Amara. "Are we ready to get out of here, or what? I don't want to stand around all day."

"You two, go," Eric said to Merida and Amara. "I'm taking her home with me."

He stopped them as they started to walk away. "Merida?"

She pivoted with her hands on her hips. "*What?*"

"Don't think I'm going to keep this a secret from Sam. He's not going to be happy with this little stunt."

Her eyes widened. "You wouldn't dare."

Ellie pulled back just in time to catch the smug look in Eric's eyes, directed at his sister. "Actually, I have no problem at all telling him how you went against his orders to wait for backup. How do you think he's going to react to this one? I guess we'll just have to wait and see."

With a defeated sigh, Merida shook her head and turned her back on her brother, following Amara to her car.

"What is Sam going to do to her?" Ellie asked as she watched them drive away.

"Probably put her on a probation of sorts," he told her. "She's a bit of a loose cannon, and she needs someone to watch out for her. I think it'll be a while before he lets her work alone again."

"That would make you happy, wouldn't it?" she asked, suspicion lacing her tone.

He shrugged. "I suppose." But the look in his eyes told her how thrilled he was. "I just want to protect her, you know. Our mother left her in my care, and I'm going to see that she's safe, even if it kills me."

He released her and she walked over to the passenger side of his car. "She seemed to do okay for herself. Maybe she doesn't need as much protection as you think."

He put his arms on the car roof and glared at her. "Why don't you let me worry about that, okay? Don't think I'm finished with you yet. Now that I know you're safe, I'm going to tell you exactly how I feel about what happened here tonight."

Rolling her eyes, she slid into the passenger seat. "Save it," she said when he got behind the wheel. "I know. You're disappointed in me. You're angry that I took off without telling you. You're—"

He put his finger under her chin and turned her to face him. "Yeah, all of the above. But mostly—and this is important so you'd better listen closely—I love you. If anything ever happened to you because you'd gone following my sister on one of her crazy schemes, I'd never forgive myself. The bottom line is, I'm not going to let you do that again. Even if I have to tie you to my bed to stop you."

She gaped at him, her mind trying to wrap around his words. She started to speak, but he stopped her with a curt shake of his head. "Whatever you have to say can wait. Right now I need to take you home."

* * * * *

Ellie was surprised when Eric pulled his car in front of her house. "This is home?" she asked. She'd expected him to drive back to where he lived, not just down the street to her little house.

"Yeah. Is there a problem with that?" He continued when she shook her head. "You were nuts to go out there by yourself."

"I wasn't alone."

"Why didn't I guess sooner what the three of you had planned?"

"Because we're smarter than you are?" His eyes darkened at her words and she gulped. She jumped out of the car and bounded up the front steps, making it nearly to the top before Eric grabbed her around the waist and hauled her back against him.

"Don't even joke about this. It isn't funny. You had me scared out of my mind." The sincerity on his face said he meant every word.

"I was fine. *I* wasn't worried at all."

"You're such a liar." He kissed her hard on the lips, grimacing as he pulled away. "You smell like smoke, and I hate to say it, burned flesh. You need to take a shower."

"Then put me down so I can go do it."

"No way. I'm going to have to watch you every second, to make sure you don't go all vigilante on me."

"I won't."

He sighed and set her down on the ground, resting his hand on her shoulder.

"Still, I'm going to stay close. I have to be sure you don't run away again." Humor sparkled in his eyes, highlighting the soft gold flecks in the green.

"Oh, all right."

She unlocked the door and ducked out of his grasp, running inside. Eric chased her all the way up to the bathroom, where he pushed her against the door and kissed her thoroughly. This time, she didn't mind being caught at all.

* * * * *

"I helped, you know," Ellie said sometime later. She opened her mouth to let Eric feed her another strawberry. There was something extremely decadent about having a gorgeous man feed her fruit in bed.

"You're still stuck on that, huh?"

"I didn't want to change," she confessed. "I didn't want any part of your life."

"I was afraid of that," Eric rubbed the berry over her lips before dipping his head to lick off the juices.

"But it's better now. I think everything's going to be okay."

"That's great." He smiled. "But now I think I'm going to have to keep an even closer eye on you than ever."

"Why is that?"

"Because now you're going to think you can walk around combating evil. That's not good for you, you know." He trailed the berry down the line of her throat. "I'm an old man, Ellie. With you out chasing trouble, I just might have a heart attack."

She swatted his side. "Ha, ha. I think this was a one-shot deal. I have no interest in doing what you and Merida do."

"Good. I'm glad. But you have to understand, there will be times that I won't be able to be home. As much as I'd like to, I don't think I can give up my job. It's too big a part of who I am."

"Maybe you could take me with you, you know, to observe and keep you company."

He sighed heavily. "Why didn't I see that coming? Okay, maybe. Maybe. But don't push it."

He was silent for a little while, his expression thoughtful. When he finally spoke again, she had to strain to hear. "I love you, Ellie."

Her heart filled to bursting with his words. She'd waited so long to hear them from him, and now that she had it was better than she could have ever imagined. She ran a finger down his chest, delighting in the little shiver that ran through him. "I love you, too."

"Even after everything I did?"

She nodded and kissed the tip of his nose. "You didn't do anything so terrible. If it wasn't for you, I wouldn't be here right now."

He caught a strand of her hair and twisted it around his fingers. "Just so you know, I don't plan to let you go anytime soon."

She laughed. "I was kind of hoping you'd say that."

His answering smile was nothing short of devilish. "In that case, sweetheart, don't plan on getting out of this bed anytime in the next century, because I plan to spend at least that long showing you how much I love you."

Enjoy this excerpt from
Midnight
Dark Promises
© Copyright Elisa Adams 2003

Chapter 1

Amara walked out of wardrobe, her thigh-high, four-inch-heeled, artificial leather boots making a horrible rustling sound with every step she took. She might as well have wrapped her legs in trash bags. It would have had the same effect.

She tugged at the top of the black vinyl bustier, trying in vain to contain her breasts. When were these people going to learn that there was a huge difference between a B cup and a D cup? *Whoever designed this costume ought to be shot.* They seemed to get skimpier and skimpier with every film.

She'd thought it was bad enough when she'd had to stuff herself into those leather pants for the first film. By the second, the pants had been changed to a mini skirt, which was later changed to a micro-mini and a halter top. It amazed her that, as the films gained popularity and the budget skyrocketed, the material used in each costume got smaller and smaller. You'd think they could at least afford something that would cover her ass.

"You doing okay, Amara?"

She turned, her hands on her hips, ready to take out her frustrations. As it just so happened, the director, Robby Baker, appeared in the hall. "No, Robby, I'm not. I can't even move in this getup. I don't understand how you expect me to run around like this. I can barely walk without some part of my body popping out."

"Come on, Amara. For your age, you have a terrific body."

Her age? She didn't realize that thirty-three had suddenly become over-the-hill.

"A lot of woman have to pay to get tits like yours. They're not naturally blessed like you, honey."

The last time she considered herself "blessed" in the breast department was in eighth grade. Then she learned how much *fun* it was to walk around all day with two mounds the size of grapefruits hanging from her chest.

"I'm not going to flash my breasts for the camera. If you want that, you can find someone else."

"Well, that's kind of what we need to talk about." He pulled her into an empty room at the end of the hall, quietly shutting the door behind them. "The new producers want to take the Midnight films in a different direction."

Shit. That was never a good sign. Were they planning to kill off her character? She certainly hoped not. It was Midnight who had made the films so popular in the first place. Well, Midnight and her human nemesis-slash-lover J.T., but without Midnight the movies wouldn't have much of a plotline. "Go on."

"Okay, what they want is to give the movies more of an...adult flavor."

She snorted. "We're not exactly making kiddie flicks here. Isn't an R rating good enough for them?"

"Well, actually, no."

She stared at him for a minute, trying to figure out if he was joking. He wasn't. "Damn it Robby, I'm not going to get involved in a porn movie!"

Robby sighed and paced the room. "Listen, Amara. The Midnight franchise isn't as popular as it was when we first started. With your face and your tits, we could make a killing if we added a little more spice. Derek agreed, the rest of the regular cast agreed. It looks like you're the only hold out."

"What is this sudden obsession with my chest?" She was looking for one good reason why she shouldn't strangle him for *that* comment. She clenched her teeth and her hands, willing herself to keep calm. "I'm not going to have sex on camera, no matter how much money it will make."

"Get over yourself, babe. There's been a couple of hot sex scenes in all five of the Midnight movies. Hell, you were only twenty-four when the first one was filmed. What's a little more skin, anyway? You'll be protected, if that's what you're worried about. Derek will wear a condom, if that's what you want. You won't have to worry about catching any diseases."

Did everyone think she had no morals? "There is a huge difference between simulated sex and real penetration." She shook her head and yanked up her bustier one more time. "It's not going to happen."

"It's just Derek, honey. You know, your fiancé? Please don't tell me you two have never had sex."

"What Derek and I do in our bedroom is none of your business, and it's most certainly not going to be exploited for the sake of making money."

Robby ran a hand through his dark, greasy hair. "Funny, but Derek didn't voice a single objection."

That stopped her cold. "He didn't?"

"No. As a matter of fact, he seemed pretty excited about doing it on camera with you."

Derek was a dead man the second she got home. "I'm *not* doing it."

"You don't have much of a choice."

"Is that some kind of a threat?" She crossed her arms over her chest, but had to uncross them when the skimpy top puckered indecently. Robby didn't miss the eyeful of cleavage she'd just unwittingly treated him to. His eyes widened and his smile grew, and she would have smacked him if he wasn't holding her fragile career in the palm of his oily little hand. Instead she glared at him, and he had the decency to look humbled.

"Of course not, honey. I would never threaten you. But face it, where would you be without these movies? Have you had any other offers lately?"

No.

Playing Midnight Morris in that first movie had been the best and worst thing for her career at the same time. Sure, the first movie had branched out into four sequels and a line of merchandise that involved everything from action figures to cereal to clothing, but it also killed her hopes of ever being taken seriously in Hollywood. To the entire population of casting directors, it seemed, she *was* the bubbly blond vampire and was therefore unsuitable for any other role.

Still, she wasn't going to compromise her principles by getting horizontal with some beefcake on film, even if the beefcake in question was the man she was supposed to marry in two weeks. It didn't matter how much money the film might gross. She'd learned that money wasn't everything, especially when her dignity was involved.

Sure, she'd spent a good portion of her adult life playing a campy, comic book style vampire with more boobs than brains, but she had to draw the line somewhere.

"I'm not doing this, Robby, and that's final."

"What can I say to make you change your mind? What do you want, more money? A bigger house? A sports car?"

"How about none of the above?" She narrowed her eyes and looked down at the little man. She wasn't overly tall, but the four-inch heels combined with his small stature gave her the advantage. He backed up, but held his ground.

"Is that your final answer?"

She nodded, her lips pursed.

"Well, then I'm sorry. I'm going to have to let you go."

"I don't think so. I have a contract." They weren't going to get away with this.

"By refusing to follow the director's and the producer's orders, technically you're now in breach of contract."

"That's bullshit! Nowhere in my contract does it say I have to fuck my costar." Right after she got out of this scrap of a costume, she was going home to call her lawyer.

"But it doesn't specifically say you don't have to, either."

The nerve of that man! To think, at one time in her career, she might have considered him a friend. "You can't do that."

"No, I probably can't." He winked at her. "But I could tell the producers about the little private party you had a couple of weeks ago in the company limo."

"You wouldn't dare!"

Robby shook his head. "What would everyone think of their golden girl then? Just you and three men in a limo with God only knows what kind of drugs and alcohol." His smile widened. "I'll bet the tabloids would have a field day with that one."

She sucked in a breath, trying to find some way out of this one. Unfortunately, there didn't seem to be any. It wouldn't matter that nothing had happened in the limo. It was just her, Derek, and a couple of his old frat buddies from college. She didn't sleep with any of them at the time, and the strongest substance in the vehicle at the time had been beer.

But it was her word against everyone else's, and she'd been known to throw a wild party or two in her day. She'd been threatened that if she had any more, she'd lose her job.

What would she be without this role? Just an aging chick with a bad dye job and a liberal arts degree from a community college back in Vermont.

"What do you want me to do?"

"Just get naked for the camera, sweetheart, and Derek will take care of the rest."

She shook her head. There was no way she could go through with this. As much as she enjoyed her job, there would be others. It was a devastating blow, but she'd get over it. After a couple of months, the hubbub would die down and she'd be able to start auditioning again. Surely someone out there would want her for something.

"This is *so* not going to happen. I have to go home and talk some sense into Derek."

"Oh, I don't think you're going to change his mind."

The hairs on the back of her neck prickled. She didn't want to hear what was next, but she had to ask anyway. "Why do you say that?"

Robby laughed. "He's not as inhibited as you, I guess. Why don't you take a look at this while you're home wallowing in your self-pity."

He tossed her a VHS tape. "What's this?"

"Just Derek's latest project. Enjoy, honey. I know I sure did."

* * * * *

"Derek?" Amara walked through the door of the townhouse they shared. She was greeted by silence. *Strange.* He should have been home by now.

She shrugged and set her purse on the coffee table, glad to be rid of the vinyl bustier. Her skin would probably itch for weeks. She poured herself a glass of wine and popped the tape into the VCR, curious about what Derek had been working on behind her back. As far as she knew, the only things going on with his career were the Midnight movies and a couple of cell phone commercials.

The title "More than Friends" flashed across the screen, followed by Robby's name as director. She blinked hard when she saw Derek's name next. Just what the hell had he been doing? He'd always thought independent films were beneath him. Why was he suddenly starring in one, and doing so without telling her?

She learned a lot more than she wanted to when the film opened and a naked Derek strutted across the screen, obviously very aroused. Oh, he was really in for it when he got home.

What surprised her more, although she should have been expecting it after Robby's comments, were the four naked women following him. When one of them, a tall skinny redhead with obviously fake boobs, encircled his cock in her hand Amara had to turn the movie off.

"That son of a bitch!"

If she hadn't been so mad, she might have heard the noise sooner. But she'd been too stunned by what she'd discovered about Derek's secret to notice. She sat on the couch, remote in her hand, for a good five minutes before the squeaking bedsprings registered as something other than the anger churning in her head.

She jumped off the couch and bolted up the stairs, taking them two at a time. She threw open the bedroom door, expecting to find Derek with the redhead from the movie. Her jaw dropped when she saw he was fucking Steve, the caterer who lived next door.

"Holy shit!" She couldn't believe what she was seeing. "What the hell do you think you're doing?"

"Hey, baby." He didn't even have the decency to look contrite. Instead he continued to thrust his cock, a cock that would *never* find its way inside her body again, into Steve's ass.

Steve, on the other hand, looked totally mortified. His entire body turned bright red and he closed his eyes, but Derek wouldn't let him go.

"Why don't you get naked and join us, Amara? I've been telling Steve all about your fabulous body."

That was *so* not going to happen. "You're never going to get the chance to see me naked again, buddy."

"Oh, come on, Amara. Have a little fun for once. It wouldn't hurt to spice up our sex life a little."

"Is that why you're with Steve, and why you made those movies? To spice things up? Geez, Derek. If you were bored you should have just said something."

"Boring doesn't even begin to describe you in bed, babe. I need so much more than you can give me." Derek's eyes rolled back and he sighed in sheer pleasure. "Steve is so much better than you are. Do you know that? He'll suck my dick whenever I want, and he doesn't get sick at the thought of swallowing."

He was actually getting off on this. "You're a scumbag, Derek."

"I just want to have fun. Come on, Amara. We could all get off together."

Poor Steve had gone beyond red. He was now a lovely shade of purple. He squirmed to get away, but Derek's huge hands kept him right where he wanted him.

"Are you high again, Derek?"

That got his attention. He stopped pumping and pulled out of Steve. The man scrambled to get his clothes and ran out of the room. Amara heard the front door slam a few seconds later.

Derek's face went ashen. "How can you even ask that? You know I gave that stuff up months ago."

And apparently he'd picked up some other bad habits. She didn't know which one she hated more—the coke or the indiscriminate sexual encounters with anything moving "I think you should leave now. Pack your shit and go. *Do not come back*!"

"We'll get through this. We've been through worse, and we always make it through okay." He reached for her, but she ducked away.

Her stomach churned at the thought of his hands on her skin. "How long have you been gay?"

"I'm not gay. I like women, too."

"Oh, yes. That's right. I watched enough of that tape to know women get you hard, too. How many times have you cheated on me?"

He gave her a solemn look. "None. I love you too much."

"*None?* What the hell did I jut walk in on, a prostate exam?"

Derek sighed, looking a lot more annoyed than he had a right to. "I've never slept with another woman, Amara. Not once since we got engaged."

"What about those women in the movie?"

"They don't count. I was getting paid for that. And the men don't count, either. That's not really sex."

Was he making this up as he went along? "How many men have there been?"

She watched him count to ten on his fingers and then furrow his brow. "I'm not sure. I lost count last month sometime."

She closed her eyes and took a deep breath, willing herself not to smack him. He deserved it, but he wasn't worth breaking a nail or two over. She didn't spend hours filing and polishing for nothing. *"Get out!"*

"That's not fair. You interrupted, so you should at least give me some relief."

"Excuse me?"

"I'm still hard. Why don't you suck me and make it better?"

"You've got to be kidding me. No cock that's been poking around in someone's ass is going to be getting within two feet of any part of my body." She lifted Derek's robe off the floor and tossed it to him. "Get the fuck out of my house. I'll pack up your stuff and you can hire someone to come pick it up later."

He clicked his tongue. "Does this mean the wedding is off?"

"Oh, I don't know. Maybe you can marry Steve or the silicone-enhanced redhead instead."

About the author:

Born in Gloucester, Massachusetts, Elisa Adams has lived most of her life on the east coast. Formerly a nursing assistant and phlebotomist, writing has been a longtime hobby. Now a full time writer, she lives on the New Hampshire border with her husband and three children.

Elisa welcomes mail from readers. You can write to her c/o Ellora's Cave Publishing at 1056 Home Avenue, Akron OH 44310-3502.

Why an electronic book?

We live in the Information Age—an exciting time in the history of human civilization in which technology rules supreme and continues to progress in leaps and bounds every minute of every hour of every day. For a multitude of reasons, more and more avid literary fans are opting to purchase e-books instead of paperbacks. The question to those not yet initiated to the world of electronic reading is simply: *why?*

1. *Price.* An electronic title at Ellora's Cave Publishing runs anywhere from 40-75% less than the cover price of the <u>exact same title</u> in paperback format. Why? Cold mathematics. It is less expensive to publish an e-book than it is to publish a paperback, so the savings are passed along to the consumer.

2. *Space.* Running out of room to house your paperback books? That is one worry you will never have with electronic novels. For a low one-time cost, you can purchase a handheld computer designed specifically for e-reading purposes. Many e-readers are larger than the average handheld, giving you plenty of screen room. Better yet, hundreds of titles can be stored within your new library—a single microchip. (Please note that Ellora's Cave does not endorse any specific brands. You can check our website at www.ellorascave.com for customer recommendations we make available to new consumers.)

3. *Mobility.* Because your new library now consists of only a microchip, your entire cache of books can be taken with you wherever you go.

4. *Personal preferences are accounted for.* Are the words you are currently reading too small? Too large? Too...ANNOYING? Paperback books cannot be modified according to personal preferences, but e-books can.

5. *Innovation.* The way you read a book is not the only advancement the Information Age has gifted the literary community with. There is also the factor of what you can read. Ellora's Cave Publishing will be introducing a new line of interactive titles that are available in e-book format only.

6. *Instant gratification.* Is it the middle of the night and all the bookstores are closed? Are you tired of waiting days—sometimes weeks—for online and offline bookstores to ship the novels you bought? Ellora's Cave Publishing sells instantaneous downloads 24 hours a day, 7 days a week, 365 days a year. Our e-book delivery system is 100% automated, meaning your order is filled as soon as you pay for it.

Those are a few of the top reasons why electronic novels are displacing paperbacks for many an avid reader. As always, Ellora's Cave Publishing welcomes your questions and comments. We invite you to email us at service@ellorascave.com or write to us directly at: 1056 Home Avenue, Akron OH 44310-3502.

COMING TO A BOOKSTORE NEAR YOU!

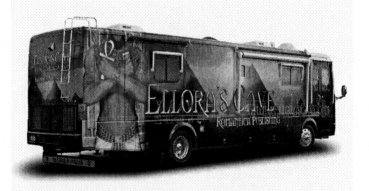

ELLORA'S CAVE
2005
BEST SELLING AUTHORS TOUR

THE
ELLORA'S CAVE
LIBRARY

Stay up to date with Ellora's Cave Titles
in Print with our Quarterly Catalog.

To recieve a catalog,
send an email with your name
and mailing address to:

CATALOG@ELLORASCAVE.COM
or send a letter or postcard
with your mailing address to:
Catalog Request
c/o Ellora's Cave Publishing, Inc.
1337 Commerce Drive #13
Stow, OH 44224

Printed in the United States
35347LVS00001B/55-96